Praise for *Twice a Quinceañera* by Yamile Saied Méndez

"Crafted in rich, beautifully evocative prose, *Twice a Quinceañera* is a bold coming-of-age story underscored by a sweet second chance romance. Readers will relate to and relish Nadia's emotional, inspiring journey. This is a triumphant story about stepping fully into your own power while fighting for the love you deserve."
—Rosie Danan, author of *The Roommate*

"YA author Méndez (*Furia*) makes her adult debut with a heartwarming romance centered on personal growth . . . It's a fun, empowering romp."
—*Publishers Weekly*

"Méndez's debut adult novel is a love letter to people starting from scratch and an ode to those searching to find their one true love . . . An enchanting novel overflowing with self-love and second chances."
—*Kirkus Reviews*

"This second-chance romance is a warm, romantic story made all the more compelling by the focus on Nadia and Marcos learning what they truly want for their lives. The details about what a second quinceañera is all about add to the vivid romance."
—*Booklist*

"Ridiculously charming."
—*Cosmopolitan*

Books by Yamile Saied Méndez

Twice a Quinceañera
Love of My Lives

LOVE OF MY LIVES

YAMILE SAIED MÉNDEZ

KENSINGTON
PUBLISHING CORP.

www.kensingtonbooks.com

KENSINGTON BOOKS are published by
Kensington Publishing Corp.
119 West 40th Street
New York, NY 10018

ISBN: 978-1-4967-3708-3 (ebook)

ISBN: 978-1-4967-3707-6

First Kensington Trade Paperback Printing: October 2023

10 9 8 7 6 5 4 3 2 1

Printed in the United States of America

To Jeffrey, the love of all my lives
And to Puerto Rico, paradise on Earth

LOVE OF MY LIVES

Chapter 1

Eighteen years ago

"I'll see you in the next round," Madi's abuela Lina whispered. "I finally return to the love of my lives. Promise me you'll scatter my ashes in the mountains and my beloved island."

Madi was only thirteen years old, and the youngest in the room of grieving family, but she didn't hesitate. "I promise, Abuela. I promise."

Satisfied, Abuela took a long, last breath, and exhaled. Her life flickered like a candle going out, but her presence lingered, warm as her laughter and hugs.

Madi didn't cry. At least not right away.

She closed her eyes to savor the last embrace they shared, so she'd remember it forever. How else would she face the world without Abuela? Besides Nadia and Stevie, Abuela Lina was Madi's best friend.

Abuela had made her life magical, pointing at little miracles even in the smallest, most ordinary places. And now in this, the darkest moment of her short life, Madi was determined to find a ray of hope. Something that would confirm that this life was worth living, even if it was too hard, too short.

A rustling sound startled Madi, but it was just her mom, kneeling by Abuela's bed.

Madi could imagine Abuela saying, "Help your mom, please. It will be hardest for her."

She swallowed her own sorrow and patted her mom's shoulder. "She'll always be with us, Mami."

Her mom turned and smiled at her through tears in her hazel eyes. "I know, mi amor. It's just that I'm really going to miss our chats and cafecitos every morning. She left us too soon. I was hoping for years and years together."

The reality of what Abuela's death meant sank in. Madi's life unspooled before her mind's eye in a flash. Eighth grade was starting next week and Abuela wouldn't be there to send her off. At least not in the flesh. As she wouldn't be there for Madi's quinceañera coming up in a couple of years.

School dances. Graduation. Her wedding.

All the happy moments she hoped to achieve, and the sad ones she knew waited for her even if she tried to avoid them, fused in a technicolor whirl that left her breathless.

Abuela would miss all of them.

Breast cancer was a monster, and Abuela never had a chance. She was only in her mid-fifties, but either her celestial friends never warned her of the illness growing inside her, or she had ignored their signs. By the time she caved and went to the doctor, it was too late. There was nothing her energy healing or herbs could do.

And now her body rested while her spirit went back to join the universe or whatever waited on the other side of the veil.

Madi refused to listen to one of the tíos who said that after death, it was only darkness and oblivion. Deep in her soul she knew there had to be something else, right? There had to be, if not, what was the purpose of this life? What was it all for?

Abuela said that after death there was love, that Abuelo

would be waiting for her. Madi held on to her words as if they were a lifesaver.

That night, the house was full to the brim with people Abuela's life had touched. Without being told, Madi served food, tended babies, and made sure everyone was comfortable as they planned Abuela's big farewell. In an attempt to be closer to Abuela Lina, everyone had gathered in the big kitchen. Her presence enveloped every surface of the room where she had hosted so many family events and one-on-one soul-baring conversations.

But Madi knew of a better place where to find her.

The funeral home had taken her body away hours ago, but Abuela's room still smelled like her, that unmistakable mixture of sandalwood incense and Florida water. The turquoise infinity scarf she'd been knitting rested by the bed, halfway through the row. Madi gently pushed the stitches all the way to the back of the needle to make sure they didn't slip. Carefully, she put the unfinished proof of her grandma's love in the tote that said *We're the daughters of the witches you couldn't burn*. Madi had brought it for her from a trip to Salem, Massachusetts, last summer.

Witches. Brujas.

There were so many meanings to the word. For Madi, a bruja had the power to connect the physical world to the spiritual sphere. She was a collector of memories, a storyteller, and a bridge.

Madi's mom wasn't into spirituality. Maybe witchery skipped generations. Madi was the granddaughter of the best bruja in their community. She hoped a little bit of Abuela's powers had lingered even though her soul had moved on, but hers were big shoes to fill and Madi was so small.

But she had observed, and she remembered.

Following the rhythm of her memories of Abuela getting ready to meditate, Madi laid a lamb's wool blanket in front of the window. It was a new moon and diamond stars dotted the dark winter sky.

New moon. The perfect planting time for seeds, dreams, and intentions.

She grabbed four candles and placed them in the middle of the blanket, representing the cardinal points. She lit them one by one. In an abalone shell, Madi poured the last moon water she and Abuela had collected during the Beaver full moon last November. She sprinkled Florida water and lavender oil in it and mixed everything with her index finger. Usually, Abuela placed a statue of the Virgin Mary or the goddess Isis with her outstretched wings in the center of the candles, but instead, Madi grabbed a framed photo of Abuela, the one from her yoga teacher graduation.

Her hands in the prayer position, she closed her eyes, and breathed.

One, two, three breaths. Then she waited for the energy to surround her.

Immediately, the air became static with electricity and warm with love. In the distance, a drumming echoed Madi's heart as if Abuela were practicing her chants with her bombo leguëro* just in the next room. Her ears couldn't quite decipher the lyrics of the lullaby, but she knew the music deep in her soul. The words perched on the tip of her tongue for an instant, but she didn't want to spend time in trying to remember them. She wanted answers.

Finally, in a determined, unafraid voice, she said, "Abuela, I can still feel you around me. There are so many things we never talked about! You said you'd guide me when the moment to recognize the great love of my life arrived, just like you guided Mami and all the tías and primas to theirs. I know I'm only thirteen, but how will I know they're the one? How will I find my soul mate?"

Her words resonated in the room. Madi breathed deeply one

---

*An Argentine drum made of a hollowed tree and animal skins that can be heard from a league away.

more time and waited for an answer. She knew it would come. Any moment now. Her crossed legs started tingling as they fell asleep.

But Madi dug deeper into her awareness, just like Abuela had taught her. She knew she'd get an answer. So she waited.

Until she felt a trickle in between her legs. Breaking her concentration, she opened her eyes, and when she shifted, she noticed the blood on the blanket.

"My period?" she said in a gasp.

She'd been so excited to get her period after her friends had theirs for a couple of years. But this wasn't the answer she'd hoped for.

"Madison, are you here, hija?" her mom said, opening the door.

Although she hadn't been doing anything wrong, Madi scrambled to her feet, but immediately, she realized trying to put away the vestiges of her ritual was pointless. She'd tipped the abalone shell, and the water had spilled on the blanket and slid to the floor. The flame of candles danced.

"I was—" she said, but she couldn't come up with a reason. With a lie.

Her mom made her way to the blanket and gazed tenderly at the candles and the photo for a few seconds, and then she gasped, just like Madi had done. She'd seen the blood.

When she looked at Madi her face was shiny with joy and pride. "You got your period."

Madi nodded because she couldn't speak. She had a knot in her throat, and she didn't want to cry. More than excitement or emotion for her period, a profound sadness that her grandmother hadn't spoken to her after all overwhelmed her.

"Oh, mi amor! Don't cry," Mami said. "How do you feel?"

"I'm okay," she said, and crouched to blow the candles.

Her mom didn't ask her what she'd been doing, and Madi didn't offer any explanations.

Later that night, when she had a heated rice pouch on her

lower belly and she had brushed the lingering taste of raspberry leaf and chamomile honeyed tea from her teeth, Madi snuggled in her bed. The soft voices in the kitchen lullabied her, and she closed her eyes for just a second.

Her breathing deepened.

When she opened her eyes just a second later, she was standing on a beach. It all felt so real. The warm breeze, the caress of the water on her naked feet, the still-warm sand underneath. But how had she arrived here? And why was she all alone?

Panic uncoiled inside her as she turned to look for a familiar face.

But then, she recognized this place! It was Flamenco Beach in Culebra Island, off Puerto Rico, where the family had gone last Christmas to visit Abuela's side of the family. This was the island Abuela was always going on about. The one she'd mentioned with her last breath. A little bit of paradise on Earth.

Madi licked her lips and tasted salt. The night sky was alight with the brightest stars she'd ever seen.

"How can this be?" she said, looking around her with wonder.

The stars pulsed with energy, as if they had a secret they couldn't contain. The ocean waves whispered but Madi couldn't understand what they said.

She started walking, not knowing her destination. Madi didn't know what she was doing here or where she was going, but she had the certainty that someone was waiting for her.

Surprisingly, now that she knew where she was, she wasn't freaking out for being out of bed, thousands of miles away from home, in her white nightgown, standing on the powder-soft sand of one of the most beautiful beaches in the world.

She must have been in shock.

But no, it wasn't shock. She was calm because she felt safe. She was supposed to meet someone important. Here. Tonight.

The soft breeze made the palm trees sway, and blew Madi's long, wavy dark hair in front of her face. When she brushed it away, she saw a star, the brightest in the sky, peel away and fall, fall, fall in her direction.

Madi held her breath, bracing herself for the crash with her arms above her head. But the crash never came. Instead, an orb of incandescent light glowed in front of her and spoke. "What do you think, Lagartija?"

She knew that voice.

The bright light softened enough that Madi could open her eyes. Her curiosity and wonder at recognizing the figure in front of her vanquished any lingering fears she might still have.

"Abuela?" Laughing, she fell into her grandmother's arms.

Abuela smelled just like before she got sick. Of agua de Florida and freshly baked bread. The warmth of her arms was the same mushiest feeling from before the cancer and the treatments wreaked havoc on her body.

"Don't cry," Abuela Lina whispered, brushing Madi's hair. Her voice was the same too, resonant and confident.

"Is it really you? Or is this a dream?"

Abuela smiled. "And who said life isn't the universe's dream?"

Madi was used to Abuela's cryptic words, but now she wanted concrete answers.

Abuela seemed to sense this because she added, "What is real? What you can touch? Well, you're touching me. What you can see? You see me with your own eyes. What you can feel? Don't you still feel the love I have for you?"

Comforted, Madi nodded and hugged her grandma again. She never wanted to let go.

"I don't want to let go either," Abuela said as if she'd read her mind. "We're stepping outside of time because you had a question, and I'm here to answer it."

Madi's heart jumped to her throat. "Really, Abuela? When will I find—"

"Shh, mi Lagartija," she said, and chuckled. "Although you're not a little lizard anymore, right?"

"I got my period . . ."

"Don't get bashful! It's just a part of life! That means your body is healthy and growing."

If only the rest of the world thought growing up wasn't a big deal either!

"I miss you already, Abuela."

Abuela hugged her. "I know. Please, remember that even if you won't be able to see me, I'll be beside you all your life. And then we'll continue our adventures in the universe's next manifestation."

Abuela had some beliefs Madi didn't completely understand. To her, this talk of the dreaming universe and its manifestations sounded like the fairy tales her friends' mothers and grandmothers told. But the strangest, most magical belief Abuela had was that of soul mates and soul companions. Abuela believed that people were souls that reincarnated time after time to try new experiences. The gender, sexual orientation, and even species changed from life to life, but what remained was the love that united the souls in a group. Abuela had told Madi they'd been together in another life because they were soul companions. So were Nadia and Stevie, her sister-friends.

A soul mate was something more.

Abuela had met her soul mate early in her life. They parted when Abuelo Elio passed away after a car crash, but their love remained. Abuela Lina told Madi that Abuelo Elio sometimes visited in her dreams, which helped not to miss him so much.

Madi's mom had met her soul mate when she was the single mom of a rowdy toddler. Madi adored Santiago, her stepdad, with her whole heart. He was her father in every way that mattered, and she couldn't wait to legally have his last name, Ramírez instead of Paredes, her mom's maiden name.

Because of her mom's and Abuela's romantic stories, Madi had always longed for her own soul mate.

Abuela placed a hand on Madi's forehead. "Close your eyes. What you see will help you find him."

"Him?" Madi's eyes flew open. "It's a he, then?"

Smiling, Abuela brushed her hand on Madi's face and Madi closed her eyes.

"Remember, the future isn't predetermined. But even if the outcome of our lives is unpredictable, the actions we take or don't take every day make it *inevitable*. What you'll see are clues. Don't go chasing that love, Madi. It'll come to you when you least expect it because it is then that you will be ready. Remember, love is energy. It's what matters the most."

"More than school?"

Abuela laughed. "Don't ask impertinent questions! School is still the most important thing, for you, señorita! If you don't continue your studies, I'll come from whatever reincarnation I'm in and pull your legs!"

"You're so extra, Abuela!"

"Now, breathe, and see, nena."

Madi breathed as she was told. The ocean waves crashed softly until a soft hum, the hum of the universe, grew in power and volume. She felt the vibrations on her skin. She got scared.

"Abuela . . ."

"Shhh, I'm here. Let go."

Madi exhaled and surrendered herself to the sound waves.

She felt she was sliding down a kaleidoscope of colors and images. Among the millions of souls in the universe, she recognized two distinct soul essences, people.

She saw the same two time after time.

They looked so different in appearance, but in her heart Madi knew she was looking at the same two souls from different time periods, cultures, religions. Sometimes they were the same sex and gender, and sometimes not. And not only people! Sometimes the souls were birds of paradise, majestic cats, pudgy little dogs, beautiful pulsating stars in a galaxy far, far away. Two palm trees swayed underwater in a world with three pink moons. But the two beings she saw in all of them were always Madi and her soul mate.

Her vision switched to a screen as wide as the purple horizon, like the one in a drive-through theater. As if it were a movie, she saw a tall man walking toward her in the middle of a snowstorm, his hands pushed into his pockets. She couldn't distinguish the color of his hair because he was wearing a green beanie hat. Gold initials on his parka glinted under the feeble light of the street: JR.

A bright light shone behind him, and she couldn't see his features, but when he looked up and noticed her, an overwhelming love bloomed inside her heart and spread all over her body. The feeling was intense and unstoppable, a force that could fuel her forever. The sun was bursting within her. Even then, she knew she'd be chasing this feeling until she finally met him.

What was his name?

She opened her mouth to ask, this man who was her soul mate, who'd be looking for her the same way she'd be looking for him until they found each other. But when she tried to speak, a rushing wind blew and plucked her words from her lips. Everything around her dimmed.

Before the world vanished, Madi struggled to speak. She needed to tell him her name, and since no words came out, she sent him a thought: *I'm Madi! Madison Paredes!*

She understood her mistake too late. By the time she met him, she'd be Madison Ramírez.

She cupped her hands around her mouth and yelled, "Ramírez! That's my last name!"

He looked up and she saw only his eyes, brown and long lashed, surprised.

The infinite love in them knocked the remaining air out of her lungs.

They both blinked and the next second he was gone.

She gulped the air hungrily.

Dry, warm air from her childhood bedroom made her cough.

"No!" she yelled, throwing the bedcovers aside, and bolting up on her bed.

She ran to her mom.

Grains of sand stained her white sheets.

Chapter 2

Present day

"Listen, I've been patient, but I'm tired of waiting. I'm tired of your excuses, your— Lies! Yes, your lies. There, I said it."

As soon as the words were out of her mouth, Madi knew she'd made a mistake. Everything she'd said was true. She was tired of waiting, of unfulfilled promises, but the delivery was slightly off target. Well, no. Very much off target.

It wasn't the poor contractor's fault that she was so stressed. At least, not only his fault.

True, the salt cave of Grounded Yoga wasn't ready yet, as he'd promised and in turn she'd promised her boss. But her problems went beyond the constant delays.

Today she was mad at the world, the universe, her long-gone grandma, but most of all, herself. Although a little voice told her that the person she was actually frustrated with was Jayden, her boyfriend.

No one took Madi seriously and the contractor's condescending tone of voice was the last straw.

A prickling sensation ran down her spine, and no, it wasn't a bolt of energy from the kundalini awakening she'd been chasing for years. It was that uncomfortable feeling of someone's presence behind her.

Madi didn't even register the chipmunk-sounding voice squeaking more excuses from the phone's receiver. Chest heaving, she turned around, and came face-to-face with her boss, Reyna Steele.

Reyna was peace, awareness, and transcendence personified. But true to her name, she was tough like a queen. A super businesswoman who owned the fastest-growing wellness studio in northern Utah Valley.

In their ultra-conservative community, the concept of a yoga center with a spiritual practice had seemed like a misguided business idea. That is, until Reyna added a full-service spa and offered retreats in exotic locations. Soon, clients started flocking, packing the classes, and filling waiting lists that extended into the next couple of years.

Come for the fun, stay for the health and spiritual benefits.

Reyna tapped her sandaled foot on the floor.

"I'm sorry, sir. I'll have to call you later. Bye," Madi said to the contractor on the phone, and hung up.

Madi waited for a telling-off of some kind. She had it coming, but instead, Reyna walked up to her and hugged her.

The gesture took Madi with such surprise that she melted in the embrace of her mentor and boss. With her parents moving to Seattle because of Santiago's job transfer, it had been a long time since someone had hugged her like this. A hug that said, *I got you. Everything will be all right.*

Jayden was kind but had the emotional wavelength of an amoeba.

"I'm sorry about the outburst, Reyna," Madi said, sniffling, breathing in the scent of lavender essential oil that enveloped the older woman. "Everything's a mess. I'm the most ungrounded person in the universe."

"Not the most. One of them, perhaps." Reyna patted her shoulder and said, "Tell me."

Someone opened the door, and Madi sucked her tears back in, turned to the newcomer, and beamed a smile. "Welcome to Grounded Yoga!"

The man didn't even look at her and headed to the massage room at the end of the hallway.

Too bad rudeness couldn't be kneaded away like a stubborn knot on the shoulder on the massage table. On cue, Madi's shoulder throbbed. She rolled it, trying to be as inconspicuous as possible.

Reyna clicked her tongue. "It still bothers you?"

Madi sighed. "All the time."

Reyna rubbed her hands and placed them on the front and back of Madi's shoulder. A warmth spread like a wave. But Madi knew the relief was only temporary.

"You're holding on to some emotional trauma and your liver, which resonates all the way to your upper back and neck, is clamoring for you to let it out," Reyna said, turning Madi to look into her eyes.

Madi blushed at the examination and had to look down at the floor. "It's just that . . ."

"Jayden?" Reyna asked.

"Everything, Reyna. I mean . . ." She twisted her fingers as if the gesture would help her untwist her confusion. "He told me he's *thinking* of proposing."

Reyna's face lit up. Underneath the granite persona, she was a sucker for romantic stories and happily-ever-afters.

"He did?" Reyna exclaimed, clapping. "That's what you've wanted for a long time, love. Isn't it? He's finally putting a ring on that finger!"

Madi wore a ring on each finger but the one that mattered the most. She'd been fanatical about saving it for marriage like she hadn't been with other parts of her body. She splayed her left-hand fingers in front of her face and tried to visualize the perfect ring, but the image eluded her. She sighed, making her shoulders and face fall dramatically.

"What is it?" Reyna insisted.

"He probably won't propose for a couple of months though. He'll be gone for his crypto business all summer, pretty much. He said he'd rather wait until he's back from his trips so he can put something special together. Which you know what it means. He'll hire someone to plan it for him."

"He'll be gone for two months? Where the hell is he going for business? Jupiter?"

Madi smiled at the joke. "I don't know!"

There was a brief silence, and then Reyna, ever the voice of reason, said, "He is growing his business. A start-up isn't a joke. And his strong work ethic was what attracted you to him the most at the beginning."

She *had* been attracted to his strong work ethic.

"But he said he'll do it when he's done traveling, right? You waited this long for the love of your lives, what's a couple more months?"

"The traveling will never end! And he already warned me that the wedding might be *smallish*."

"Why?" Reyna's eyes were wide like galaxies. Through the years of friendship, she'd learned that one of Madi's love languages was celebrating, throwing-the-house-out-the-window kind of parties.

"He said it has to be within the fiscal year to take advantage of tax write-offs, or whatever, so there's no time to plan a big thing."

"Oh, Madi!" Reyna exclaimed, patting her hand. "Tax write-offs?"

Madi clicked her tongue. "Now that I hear myself saying this aloud, it doesn't sound romantic at all."

"Everything doesn't have to be romantic to be perfect or

right, and vice versa. When you met him, you didn't think he was super romantic, but here you are."

"Here I am . . ." Madi huffed the hair out of her face.

Reyna shrugged. "With your soul mate, right?"

Soul mate . . .

She'd been obsessed with the concept of meeting the love of her lives, her soul mate, for as long as she could remember, especially after that dream, that vision, she'd had the night Abuela had died.

When she met Jayden at the ski resort last year, she had thought that search was over. She'd kissed so many frogs (all with the initials JR), but finally she'd met her prince!

That day, her friend Stevie had pretty much forced her to come along, claiming that no person born and raised in Utah could go throughout their lives without ever setting foot at the top of a ski lift. They had, after all, the "best snow on earth."

Stevie, along with Nadia, were Madi's soul sisters. Nadia was a lawyer whose double-quinceañera was the event of the season two years ago. During that fateful, snowy weekend, she and her fiancé, Marcos, were in Australia visiting family, and that's why Stevie had roped Madi into going along.

Stevie was a daredevil adventuress who put Indiana Jones and Lara Croft to shame. She never took no for an answer, and besides, Madi had nothing else to do and had wanted to spend time with her friend.

Madi had caved, but she'd complained the whole time. Unsurprisingly, everything went wrong. The ski rental place didn't have her sizes. The boots were so tight they cut the circulation to her legs. She couldn't even slide down the bunny slopes alongside three-year-olds and not an hour had gone by when her face became so numb with cold, she couldn't even fake smile.

"Come on, Madi! At least you can try to enjoy it!"

"I'm trying but staying unfrozen is taking all my concentration and effort," she said, sniffing because she was so cold.

"Wait for me here," Stevie told her, not hiding her frustration. "I'll run down that black diamond and then we'll go home if you're so miserable." She'd left before Madi could stop her.

Madi had waited, embarrassed tears frozen on her face. She felt guilty for ruining her friend's day. She decided to try one more time and headed to the lifts.

Maybe it had been the bad vibes still clinging to her, but when she was ready to get off the gondola, one of her skis fell. She hadn't known *that* could happen. What was she going to tell the rental place? What if she lost the other one? She never intended to go skiing ever again, and she didn't want to pay full price for a set, or a half.

What if the other one fell on someone's head? The thought made her nauseous.

With all the powers of her mind, she tried to hold on to her remaining ski while she held on to one of the handles with her gloved hands. Looking down at the abandoned sky, she got dizzy.

She scuttled back. What if *she* fell?

Terrified, she looked in all directions as if hoping a spirit guide would pop out from the arctic clouds enveloping the mountain and help her out of this nightmarish situation.

Instead, a voice, a man's voice, told her from the gondola behind her, "Get off on this one stop! The next one is a black diamond, and you can't go down on one ski!"

She couldn't ski down a black diamond at all. Not if she wanted to live to tell the tale.

Frazzled, she'd jumped off the lift before she could think about it. With all her might, she had tried to balance on the foot that still had a ski attached.

"Watch out!" the man exclaimed, taking her out of her thrilled focus.

Before she crashed against the tree coming at her with surprising speed, her survival instinct took over, and she plopped to her side. Her shoulder throbbed.

The man skied down to where she lay, humiliated, imagining how pathetic she must look. But at least she was alive.

"Are you okay?" he asked.

She looked up to mumble a thank-you and send him on his way, but at the sight of him, she went breathless. He was tall and had a smile brighter than the snow surrounding them. He wore a beanie and a black parka with the initials JR on top of his heart.

"You," she'd said with a sigh. She was acting like an airhead, but who could blame her? This had to be a sign that she had finally found "him," the one, the love of her lives, after years of dating jerks with the right initials but totally wrong personalities.

His name was Jayden and he was a true gentleman, like, in every sense of the word. His tone of voice was gentle and kind. He even went back to retrieve her lost ski, and then seeing how her shoulder was injured, he refused to leave her alone.

In typical Madi fashion, she clung to him immediately. And he clung back. By the time Stevie found Madi, she and Jayden were snuggling by the fire of the ski resort like they'd known each other forever.

But the next day, when they went on their first date . . . the spark had kind of dulled.

Their kisses, including the first one, had never really inspired any kind of replays that would make the area of her root chakra ripple with pleasure.

Where was the consuming passion the romance paperbacks that she loved promised?

But what did it matter after all?

He was handsome. He was kind and attentive. He was driven. And he liked her and he seemed to like no other people.

After a few weeks, he had said the actual L word. Even though he wasn't affectionate, she knew he loved her. In his own particular way.

When he'd started talking about proposing, she was thrilled. She really was. But a voice, annoying like a weather warning announcing an incoming disaster, told her she was making a mistake.

She told the voice to shut up.

That hesitation, that heartbeat of a pause when she decided not to listen to her gut, kept her up at night. If he had just done it, she'd said yes. But waiting for two months or more to make things official? A part of her told her they might as well walk their separate ways.

But if she did, what would she claim were her main reasons for breaking up with him? That he never inspired that world-stopping feeling she'd experienced once, at thirteen, and during a dream, at that? That Jayden wasn't super passionate? He was head over heels for her. He never gave her reasons to be jealous. He had two modes: work and Madi.

Was she going to be jealous of work? In the past, she'd dumped boyfriends for not being driven enough, for not having ambitions. Who could understand her?

She wasn't perfect either, after all.

Jayden always complained she was too dramatic, too loud, too much of everything. He always said it as a joke, but would a real soul mate even joke about those things? Would *she* be having second thoughts if he were really the love of her lives?

She was so confused.

"Don't mind me, Reyna." Madi sighed. "I don't know what's wrong with me. Maybe something's in retrograde?"

Reyna shook her head. "You're in retrograde. And it's only natural! But you just barely turned thirty-one, and—"

Madi made a disgusted expression. "Ay! Don't remind me of that!"

"What are you so afraid of growing old? I'm forty-seven, and I feel better than ever. Before you interrupted me, I was going to say that you're still a baby."

Reyna had three kids, and looked her age, but in such a radiant way that she outshone people of all ages, even younger—people like Madi.

"What you need is a vacation."

"I can't take a vacation. The studio needs me," Madi said with an urgency in her voice that took her by surprise.

"Well . . ." Reyna paused, choosing her words carefully. "The studio doesn't need you all frazzled and struggling, love. Remember, Jayden will be gone too. Maybe you need distance and time to put your struggles with him in perspective."

There was an awkward silence.

"*I* need the studio though."

"And the studio needs you too, just in another capacity."

"What are you saying?" She paused, seeing the conflicted expression on Reyna's face.

Reyna didn't reply right away. Instead, she walked around the front desk and stood in front of the electric kettle on the counter. She poured herself some tea in a cup, and looked at Madi, who nodded. Reyna poured her a cup and handed it to her.

Reyna blew on the tea. The soothing scent of lavender chamomile blend reached Madi, but it wasn't powerful enough to melt her tension.

"Actually, this whole thing with the salt cave not being finished yet is getting to me too."

"Sorry," Madi said. "I promised you it'd be ready in the fall, and now . . . I'm not so sure we'll get it in time for winter."

Reyna sipped from her tea, and then said, "I always believe things happen—or don't happen—for a reason. And there's obviously a block of some kind with the cave."

Madi's mouth went dry, but she forced herself to say, "Reyna, if you want me to present my two-weeks' notice . . ."

"¡Mujer! Don't take it like that!"

Madi could've cried from relief, and then Reyna added, "I do think you should leave, though."

It was as if someone had pulled the rug from under Madi's

feet. She'd heard the expression multiple times in her life but had never understood the meaning until this moment. She tried to remain balanced on the tall stool on which she sat, but she was light-headed. If it hadn't been for Reyna's lightning-fast reflexes, Madi would've ended up on the floor with more than a hurt shoulder.

Reyna fanned Madi's face and said, "Whoa! I underestimated how frazzled and not like yourself you really are. I'm sorry for scaring you."

Madi took a sip of her steaming tea so quickly, she scalded all the soft tissues from her mouth all the way to her stomach. "You *are* firing me! How else am I going to take it?"

Reyna stared at her, and when she had Madi's attention, she rolled her eyes. "Seriously? Why would I fire you?"

Madi's chin started quivering, as if she were thirteen years old.

Reyna patted her cheek. "You're an excellent instructor. Everyone wants to take a class with you. The clients tell me their lives take new meaning after meeting you. Everyone is thriving. Everyone but you. And so, I had an idea."

"I'm all ears," Madi said, sipping some tea to settle into Reyna's words. She was a sucker for compliments.

"The retreat in Bali is a no-go."

"I'm sorry," Madi said.

The retreat in Bali had consumed Reyna for months, but she hadn't found a venue she liked because of ethical reasons like the use of elephants for entertainment, shady employment of underage "massage therapists," and security concerns.

"But here's what we're going to do instead."

The "we" grounded Madi better than the tea.

"What about Puerto Rico?" Reyna asked.

The effect was immediate.

Madi felt like she could finally take a full breath she didn't know she'd been struggling to inhale. The sight of an endless white-sanded beach almost made her groan with longing.

"What about Puerto Rico?" Madi's voice was raspy with a mixture of excitement and anxiety.

Reyna had a cryptic expression on her face. "I was going to wait for Audri to get here and tell you herself, but I feel this is the right time."

Audri was Reyna's ex-girlfriend. Madi's roommate and friend. She was Reyna's business partner and taught hot yoga at the studio.

"She's had a secret? Is that why she's been acting so weird lately?" Madi asked, thinking of Audri's awkward silences and stares.

Reyna laughed. "I asked her not to spill, and I'm proud she hasn't. But a couple of weeks ago I told her my plans . . . What if you two went to Puerto Rico, and checked out a couple of locations for our retreat?"

Madi's eyes filled with tears. She hadn't been to Puerto Rico, where her grandma had been born, since she was eleven. Her dream at thirteen didn't count.

"I've been talking with a few places, which look great online. But a set of eyes there would be fantastic. The universe is sending us the message that the salt cave is a no-go. For now. Why do we keep ramming against a wall? Besides, you need some time to get things clear in your head and in your heart. I can't travel now, and you still need to go to keep your promise to your grandma."

Abuela's only request had been for part of her ashes to be sprinkled in the Utah mountains *and* the island that she loved. For one reason or another, neither Madi nor her mom had been able to fill this last part of her request. Now this was her chance.

"Unless you're saving Puerto Rico for your honeymoon . . . ?"

"Jayden's allergic to humidity and heat," Madi said, waving a hand in front of her face. When she caught Reyna's eyes, she burst out laughing. Then, she added, "Besides, I'm not the best business-minded person to do this, Reyna . . ."

"You are, Madi," Reyna replied. "You have to stop putting yourself down."

Right then, the main studio door opened, and smiling, flushed-faced people started streaming out. Audri, a statuesque Black woman with long twisted braids, came out of the class-room last, a satisfied smile on her face.

"Oh, you look like a cat that ate the cream!" Madi said.

Reyna and Audri looked at each other and snickered.

"Madi! You're so innocent, mama!" Reyna said, wiping the sweat off her forehead with the back of her flowy white shirt.

Madi didn't know what she'd said, but she loved to make other people laugh.

"You told her?" Audri asked Reyna, who added, "Well, not all of it."

Madi's cheeks flushed. "What else were you going to say?"

"Be our partner," Audri said without preamble. "You're the Puerto Rico expert."

"Me? A partner like, an owner in the studio?"

"Of course," said Reyna. "Why not?"

Why not indeed? Madi had thought about buying into the studio for a couple of years, but never had the guts to actually do it. This was her chance to prove that she was capable of be-ing successful.

"So?" Audri said, bumping Madi with her butt. "What do you think?"

"I love the idea, but . . . what's Jayden going to say?" Madi asked, biting her lip.

Madi knew what he'd say, that she wasn't really a business-woman, that her view of things was always rose-colored be-cause she was such an optimist.

Once again, Audri and Reyna exchanged a look. Madi never knew if the fact that they'd been lovers had connected them in a way that she would never share. She'd never experienced the level of intimacy with any of the men she'd ever dated or slept with. She craved that, the exchange of looks, the inside jokes, the mind reading . . .

Was she asking for the impossible?

But no, her mom and her stepdad shared that too. She wanted that. But she and Jayden weren't really in the same bandwidth, although she had tried to adjust her vibes to him.

"What does your gut tell you?" Reyna asked. "Remember, if you make a decision after nine seconds, then the head takes over and you start rationalizing."

"Puerto Rico for a week, scoping the island for retreat spots?" She scratched her head. "It's tempting. So tempting!"

Madi closed her eyes. Her gut told her to take this chance and run. But wasn't that her lizard brain speaking?

You're a lagartija after all, she heard Abuela's voice so clearly, her eyes prickled with emotion.

"I think I need to go," she whispered.

"And who knows?" Audri asked, draping an arm over Madi's shoulder. "By the time you come back, you may have confirmation that Jayden *is* your soul mate after all, that you can't live without him. Or, you may finally see that he's not . . ." She wiggled her eyebrows like a dork and stuck her tongue out.

"There's no *or*," Madi said, shrugging off the embrace. "I'm going to celebrate the end of my life as a single woman, and by the time I come back, I'll be ready to become Mrs. Randall."

This time, Reyna and Audri didn't look at each other, but they didn't need to for Madi to catch the negative vibes of their opinion.

She shrugged them off.

All she needed for her relationship with Jayden to bubble and erupt like the volcano of passion she'd always expected was a little time apart from each other, like Reyna had said. Becoming a successful businesswoman would for sure make him see an aspect of her he'd always underestimated. And it would help her self-esteem for sure too.

The distance would help Jayden liberate the love he surely felt for Madi. And it would be great to clear her head of the annoy-ing doubts that kept pestering her.

It was a perfect plan.

Once she came back from Puerto Rico, her eternal love story with Jayden would make everyone jealous. She just knew it.

Chapter 3

Later that day, Madi's watch beeped and startled her so hard she almost fell off her chair.

High heart rate. Take deep breaths or go to the nearest emergency room, flashed on the tiny screen.

"What?" she asked aloud, but no one replied, thank goodness since she was the only one at home. She tapped the notification, and once again, her watch beeped. At the exact same time her doorbell rang.

It must be Jayden.

Her heart rate skyrocketed again.

"Breathe, Madi," she told herself. "It's only dinner with Jay-Jay. What are you so nervous about?"

They were going to dinner to Cancún Querido, her favorite place. Even though it was just a hole in the wall, she felt at home there. She was excited for Puerto Rico and her new role at the studio, but also, she secretly hoped that he'd fall on one knee and propose tonight.

If he did, then she could go to Puerto Rico another time, and she wouldn't be so scared to make a mess of Grounded Yoga.

Everyone's future depended on Jayden reading her mind. No pressure.

Maybe he would snap out of his obsessive need to plan out his life down to the minute and invite her to go on his trip. Or she would invite him to go to Puerto Rico to scout locations.

She shivered and not only for nerves. The apartment's temperature was gelid, but that's how Jayden liked it and she wanted to make sure he was comfy tonight.

"Coming!" she said brightly when the bell rang again.

Because she shared the apartment with Audri, Jayden never just walked in. She was grateful for the few seconds to collect herself.

She fixed a dazzling smile on her face and opened the door dramatically.

"Hey, love," she said airily.

For a moment, he didn't say anything. Then, his green eyes widened, and the blood drained from his face. His Adam's apple bobbed up and down, and then he cleared his throat.

"Wow."

The mixed effect of a good halter sundress and matching shining smile was infallible even after more than a year together.

She laughed and fell into his arms. "I've missed you!" she exclaimed although they'd seen each other just a couple of days ago.

His soft chuckle rumbled in his chest against her ear, and he hugged her back with one arm. In the other, he held a plastic bag.

The scent coming from it made Madi's stomach rumble embarrassingly.

"I guess I did well in switching up the plan," he said, softly extricating himself from her arms. He didn't like showing affection in public other than holding hands and a chaste peck on the lips—for special occasions like during Fourth of July fireworks. Not on the landing of her apartment where the teenage neighbors sat, pretending not to gawk at them.

"What do you mean change of plans?" Madi asked, winking at the girls and then turning back to Jayden. "You brought food?"

She had spent a lot of time getting ready, anticipating a proposal. But this detour could only be a sign of good things to come.

After he asked the most important question anyone would ever ask her, and she said yes, then they could come out and ask Sadie and Carmen to take a couple of pictures to document the occasion. The Wasatch mountains across from them were the perfect backdrop, even if they were hazy with smoke from the wildfires. Still, she'd have a chance to geek out with the neighbor girls who thought Madi's life was so perfect and romantic.

For all his talk about investments, Jayden wasn't very taken by the neighbors' interest in their relationship, though.

He glanced at the girls briefly but didn't even say hi.

He turned to Madi. "The food's getting cold. Let's go inside."

Madi's cheeks reddened at how rude he sounded to the girls, who always complained that Jayden was so intimidating. To make up for his behavior, Madi smiled at them, and once Jayden had stepped in, she whispered, "I'm sure he's going to propose tonight!"

The girls' faces lit up like Christmas trees as they did jazz hands.

"Oh. Em. Gee, Mads!" Carmen said. She lived next door.

"Tell us *all* about it later," Sadie added with a mischievous glint in her eye that made Madi blush. Sadie lived upstairs. "I mean, *all*."

"Sadie!" Carmen playfully slapped her arm.

Sadie made a show of rubbing her arm, but she was full-on laughing now. "I'm eighteen! It's not like—"

"No," Madi said, putting a hand up to stop any words that might be coming out of her neighbor's mouth. "You *just* turned eighteen, but in my eyes, you're both babies. Stop!" She laughed, and then bit her lower lip with excitement. "Okay! I need to go. See you later!"

"Be good!" Carmen said.

"And if you can't be good, be careful!" added Sadie, and then they laughed like the kids they were.

Madi was smiling so hard her cheeks hurt when she closed the door and stood with her back to it to collect herself.

In the kitchen, Jayden was plating their meals. She noticed he hadn't taken his shoes off at the entrance, although there was a polite sign that Madi had painted herself.

But he looked so handsome with his perfectly pressed charcoal shirt and dark European tailored pants, that she didn't have the heart to remind him for the millionth time to remove his shoes. Besides, she didn't want to ruin the aesthetic. Every one of his movements was precise and measured. Feeling her eyes on him, he looked up and a corner of his mouth twitched. For Jayden, that was like a full-on grin.

"Let me help," she said, running on tiptoes to grab one of the plates where he'd carefully arranged a sweet pork enchilada. She was so short next to him, that without the couple of inches the high heels placed at the door provided her, she felt like a hobbit.

He shook his head. "Get the drinks," he said, pointing to the fridge with his puckered lips.

Madi smiled at his gesture. Spending so much time with Madi and her family, he'd caught a few mannerisms. She grabbed two bottles of a local beer he liked and joined him at the table, where he was waiting to push her chair in.

"Wow!" she said in a playful voice she hoped was seductive and not mocking. "Is this a special occasion?"

"It's always special with you. But even more so tonight." He sat across the table from her and placed a paper napkin on his lap. Noticing that Madi was frozen, he added, "Eat. Don't let it get cold. Or colder, I should say."

Madi's stomach was twisted in knots of nerves. She had been hungry, but if he was going to pop the question, she didn't want to get bad breath. But what if Jayden had hidden the ring in the food, and his plan of making her dreams come true fell apart because she refused to eat?

She grabbed the fork, and they ate in silence. At first, Madi chewed each bite carefully, but then, she stopped. Something didn't seem right.

For one thing, Jayden ate while scrolling through his crypto apps on his phone. If he had hid the ring in the food, wouldn't he be watching her expression for when she got the surprise?

And second, she was halfway done with the meal she'd eaten mindlessly and now her mouth was on fire. The sauce was way spicier than usual.

Trying not to butcher her enchilada, she poked the rest of it, hoping to find the treasure buried under the tortilla and the most delicious salsa verde in the world.

Jayden chuckled, and when she looked up, she was so disappointed that he was still hypnotized by his phone that she clicked her tongue.

"What? Everything okay?" he said when he finally looked up at her, his green eyes warm with worry. She didn't know how he did it, but every time he looked at her this way, her insides melted, and she forgot she was even mad at him.

But today there was a difference.

Her insides melted all right, but she didn't forget that she was hoping for *more* tonight. That he didn't seem to realize that so much hung in the balance. A small move, and this dinner would be the rolling stone that sent the last months of bliss into history. Or it could be the one that sent them into a happy eternity together.

He saw her plate then and chuckled again. "You were hungry, huh?" Placing his hand on hers, he said, "I'm sorry I was on the phone. I had to finalize a deal. And when I glanced up, you were busy eating. You seemed so hungry I didn't want to interrupt. Look. You almost finished your food."

She looked at him with an attention she hadn't allowed herself since she first met him.

That time on the slopes, once she made sure he wasn't married or in a relationship with someone else, and that he seemed like a decent human being and not a perv pretending to be one, she'd found out his birthday, birth time, and location. She'd wasted no time in looking up his zodiac signs. When things got more serious, she crafted his natal chart and compared it to hers. At first, the journey that the stars had sketched for him looked simple and straightforward, like him. But in its simple lines, there was a complexity that complemented her chart. She'd loved that about him. Their journeys intersected in the perfect place. They had been meant to meet and change each other's life.

Jayden picked up the last morsel on her plate and swallowed it. "Delicious."

She watched him to make sure he wouldn't choke. Maybe he'd pretend he had bit something hard and then take out the ring from his mouth? It wasn't really that romantic, but it would be a surprising turn of events.

But he didn't. He swallowed, drank his beer, and watched her.

Madi sighed, all the pent-up anxiety boiling inside her body.

"What, babe?" he asked, stroking her hand with his thumb.

"Jayden . . . Reyna needs me to go to Puerto Rico for her," she said, surprised at how her words had swerved at the last second and how composed her voice sounded.

"When?" he said, sipping from his beer.

"Next week," she said. "When you leave for your trips."

The silence between them felt heavy with so many unsaid things. Her yearning for a grand gesture took up most of the space. She'd settle even for a small gesture at this point.

What she wasn't expecting was having to settle for what he said next.

"Oof, that's wonderful timing."

Madi wasn't sure if he was being sarcastic or not. "Why is it good timing?"

"Well, with you busy on your job, if that's what we keep calling teaching yoga." He scoffed and she pulled her hand from his.

He made snide remarks about her yoga teaching all the time, saying Reyna's business model was flawed because it was so ambitious, which was code for impossible. But were they having this conversation right now?

"If you wanted to invest your money, I've told you a thousand times, crypto is the way to go," he said.

Madi recoiled at the suggestion. It wasn't the first time he made it. She had a little money stashed away that she'd saved over the years. She wanted to invest it in something that was hers, something yoga-related, perhaps. Maybe become partner in the studio, that is, if the trip to Puerto Rico worked out and she didn't make a mess of things.

"You know you don't have a good head for numbers, babe. Do your yoga, I can help you invest."

There was a pause and then she got the courage to say, "Maybe I can invest in the studio . . ."

He rolled his eyes and ignored her words. "Actually, let's talk about something important. Since you'll be gone . . ." He took her hand again. She was either unusually cold or his skin seemed scorching. Was he nervous?

She held her breath, hoping to remember this moment for the rest of her life.

When later she looked back on this conversation as she replayed it a million times in her mind, she guessed her body had known before her mind had even suspected what he would say next. But her heart? Her heart was oblivious.

"What, JayJay?" she asked with a thin voice.

"Don't look so nervous, babe. But . . . I've been thinking

that . . . Okay, I'll say it: Since you'll be gone and I'll be gone too, it's better if we take a break this summer."

If this were a movie, there would be a record scratch in this exact second. But it wasn't. The scratch sound must have been the U-turn Madi's soul did coming back to her body to hold her before she fell to pieces.

"A break?"

"Yes, a break. Proposing now is out of the question. There's no time to plan the kind of production you've been dreaming about your whole life. And the next couple of months I'll be consumed with work. I don't want to have to worry about calling you, or checking in, or— You get what I mean, right? And you'll be busy with this little endeavor."

Madi snatched her hand away. "You're breaking up with me."

He'd said he'd been thinking about it; what he meant was that he'd already decided. She'd tackle the problematic comments about her job later.

"Don't look at it like a 'breakup,'" he said, sounding like a person trying to calm down a dangerous creature. "It's not like I'm doing this to date other people without feeling guilty for cheating, or even—"

"What is it then, Jayden?" she asked. She must have looked serious because the little color he had drained from his face. He'd never seen this serious side of Madi before, and now he realized he'd made a mistake.

"I thought this would be the best course of action."

"The best for whom? You're breaking up so you don't have to worry about me? So you don't have to put up with me calling you or dropping by to surprise you wherever in the world you may be?"

Unexpectedly, he blushed.

"Is that really what you thought? That pressing pause on our relationship now would free you up for work? That you can then come back when it's convenient for you and resume, get engaged, and continue as if nothing happened? What's going to happen when you have to travel for work again and we're already engaged, or, heaven forbid, married? We're going to break up or get divorced so you don't have to waste emotional energy on me?"

His silence was answer enough.

Madi's mind boomed with the echoes of her words.

"Do you even love me?" she asked.

"Of course I do," he said, but his reply sounded hollow.

She wished she could look inside his heart and mind and get a clear answer.

"So why not propose now? I can respect your boundaries, you know? If you don't want me to call you every day, I won't. I won't even surprise you with a visit. But 'take a break' and live our separate lives and then in two months pretend we can pick up right where we left off? Love doesn't work that way, Jayden."

She was romantic, spontaneous, and naïve sometimes. But she wasn't clueless. She loved and respected boundaries, and by the way the evening had gone, she realized that their relationship had never been what she thought it was. It wasn't what Jayden thought either.

"You can't pause love, Jayden," she said, pushing her plate from her as if she were pushing him. "You can't stop it or erase it when it's not convenient. I would've been happy with a ring pop, you know? I'm sorry I gave you the idea that I needed a big production to be happy. All I wanted was you. I would've been happy with *you*."

Jayden's eyes were shiny, and the vein in his forehead throbbed. If she fell into his arms, she would feel his heart trying to break out of his chest.

Just like hers.

If he couldn't find the courage to follow his heart, then she'd have to show him the way, and hope that he would then follow her.

Carefully, she rose to her feet, her hand still in his, and then she knelt in front of him. She hoped that one day in the future, they would laugh and laugh about this, but for now, she was serious so he knew she meant every one of her words when she said, "Jayden, will you marry me?"

To hell with tradition and expectation. Why had she waited for him when she had every right and opportunity to take charge and propose to him?

She gazed up adoringly into his green eyes.

His lips parted. He was going to say, *Yes, yes! A million times yes!*

But then, he closed his eyes, as if he wanted to block her.

"Madi . . . I . . . I'm not ready to commit yet."

"You're not ready?"

"Not now. Not today. I made the decision to take a break and resume when I come back from the summer, love. I don't want to go back on that."

Who knows how long she knelt in front of him, looking at him, hoping that when he opened his eyes there would be a mischievous spark that would reveal he'd been joking with her the whole time? But it wasn't a joke, of course.

Jayden didn't joke.

She stood up, feeling so small beside him.

"The answer's no, then?"

"For now, Mads," he said.

"Don't call me that," she said, the fury finally rising in her.

"Madison," he said, standing up too and trying to hug her. "You're taking it the wrong way—"

"You made it very clear I'm not your love, Jayden," she said, walking to the door.

Jayden scoffed. "What? You're kicking me out? I thought we could—"

"What, Jayden? You thought we could fool around as a last hurrah?"

"Why are you so crass, babe?" he said, sounding disgusted. He grabbed his jacket from the sofa, swung it over his shoulder, and walked to the door.

Every cell of Madi's body clamored for her to take back everything she had said. Go along with his plan even if every part of her recoiled from it. But what if living with the love of your lives meant always hiding part of who you really are? If she had to be someone she wasn't to keep the peace, was Jayden really the one?

She stepped out of his way, and he opened the door.

"Call me when your thoughts cool enough for you to act like an adult, Madison," he said.

Outside, a shower of confetti, an explosion of firecrackers, and party horns waited for them.

Sadie's eyes widened when she saw Madi's expression. She tapped Carmen on the shoulder, and they jumped out of Jayden's way.

"What happened?" Sadie asked, perplexed.

The three of them watched as Jayden raced downstairs, got in his car, and left the parking lot. He never once looked back.

For all she knew, he'd already gotten over her, so cold and calculating he was. He might even be relieved.

When his car turned toward the freeway, Sadie and Carmen asked in unison, "What happened?"

Madi looked at the girls and said, "We broke up."

The girls exchanged a look that made Madi long for her own besties with all her heart. She needed an intervention. If there was one thing she had learned in this life, it was that help was only a few clicks away.

She fished her phone from her dress pocket and texted a bat signal to her soul sisters.

Chapter 4

Madi was an expert in giving out advice on love and life, but applying it was a different matter. None of it seemed to work for her.

Good thing she was surrounded by friends who kept reminding her that she was worth being loved how she wanted to be loved. Nadia and Stevie called and texted memes and TikToks constantly to remind her not to run to Jayden. Sadie and Carmen brought her cookies and her favorite drinks from the soda shop where they worked. Reyna and Audri were more determined than ever to help Madi succeed in her career, and of course, she didn't want to let them down.

She even had a dream of Abuela Lina shredding Madi's phone so she wouldn't cave and call Jayden back.

Still, she second-guessed her decision all the way to the following week when she was leaving for Puerto Rico.

Although she knew better than to hope for impossible things, Madi gazed toward the airport exit and sighed. Obviously, Jayden wasn't coming to take her back or even say goodbye. His flight was in the evening, and he wasn't going to make the hour drive to the airport twice. But, truth be told, if Jayden pulled a romantic move and came running to her with a bouquet of flowers, she'd elope to Las Vegas with him without hesitation.

"If we don't go through security now, we're going to miss the flight. If that happens, I swear to the Goddess, Madi, I'll kill you," Audri said through gritted teeth.

Madi doubted her friend would actually follow through with her threat, but something in Audri's tone or murderous expression told her she didn't want to test her. But even if the threat held a pinch of truth, it didn't hurt as much as the sense of disappointment and betrayal weighing down her stomach all the way to her toe chakras.

"I thought he'd at least try to fix things," Madi said, getting on the TSA line to go through security.

A drug-detecting dog sniffed past her, and although she didn't carry any drugs—her essential oils kit didn't count as such—she always flinched. She'd called the airline to make sure that the urn with her grandma's ashes was okay to bring along, but she was still nervous.

Maybe because she was attracting the attention with her anxiety, the dog handler eyed her suspiciously.

"Hey," Madi said with a nervous giggle, waving at the officer.

"Stop it," Audri whispered, and gently elbowed her before they got in trouble for looking suspicious. Pale as she was, Madi could pass as white. But Audri, with her luminous dark skin and coily braids piled on top of her head, was anything but inconspicuous.

Madi placed her treasured Louis Vuitton weekender on the X-ray belt and went through the metal detector. The light blinked red and an alarm went off.

"You've been selected for a random check," the TSA officer said, sounding bored.

"Of course," Madi said, and submitted to the indignity of

getting extra patting on her legs. Seeing as she was only wearing leggings and a tunic shirt, she said, "I must have Wolverine legs or something."

The TSA woman didn't even smile. "You can go," she replied.

Next to her, Audri was getting *randomly checked* too. Lucky that they both got the random check lottery. What were the odds? Madi's mind tried to come up with the number but got distracted with how thorough the patting on Audri was.

The officer was checking her braids. Madi could see that the Zen attitude that was Audri's trademark state was about to vanish soon. And if her friend lost it and snapped at the agent, they'd be delayed even more, and they would miss their flight.

All because of her.

When the tension was reaching a solid level of discomfort, the TSA officer said, "Off you go." She sounded a little disappointed there was nothing for her to complain about.

Madi held Audri by her elbow and got them away from the line so fast she almost forgot her purse and weekender. Audri's things were waiting at the end of the belt.

Frazzled, like they'd been through a war zone and not the airport security line, Audri and Madi headed to the Starbucks counter without consulting each other. They hadn't even left Salt Lake City yet and they were already emotionally exhausted.

"One thing I wish the mind could do was teleport us. I hate this shit," Audri said.

"You can say that again," Madi replied.

"I hate this shit," Audri said louder and a young mom with a toddler in a stroller sent them a pointed look that made Madi laugh.

"Ladies and gentlemen, we're boarding flight TL93 with destination to Orlando . . ."

"That's us!" Audri exclaimed, grabbing Madi's hand.

The barista handed them their chai lattes and they headed to the gate. Madi's heart pounded hard against her chest, and she inhaled deeply to slow it down. Ever since the episode with

Jayden, her heart rate had been scarily high. None of her calming techniques worked but she had to keep trying if she didn't want to have a heart attack.

For the first time in days, though, she was excited. Excited to get away. Excited to be in Puerto Rico. Going back to one of her family's ancestral lands might be just what she needed to ground herself again. To recover from the sting of rejection. To screw her head back on so she'd start thinking instead of following her foolish, romantic heart.

Electricity tingled all the way from her feet to the crown of her head as she checked the boarding pass on her phone, and she scanned it. The machine beeped.

"Have a good flight," the airline guy said. He was short but had a sweet boyish face, and amazing dark blond hair.

"You too," she replied.

He winked at her, and an adorable dimple flashed in his cheek when he smiled.

"See? You still got it," Audri told her as they headed through the tunnel toward the plane. "Jayden will regret this. Letting you go is the biggest mistake of his life."

Madi blushed as she shrugged.

Jayden hadn't let her go. She'd practically kicked him out. Had she been too impulsive? Nadia and Stevie had reassured her that she'd done the right thing. But she wasn't so sure.

She placed her weekender in the overhead compartment and plopped on the window seat in the comfort section. She gazed out the window, her heart breaking into even smaller pieces as she realized Jayden wasn't coming at all. Her eyes filled with tears she tried to will away before they fell.

"Oh, honey. I'm sorry." Audri placed a hand on hers.

Madi shrugged because she couldn't talk.

"Mads, when people tell you who they are, believe them," Audri said. "Jayden told you very directly that in his mind he's done."

"But if he loved me, he'd have tried to fix things, right?"

Madi whispered so her disappointed voice wouldn't carry to the passengers already packing the aisle.

Audri sipped the tea she'd brought on board. "He loves you in his own way. There are different kinds of love, after all."

"But the way he loves me is not enough to change his mind. I visualized a happy ending for both of us. Is my life just a fraud? Are all those sayings about manifestations and the power of thoughts a lie?"

"Absolutely not, but some things can't be manifested with the power of thoughts." Audri hesitated and then added, "Maybe it's not him you really want? Maybe you're in love with being in love?"

"Of course I love him." But even to her ears she didn't sound convincing. Madi sighed. "Maybe after the summer, we can start all over?"

"Maybe . . . You have a shared history, after all. It's already there between you, and you can work to build something better from this, or . . ."

"Or what?"

Now Audri was the one who sighed. Madi could tell she was choosing her words very carefully. "In any case, you must examine if building on this foundation is a good idea, you know? It's not fair to expect someone else to change."

Madi's heart fell. Because she did want to change him.

She took out her phone from her purse and she stared at the screensaver photo of her and Jayden. They were hugging at the top of the ski lift where they had met and gone back to on their first anniversary. Pristine snow glittered around them. A faux-fur hoodie framed her pale face. Her brown eyes were highlighted with super-volume eyelash extensions, and the pink of her lips had made her smile shine brighter. What the picture didn't show was the niggling voice in the back of her mind telling her something was missing. She'd ignored it for too long.

Jayden was a good man, but sometimes he was cold like he was the Snow Queen's brother. When Madi had told him that sometimes she felt like a checked item on his bucket list, he'd apologized but hadn't denied it. The hurt had remained like a thorn in her heart. He'd tried to make it up in so many ways, but late at night, she'd wondered if she wasn't forcing things only because he had the right initials: JR.

Had she brought this heartache upon herself?

She brushed her thumb over his sharply sculpted face on the screen, imagining she felt the sexy scratch of his reddish-brown stubble. His green eyes were hyper focused—always on the future. He never even considered the past. He was never fully in the present. He said his biggest talent was getting over things—and people—quickly.

But gosh, was he gorgeous.

The plane hadn't taken off and she missed him already.

Her finger hovered over the DIAL button, but before she made a mistake she later regretted, Madi tucked her phone in her pocket.

The airplane doors closed, and the flight attendant was doing the safety demonstration. The thundering sound of the plane engines couldn't drown the echoes of Audri's words still reverberating in Madi's mind and heart. But it was also true that she loved him. Because she did, didn't she? And wasn't love worth any obstacle? Any sacrifice?

She wasn't so sure anymore. She didn't even know what love was at this point.

Madi turned toward her friend, but Audri had put her headphones on and placed a mask on her eyes to deal with her flight anxiety. Madi went back to gazing out the window. Salt Lake City and the beautiful still white-capped red rock mountains that surrounded it grew farther and farther away.

The man she had thought of as the love of her lives stayed behind.

Did he feel a tug in his heart like she did? Would he miss her or relish that they'd broken up?

She too put her headphones on but kept looking at the clouds as if in them she could read her future or receive any advice from supernatural beings: She loved Jayden, but if she decided to get over the rejection and went back to him in two months' time, could she live the rest of her life craving more affection from him? And if the answer was no, was that dream from long ago all a lie?

Only time would tell.

Chapter 5

As soon as she stepped on the walkway from the airplane to the airport, the humidity struck Madi with such force, she had to pause a couple of seconds so her breathing could adjust from so many years in desertic Utah.

It was just as she remembered. The heat and humidity. The denser scents. The throbbing hum of the island that called to her with an intensity that had made her cry with yearning for having been apart for so long.

"We're here, Abuela," she whispered while people surged around her.

She took another deep breath, and envisioned the oxygen reaching all the way to her toes and the last tip of her long hair. She could practically feel her skin rejuvenating itself and her split ends sealing back at the first gulp of island air. She'd been to other tropical locations, but there was nothing like Puerto Rico. Nothing.

It must have been the call of the blood.

"Madi!" Audri waved her over from the closest women's bathroom several feet behind.

Madi shook her head as if to reset her mind and followed her friend.

"If I don't take this off immediately, I'm going to combust," Audri said, wrestling out of her navy hoodie. She ran into the first stall and Madi headed to the second one.

She had packed an outfit to change into as soon as they arrived on the island. She always had when she was little. Her mom had made her pack an extra outfit for any kind of emergency on the airplane, and then a summery one to change into before they saw the family by the luggage carousels. By now, her tías and cousins had moved to Orlando, New York, and Utah. There would be no familiar faces crushing her with hugs contained for years and commenting on how much she'd grown, or how gordita she looked. Although she wouldn't mind not hearing comments on her weight or a bout of acne, Madi would miss this reunion.

She had always loved the ritual of leaving her wintery clothes behind and changing to her island outfit. Everything had to combine. Everything had to be perfect. At first, she'd complained, but now, so many years later, she had to swallow a knot in her throat at the rush of memories hitting her like waves.

She missed her grandmother so much she could practically feel her presence—outside the stall.

She took off her cardigan and long-sleeved shirt and put on a fitted tan halter top. She changed her leggings for a flowy white tunic, and her Nike Airs for jeweled sandals that showed off the beautiful marble-polish pedicure that made her feel like she was wearing turquoise crystals on her for protection. Turquoise to match the scarf her grandma had left unfinished, and that Madi had painstakingly kept going until she completed it. The line that showed the transition of stitches from Abuela's to hers was blatantly obvious, but she was proud that she'd brought the project to an end.

It was her favorite accessory. She tied her hair back from her face with the soft, gauzy scarf.

When she came out of the stall, Audri was washing her face and refreshing her hair with dry shampoo. She had changed into a pink tie-dye halter dress and platform sandals.

"You look gorgeous, Auds," Madi said.

"It's the ocean cleansing my aura. I tell you, I don't even know why we stay in Utah. I want to move here."

Madi laughed. "We haven't even left the airport yet!"

Audri pressed her lips and shrugged. "So far, I like what I feel. And at the end of the day, isn't that the most important part? What we feel?"

"But what does Reyna say all the time, Auds? That sometimes we need to heed our mind, too," Madi said, as she splashed water on her face. Her skin already looked more glowy than if she'd applied the most expensive moisturizer.

Audri caught Madi's eyes in the reflection of the mirror, and nodded, impressed. "Wow. Island life agrees with you!"

"It's my natural habitat." Madi smiled as she applied her nude lipstick and fixed her scarf. Her hair coiled with a life of its own, and she tossed it over her shoulder, relishing the sensation of how it tickled down her back through her barely there top.

It was an island miracle. Their luggage arrived perfectly on time, and the two amigas made their way outside to wait for their ride.

"Our driver's supposed to be a silver Camry. Be on the look-out," Audri said. For all her instalove with Puerto Rico, she was gasping for air and a thin sheen of sweat beaded on the bridge of her nose.

Madi loved the humidity, but her lungs were still trying to adjust to this much oxygen. She fanned her face and looked around for their car. A man lit a cigarette beside her, and she sent him a pointed look. But he seemed unfazed. She moved to a different section. And then she saw their ride.

"There, Audri!" she exclaimed, pointing.

Audri nodded, and they crossed the street behind an elderly lady carrying a cart so full of suitcases she couldn't see she was heading right into a black car whose driver was staring at his phone. Audri ran to help the woman, and Madi took her suitcase and stared down at the distracted driver.

"Thank you, linda," the woman told her. "Dios te bendiga."

The blessing was touching.

"Thank *you*," Madi replied as the woman walked away.

The pinging of a notification on her phone startled Madi. When she looked at her screen, she almost dropped the phone.

It was a Facebook memory that said, *Lina Paredes loved your picture.*

First of all, Madi hadn't used her Facebook account for more than ten years. Second, she'd never had notifications turned on.

Third, Lina Paredes, her abuela, had been gone for longer than that. And for all she knew, they had no social media in heaven. Maybe in hell, but Abuela wouldn't be there.

Feeling like she was having an out-of-body experience in the middle of the San Juan Airport pickup lane, Madi clicked on the notification to see what picture her abuela had loved from the afterlife.

It was a shot of hers she'd never seen. She had just graduated from her first yoga certification program and her family surrounded her. Madi remembered the longing for her grandma, and all the dreams she had of being true to herself, savoring each moment of her life without having to rely on anyone else to be happy. The most surprising thing in the picture was the column of light falling on Madi like a blessing from heaven, and the dots of bright lights haloing her head. She had never seen glitter beetles in Utah, but it looked like she was surrounded by them, cucubanos.

A car honked and brought Madi back to the present. The combination of jet lag, too much oxygenated air in her brain, and affection deprivation were making her hallucinate. That could happen, right?

She took off, her pace tight as she tried to find Audri across the street on the opposite sidewalk.

Audri waved to her from a silver car, her face alarmed. The driver, a woman, had finished placing everything in the trunk and closed it with a *thunk*. Madi ran to them, dragging her suitcases.

"I got you," said the driver.

"Thanks," Madi said, and joined her friend in the back of the car. "Sorry," she said, still clutching the phone like it was a lifeline. Trying to ground herself into what her dreams had been once upon a time.

"What is it?" Audri asked, placing a calming hand on Madi's arm. "You look like you saw a ghost."

Madi shivered. "Close enough. See for yourself."

The driver got in the car and maneuvered out of the airport. An old-style salsa that, in other circumstances, would have Madi dancing already sounded from the car speakers.

"What is it?" Audri squinted at the phone as if she were trying to understand what had affected Madi so much.

"You won't believe me! I got this notification from an account I never check. My grandma liked a picture! And not just any random photo, but this particular one. I feel like she's trying to tell me something."

The driver turned the music down, so the last of Madi's words were louder than she'd expected.

"Sorry," she said, and the driver smiled to her in the rearview mirror. She was white-skinned but had a red afro. Puerto Ricans came in a variety of colors, but they shared one thing: the ability to connect with just a glance.

How else could Madi explain the need to share the surreal

experience she'd just had without fear of a stranger overhearing her and thinking she was insane?

"I believe you," the driver said. "The day my divorce was final, I felt the ghost of my cat lie in bed next to me. She'd passed away a year before when my ex-wife forgot to bring her in."

"No way!" Audri exclaimed, clapping a hand over her mouth.

"I feel like as soon as I arrived here this veil cleared from my mind. This must be a message from Abuela Lina that this was the right move for me." Madi fanned herself. Now that the adrenaline had left her, she was sweating again.

"I told you the distance from Jayden would help you see things clearly," Audri said, and then she added for the driver's sake, "Jayden's her ex-boyfriend."

The word "ex" was like a knife twisting in Madi's stomach. But maybe she was just hungry. She hadn't had breakfast in Orlando. Now, her stomach, like the rest of herself, wanted to consume everything. The air. The food, the drinks, the people, the music, the feelings.

The feelings were overwhelming.

Sensing Madi's vibe, Audri handed her a chilled bottle of water that sat in the middle console between them.

Madi drank the whole thing. It was just what she needed.

"Wow, everything looks so different but also nothing has changed," she said, looking out the window at the tourists doing standup paddle in La Laguna del Condado as the car crossed El Puente Dos Hermanos.

"That's San Juan for you, love," said the driver. "How long has it been since you've been here?"

"Too long," said Madi as Audri said, "First time."

"Ooh! You're in for a treat!"

"Are you from here . . . ?" Audri asked. "Sorry, I didn't get your name."

"Mariela," the driver said. "Mariela Rodríguez, at your service. But you two need to be more careful and never ever get in a car without double- and triple-checking that you know you have the right driver."

Audri and Madi exchanged an appalled look.

"You're right," Audri said. "Small-town living has us lowering our guards."

"I feel like a little country mouse," Madi said in a small voice, shrugging.

Mariela smiled and shook her head. "Where are you ladies from?"

Audri took the reins of the conversation, and Madi looked out the window, enchanted by the beauty she saw in spite of the scars left from hurricanes and earthquakes hitting her beloved island. Thousands upon thousands of Boricuas had left the island for homes in the US after a financial crisis that spanned more than a decade and natural disaster after natural disaster. Her abuela had said that living on the island had a steep cost. But leaving did as well.

It was an excruciating choice either way.

Now, seeing in real life the beauty all around her, she understood how hard it would be to leave the island behind, and why her grandma's last wish had been for her ashes to be scattered here.

The drive from the airport to their hotel—Casa Grande Hotel—wasn't long, judging by the directions on her phone, but traffic was wilder than anything she'd ever seen before.

"Is this rush hour?" Madi wondered aloud.

Cars, motorcycles, and buses honked, adding their pulse to a cacophony of sounds that created a kind of music, once her ears got used to it.

Mariela, the driver, expertly dodged behind a police cruiser with the lights on. The street slowly made way for it, and Mariela rode behind it.

"Why's that car in front of it not pulling over?" Audri asked.

"Pulling over for what?" the driver asked.

There was a moment of confusion as Madi tried to understand. And then the driver said, "Oh! It's not like in New York. Here the police cars have the lights flashing at all times."

"And how do you know they're pulling you over?" Madi asked.

Mariela shrugged. "They call you out on their speaker."

Audri and Madi exchanged another look. As for Madi, she'd never been happier than now when she thought of how she didn't have to drive in this chaos.

Soon, they arrived in the old city.

"Here's where the cruise ships dock," Mariela said, sounding like a tour guide. "At night, the street will be bubbling with life. You can walk all the way here, but be careful going past this point, there's a residencial, a caserío, and it might not be the best idea to walk on your own. And for all that's holy, don't try to step in La Perla without being invited. It isn't the 'Despacito' videoclip, after all."

San Juan was just like any other big city in the world. Even Salt Lake.

The ocean glinted like diamonds dipped in turquoise. A boat crossed to the opposite coast where industrial-looking pipes sawed through the horizon.

"What's on that side?" Audri asked.

"Oh, that's the Bacardi plant in Cataño. The water taxi can take you there, or the party boat. It leaves every half an hour or so from la Plazoleta."

"Wow, so many things to do in Old San Juan," said Audri.

"It's an UNESCO site," Madi said, in a tour guide voice that made Mariela smile.

"The magic goes beyond the old city, though," Mariela replied. "There's plenty of charm out in the island too. Do you have excursions set up already?"

"Yes," said Audri. "We have a bunch. Our guide was super helpful."

Madi was heartbroken when she'd found out the observatory in Arecibo had fallen. Literally. Now she'd never get to see the stars from there like she'd dreamed as a little girl.

"Javier's a cool guy," Mariela said. "You'll like him a lot. He knows every corner of Borinquen."

"Javier?" Madi asked.

"Javier Rodriguez, our tour guide." Audri had done the arrangements with the tour company, El Isleño Adventures. The last few days had been so hectic, what with breaking up with Jayden and finding subs for her classes, that Madi hadn't even looked at the itinerary. She'd packed last-minute too.

And now they had a whole week planned with someone whose initials were JR.

JR! Like the initials she'd seen on the jacket the love of her eternities wore. In a dream, but still . . .

Madi's whole body tingled with magic and possibility.

"Javier Rodriguez?" Madi repeated, trying to make sure her ears didn't deceive her.

"Like I said, he's super cool. We go way back. We're second cousins, actually. What else do you have lined up?" Mariela asked.

Audri told her about their plans, and Madi, her mind still in the clouds, added, "We'll end in Culebra."

Culebra, a small island off Puerto Rico, had suffered greatly after the hurricanes, and it was still trying to recover from the wreck the storms left behind. But it was where Abuela Lina wanted her ashes to be scattered. Madi had to make it there no matter what.

It was also the beach of her dream with JR. And now she found the tour guide's initials were JR? What were the odds?

"Culebra is a whole weekend event," Mariela said. "Even that's too short to see the whole magic of it, but something's something."

Audri and Madi beamed at each other.

After a slow climb on the cobblestone streets, Mariela pointed at a white church, and said, "Here's the cathedral. And there's the hotel. Casa Grande Hotel. It used to be a convent for nuns." She parked in a super-narrow street that was perpendicular to the church.

Audri pressed her lips in amusement. "We can pretend we're little nuns," she said, making Madi laugh.

Mariela helped them unload their bags, and handed Madi her card. "I'll see you tomorrow for the first excursion, but in case you need a driver—or a friend"—she said this looking at Audri—"text or send me a WhatsApp and I'll be here. There are plenty of títeres around, but you'll be safe with me."

"Thanks," Audri and Madi said in unison, and finally Mariela waved and drove off.

"She's super nice," Madi said.

Audri nodded. "Everyone's nice to you, country mouse. But you're right. She's nice. I love getting to know people right away, especially as we scope future possible venues and personnel."

"Yes, that's something Reyna mentioned," Madi said, hoisting her backpack on her shoulder as the sound of the nearby waves soothed her nerves. There was so much to do, and so little time.

Puerto Rico was only one hundred miles long and thirty-five miles wide, but once on the island, distances expanded. One could spend a life and never get to know all its mysteries and beauty.

"Mariela's a good contact to connect us to other services," Audri said, rolling her suitcase inside the hotel. "Maybe she can point us to more out of the radar places to set our retreats."

"Or that guy Javier," Madi said, hoping she didn't sound too eager, and they walked into the hotel lobby.

Chapter 6

"First lunch, and then, I need a nap," Audri said, when they met by the elevator a few minutes after checking in. The air was hot and humid and smelled of a heavy bergamot candle. "How are you, Madi?"

Madi had changed into a white bambula dress and a yellow headwrap to try and tame her curly hair. She wasn't going to waste this look.

"I'm a little tired," she said. "But I don't want to sleep the day away now that I'm finally here."

The elevator chimed and they both got in. Inside, the scent of cologne from a previous person lingered, and not unpleasantly.

In fact, it was comforting.

The truth was, Madi didn't remember ever being this exhausted, but she wasn't surprised by the way her body was shutting down. When she was little, her parents always needed the first day to decompress and acclimate while she and Abuela hit the road to find the next adventure. The hours were never enough for them. Every time she went back to Utah, Madi wished she had more time on the island.

Before Abuela got so sick, they had been planning on coming back on a girls' trip. The plans never went beyond hopeful scribbles in a notebook. Little Madi never imagined that she wouldn't breathe this salt air for more than twenty years. Had anyone told her that she'd be here again but without her grandma, the sorrow would have been too great to bear.

Since losing Abuela, a couple of her friends had lost theirs, and they didn't understand why she couldn't get over her grandma's death. But they didn't get that she'd been more than a grandma. She'd been a friend, a mentor, and a guide. Although her grandma would remind her there was no guide like one's own heart.

Madi couldn't boast her flighty guide, though. All these years, her heart had led her only to dead ends. She'd given up on looking for a soul mate who had the initials JR.

But what about Javier Rodriguez? What if she had to go through all the noes before she found her yes?

What was she thinking?

She didn't even know if the guy was straight and/or available. She should put the thought out of her mind and start acting her age instead of . . . what she'd always done: Dive headfirst into instalove that had no foundation in any logical explanation.

She was done with love. She was done forever.

The thoughts circled her mind, but she didn't say the words aloud. Everyone knows words have power, and once they're out, the universe will conspire to make them a reality.

No. Madi was disappointed in love, the romantic kind. But deep in her essence, she couldn't deny that it existed.

Hopefully, it could exist for her, too.

The elevator halted to a false stop and then stopped all the way.

"Yikes!" said Audri. "That was intense."

"I'm glad I wasn't alone, or I would've freaked," Madi said, placing a hand over her racing heart.

They headed to the restaurant nestled in the hotel's internal patio where a young hostess led them to a small table placed under a canopy of ferns and orchids. The gurgling sound of an ancient fountain covered in moss serenaded them, but even before they were done with their meal, Audri yawned.

"I'm going to have to rest for a bit. Do you mind?"

"Don't worry about me," Madi said, patting her friend's hand, although she didn't like being alone.

"Are you sure you'll be okay on your own?"

Audri knew her, after all. How many times had Madi stayed late at the studio just so she wouldn't have to go back to the apartment alone? She didn't like to venture out like Stevie would.

But now, she felt a tingling all over her body. She felt her abuela nearby.

"I promise," she said, and she wasn't even lying. "I'll just go explore around the hotel and then come back."

"Text me, okay?"

"It's the daytime!"

"Still," Audri said, and headed back to the room.

For a second, Madi was tempted to follow her, but the ocean was calling her.

There wasn't a beach here in Old San Juan except for a small section by El Paseo de la Princesa, but people didn't bathe in that area. The hotel was literally a few feet from San Juan's gate, the entrance into the old city, and a few steps from the city wall that protected San Juan from the ocean. Or she could walk a couple of blocks to the Old San Juan cemetery abuela had loved visiting each time they came to the island. She had a strange fascination for the marble statues and mausoleums their humble family never had access to.

Madi almost went back to the room to gather the urn. But Abuela had asked for her ashes to be scattered not only in Puerto

Rico, but on Flamenco Beach in Culebra. Madi wouldn't have the chance to visit Culebra until the weekend. She'd waited so long and come from so far to fulfill her promise only halfway through?

"Just a little longer, Abuela," she muttered, walking through the hotel's hallways. "I promise you it'll be worth the wait. We're home!"

Home.

How interesting that she felt so connected to her abuela's ancestral land. Her biological father and her stepdad were from Argentina. Although she loved fútbol, *mate*, and asado, Madi never really felt the pull of the land like she did with Puerto Rico. Maybe because her grandma and mom had been the home "makers" and had brought the island to their home in the mountains, Madi clung so much to this part of her family tree.

She wasn't sure. But she felt at home as she walked along the cobblestones. The sun beat furiously on her neck as she leaned over the city wall and gazed out to the sea. She went down the path along the wall all the way to El Paseo Princesa and bought a coconut piragua from the same man who had sold the ice cones since time immemorial.

"¡Provecho!" he said when he handed her the Styrofoam cup full of sugary shaved ice.

With a smile, she headed toward the Raíces Fountain that honored the European, African, and native Taíno roots of the island. It wasn't the Trevi Fountain in Rome where Stevie had made a marriage pact with a random guy she met there (to her defense, they were both drunk), but it was beautiful all the same.

Silver and copper glinted in the bottom of the fountain from the coins people had tossed.

So many wishes.

Which ones had come true? Which had been forgotten?

She'd always felt like wishing to find her soul mate was a sacrilege. You had to work at finding the love of your lives, your "media naranja," like Abuela Lina had called her other half, Abuelo. The disappointment over Jayden had left Madi tender and wounded. She had worked hard at it.

Perhaps too hard though?

She'd told Audri she'd given up on finding real love, but Madi couldn't help herself. It was a tiny, meaningless gesture. She rummaged in her purse until her fingers found a nondescript quarter.

She looked at it for a few seconds, feeling silly. Was it wrong to wish that the JR of her dreams was the tour guide? Wouldn't that be the most romantic thing ever?

Or the most desperate?

She closed her eyes like every time she wanted to listen to the voice of her heart.

What did she want? If fear of ridicule or heartbreak weren't the leading factors to consider, what did she really want? In spite of what she'd said after breaking up with Jayden, she knew what she wanted.

"I wish . . ."

The wind snatched the whisper from her lips before she could complete the sentence. She didn't dare say her greatest wish aloud, but she kissed the coin and threw it over her shoulder hoping destiny could read her mind and her heart.

It wasn't like in the movies.

The coin plunked into the fountain but nothing magical happened.

A toddler chased pigeons while her mom patiently trailed behind her, watching she wouldn't fall or cross the street. Teenagers made TikToks to the side of the fountain, and a young couple who looked local kissed languorously against a palm tree, uncaring of the curious glances a group of elderly, white-haired tourists sent their way.

With a sigh, she stood up.

Flamboyán trees lined the sidewalks and she headed back to the hotel as the tourists bargained with the artisans who had set up shop early. Two cruise ships sat like monstrous beached whales on the dock and three more approached the port in the distance. A constant stream of people descended on the city.

San Juan was usually crowded, but she didn't remember it being busy like this in the middle of the day.

"Excuse me, what's going on in the city? Is there a festival?" Madi asked a woman standing outside a cigar store. The scent of tobacco stirred memories buried deep in Madi's mind. So deep in fact, she couldn't unroot them before the woman started answering her question.

"It's la Noche de San Juan, m'ija!"

M'ija. There was something about that endearment, a contraction of "mi hija," that never failed to move Madi. She felt an instant connection to the slender woman who seemed to be around her mom's age.

"I've never heard of Noche de San Juan!" she said. "What is it?"

The woman's eyes lit up like she'd been waiting all her life for someone to ask her this question. And here Madi had come.

"Let me tell you the short version. Noche de San Juan, St. John's Night, is, in theory, a festival for the patron saint of Puerto Rico. St. John. Now . . ." She raised her eyebrows conspiratorially and pointed up with her index finger. "The real roots are pagan. Think of Midsummer Night." She opened her hands like there was a mini explosion between them.

Madi had the flash of a vision of a girl with a crown of flowers, screaming, and her boyfriend stuffed inside a bear somewhere in Scandinavia.

She must have made a face because the woman said, "No, chica! Don't be alarmed. Think of Stonehenge and stuff."

The blood returned to Madi's face. She waved herself. "Oh! I get it!" And now she remembered that she'd read about Noche de San Juan before, but only vaguely.

The woman laughed and patted Madi's shoulder. "Noche de San Juan is a night of fire and water. People build bonfires on the beach, and then at midnight, they plunge into the ocean, seven, nine, or twelve times—numbers vary depending on who you ask."

"And what do they do that for?"

"They throw themselves backward, to symbolize trust, and then ask for a wish."

"Any wish?"

It seemed destiny was determined for her to make her wish once and for all.

"Any wish," the woman said. "The city's crowded now, but it's nothing compared to what it will be tonight. If I were you, I'd take a nap to gather energy. Tonight the real party will start."

Madi wasn't sure if it was her imagination or a memory, but she thought she remembered being a little kid in the plaza and the pedestrian way packed with people dancing bomba and plena, the Afro-Caribbean dances that had survived colonization, occupation, and exile. Artisans and food vendors dotted the esplanade and fireworks exploded in the distance.

"You should come," the woman said.

"I don't know . . ."

She wasn't sure why she was hesitating. Seeing the festival traditions firsthand would be fun. Especially one that hadn't survived in their family after the move to Utah. Perhaps the lack of access to a body of water and the fire restrictions in their area had killed this particular custom that seemed like something Abuela Lina would have loved.

Besides, the festival would be a nice opportunity to find a new nativity for her mom, who collected them. And the food . . . Everyone knew Puerto Rican street food was the best kind. Maybe they could time the yoga studio retreats with the solstice and midsummer. Reyna would love that.

A couple of elderly men in elegant linen shirts, guayaberas, and Bermuda shorts walked into the store.

The woman said, "I need to go back, but I hope I'll see you at the party tonight."

She left and Madi walked back to the hotel, feeling an electric charge all around her. Maybe the electricity was inside her. Or maybe the heat was starting to affect her. In the distance, the seagulls dipped into the sparkling crystal water, and Madi sighed, imagining the coolness of the water settling her thoughts.

She loved it here. She wanted to move here.

Why had it taken her so long to return?

Jayden refused to go to a tropical location after suffering an aggravating sunburn in Hawaii. He claimed that in Costa Rica, he'd been eaten alive by mosquitos.

"Warm weather and I don't go well together. Besides, I have my own sun made into woman in you," he told her once.

He'd meant it as a compliment, but the prospect of never sharing the island with him had filled her with despair. She went with him on his skiing trips, and when they talked about getting married *someday*, she'd agreed to a honeymoon in Iceland. But to give up this? The prospect of such a big part of her having to be totally separated from him had always filled her sadness.

She had nothing else to complain about. He wasn't a cheater or even a flirt. But he wasn't *it* after all.

Any other woman would be kissing the ground he walked on. He was *that* perfect on paper. And yet . . . What else did she want from life?

If Reyna found an acceptable place for the retreats, then Madi would have the chance to come here to head those. Maybe she could make a proper Noche de San Juan wish then.

When she passed one of the garitas, the sentinel lookouts posted along the wall where soldiers had guarded the city since the time of the conquest, she snapped a selfie. She looked good. She was tempted to send it to Jayden along with the words: *This is what you lost, fool.*

"But what for?" she wondered aloud. Besides, it was settled that she didn't really want him either. He just had the right initials. How shallow was that?

The crashing waves on the wall and the cry of the seagulls told her it was super shallow.

Now that the effervescence of the preparations for the festival were behind her, she arrived at the hotel with a heavy heart.

Audri had left a note stuck on Madi's door: *Tried calling you, but my phone is acting up. I'm getting a massage. See you later!*

Madi laughed. Audri never lost time in checking out the spa in any place they visited. As she walked into the room, her phone chimed with a series of texts from her friend. She hoped she wouldn't have any issues with her signal while in Puerto Rico. Still, she texted to let her know she was back.

Exhaustion fell on her.

The combination of the heavy, hot air outside, the AC in the room, the jet lag, and the emotional turmoil of being back on the island finally took a toll on her. She kicked off her sandals and shed her dress and got in bed, relishing the luxury of taking a nap in preparation for a night out. The AC dried the sweat on her skin, and she shivered, burrowing deeper in the covers.

Maybe she should set an alarm, but she brushed the thought away.

It was just a few minutes.

She closed her eyes and took a long breath. Next thing she knew, she found herself on the magical beach from that night long, long ago.

Unknown galaxies swirled in the sky making it look like the covers of Madi's favorite new age meditation albums.

Next to her stood Abuela Lina. "It's good to be back."

"Abuela!" she said, turning to hug her. She smelled the same as always, agua de Florida and baby powder.

"I just came to remind you to follow the signs, and to remember the rule of three: Three witnesses will show you the way, but above all, trust yourself."

"What?" Madi had so many questions. "No, don't go yet, Abuela!"

She blinked and she was back in bed.

On her lips, she still tasted the ocean's gritty saltiness.

For a moment, she was confused at how dark the sky was. She sat up, sensing that she was missing something. It had been a dream. She wanted to go back to the beach, but she also knew she was supposed to be somewhere.

La Noche de San Juan.

She looked for the blinking clock on the nightstand and to her horror, she realized she'd slept for four hours.

"What in the world?"

She checked her phone and saw a string of messages from Audri, the urgency escalating with the passing of time and the lack of response. The dream had been so short, but she'd been out cold for hours.

Four hours!

Instead of texting her friend, she dialed her number.

Audri picked up after the first ring. "Mads? Are you alive?"

Madi sat up and rubbed at the lines the pillow had left on her face. Her shoulder throbbed in pain, making her wince. The curtains fluttered with the blast of cold air from the AC. She peeked at the waxing moon shining up in the sky, and although math wasn't her talent, she quickly calculated that next week, when they made it to Culebra, it would be a full moon.

The solstice, midsummer, the moon sent her emotions all over the place. No wonder she was exhausted and disoriented!

"Sorry, Audri! I don't know how I could sleep so much," she said, and her voice sounded like she hadn't used it in years. "Did you try to wake me?"

"I knocked on the door, and you told me you were tired, so I let you sleep, but it's been hours and you're missing all the fun. I know you'd hate me if I didn't at least try to get you here. You wouldn't believe the bonfires all over the beach! The vibes in the air are electric!"

Music blared in the background from the other side of the line, and Audri's voice distorted, sounding like a robot.

Madi looked at her screen. She only had one bar.

"What? You're cutting off."

Audri mumbled a curse and then she said, "Meet me at this canto bar. I'm with Mariela." It sounded like she was cupping her hand over her mouth.

"Mariela?" Madi asked.

"Our driver? Meet us at the bar. I'll text you the address."

Audri hung up and Madi got a location pin for a place not too far from the hotel.

Then, noting the time again, she hesitated.

She was in a strange city. Well, not really, but she'd never been in San Juan on her own at night before. But she was a grown-ass woman, and she was single.

She wasn't about to spend her first night in paradise, especially la Noche de San Juan, doom scrolling through her social media hoping to see a glimpse of her ex or a sign from a supernatural being.

She flung the covers aside and headed to the shower.

Chapter 7

Without breaking her brisk stride, Madi pulled back the strap of her dress that kept sliding off her shoulder. Her sleek high-heeled sandals echoed against the cobblestones like the rhythm of the Bad Bunny song blaring from a window in one of the colorful houses. Her heart whispered of possibilities and adventures. It wasn't Las Vegas or New York, but there was a magic in the air of Old San Juan that made her feel invincible.

"Mami, esas curvas y yo sin freno," a man called out from the passenger seat of a black Mercedes. His friend in the driver's seat countered with "Sorry! He's a little tipsy. But who can blame him? You look lovely! Careful!"

He sped up before Madi could react. Self-doubt assaulted her. Maybe she shouldn't have worn this little silver dress, with its watery silky fabric and plunging neckline. But when they were out and about exploring the island, like the Boricuas called anything not in the capital, she wouldn't have another chance to wear it. And the truth was that Madi felt like a goddess in this dress. It made her feel like she was naked. And powerful. Her hair tickled her back and every few steps, she had to double-check that her skirt hadn't crept as she climbed uphill in the old city.

No sign of the country mouse anymore.

Her eyes scanned the signs for La Sirena Canto Bar where Audri said she'd be waiting with Mariela.

The coquís sang from the trees, and the Caribbean Sea lapped against the city wall, its murmur just a background sound. The stars blinked furiously, telling Madi to keep going.

"But where?" she asked aloud, looking at her phone that had frozen in the map app.

She tried refreshing it to no avail, and when she restarted it, the pin that Audri had sent her vanished. Madi stopped by the stoop of one of the enchanting colonial homes painted orange and yellow and dialed her friend's number.

"Audri here! Leave a message!" the voicemail message said.

Madi groaned in frustration. She was missing out on the party!

Audri had given her express directions. Madi was sure she'd walked by La Sirena this afternoon. But after circling the same block three times, she couldn't find it.

"I'll just go back to the hotel and ask the concierge," she muttered to herself, aware that the *tipsy* passenger of a few minutes ago was now heading in her direction.

On foot. She recognized the Yankees hat.

Panicked, regretting walking out on her own, she headed to an open bar from where the sound of a Karol G remix pounded all the way to the sidewalk. The audience blared the lyrics at the top of their lungs.

"Good night, preciosa," the bouncer said. He was one of the largest men she'd ever seen in her life. Sized like The Rock, with skin dark and eyes bright and that same alluring smile. "Meeting your party?"

She smiled back at him and looked over her shoulder but

there was no sign of her stalker. "Actually," she said, "I'm looking for La Sirena."

The man made a melodramatic frown. "Aw. But why are you going to our competitor, linda? We have wonderful Noche de San Juan specials."

Madi flicked her hair off her shoulder, and the bouncer's eyes traveled to her deep neckline, but promptly climbed back to her face.

"My friends are there," she explained.

He shrugged. "Mira, follow Calle del Sol all the way to the top. When you see the sign for the hamburger place, go inside that little passageway and you'll see the sign for La Sirena. It's a hole in the wall, but you can't miss it," he said. Now she recognized the Brooklyn accent.

She could see the sign of the bar in her mind's eye from this afternoon. She hadn't been wrong. But now she was afraid of heading back in the street with that man lurking around looking for her. A couple came into the club and before turning to them, the bouncer winked at Madi and said, "Come back here after La Sirena."

"We will," she said knowing that chances for that were nil.

A voice in the back of her mind told her to go back to Casa Grande Hotel and settle in for a bath and a night of Netflix and room service. But she didn't want to waste her looks and seeing the bonfires at the beach. Stubbornly, she headed to the sidewalk.

After checking her phone one more time, she puzzled over why it wasn't working at all now when she needed it the most. Her mind was so clouded! She would've asked the bouncer to let her use his phone, but unfortunately, she couldn't even remember Audri's number. Months ago, Madi had caved to peer pressure to join the twenty-first century and she'd taken out her old-fashioned phone notebook from her purse.

When she was about to turn back to the pub, ominous footsteps echoed on the cobblestones behind her. Suddenly, she felt the five hundred–plus years of history that thrummed from the city, the houses, the streets. For anyone looking from above, she must have looked like the clueless girls in scary movies, the first one to die.

She regretted watching *Interview with the Vampire* and boasting that in Louis' place, she'd have turned and faced Lestat without hesitation. Now she wanted to run back to the safety of her hotel room.

When she'd woken up from her nap, she'd been so sure magic awaited her. But for all her obsession in high school, she didn't want to be a vampire!

"Help me, Abuela," she muttered, and looked over her shoulder.

No one followed. Only a skinny black cat sauntered on the thin stone wall in front of a house. When she turned to continue, she caught sight of the drunk man from the car, standing on the corner.

"There you are, bombshell!" he exclaimed, and stumbled toward her.

Vampire or no vampire, she turned around and tried to run in the opposite way. Tried because she could hardly walk with her pointy heels on the cobblestones.

A sob rose in her throat, and when she could almost feel the man catching up with her, she saw her grandmother beckoning to her from the corner. For a second, the air disappeared from Madi's lungs. Her grandma looked the same as always, with her hair braided in a crown and wearing a billowy white dress.

If she hadn't been terrified about the drunk guy, she would've screamed at seeing the ghost of her grandmother. But since when was she scared of her abuela? She'd never been afraid of spirits, and there was an intoxicating scent in the night that had probably made her imagine her presence. But the man chasing her was real.

She kept walking toward the apparition, her heart drumming

hard against her ribs. And when she turned hard at the corner, she collided with someone.

She screamed so loud her throat hurt, as she turned around to run. Her ankle twisted, and the heel of her sandal snapped.

"Tranquila. Madi?" the man she'd crashed into said in Spanish. "Are you okay?"

Of course she wasn't okay. She was seeing her grandmother's spirit, and a man was following her. What was this guy saying or . . .

Were the two guys working together to get to her?

"Let me go!" She pushed him as hard as she could and broke a nail. The sudden pain made her snap out of her panic. She saw his expression, wide-eyed and worried.

He lifted his hands in the air. "I'm a friend of Mariela's, one of the tour guides? I came out to look for you," he said softly. But when his gaze traveled beyond her, to the guy who'd been chasing her, his expression hardened. "Who are you? Are you following her, sendo cabrón?"

The man turned around and stumbled away.

"Jodí'o borracho!" her savior said.

Madi could've cried with relief. One of the tour guides? Was this Javier Rodriguez, JR? *Her* JR?

She quickly glanced at his hand. He had no ring, which didn't mean he wasn't taken, but she'd consider this as a good sign.

But nerves got the best of her. She laughed. "Sendo cabrón?" she asked, pounding against his chest again. A part of her brain registered how rock hard his pecs were. "What kind of insult is that?"

The man ruffled his lightly gelled dark hair and smiled.

As she took in his presence, Madi's body tingled. He was gorgeous. He was beyond anything she'd ever imagined her soul mate would look like.

He had perfect white teeth, except for one on top that was a little crooked, adorable. His beautiful long-lashed brown eyes seemed to reflect the whole starry sky. But the most impressive fact about his eyes was his gaze, deep and velvety. Safe. She felt as if she'd known him forever.

Involuntarily, something tickled below Madi's belly button. Was she ovulating or something that her body was out of control? She'd never had this kind of reaction, even to attractive men, but especially not a stranger after she'd been worried about her safety just a second ago. It must have been that survivor's instinct she'd once read about that wanted the body to reproduce after a life-threatening situation. Or it might be some part of her recognizing the love of her lives.

She became aware of the music ringing in the place, and the fact that she'd been staring at him for a full minute without saying a word. But then, so had he.

"I'm sorry," she said. "How did you know who I was?"

He seemed to come off a trance too. He brushed his fingers through his hair again and she couldn't fail to notice the corded veins in his muscular, tanned arms. His whole body seemed tight under his dark button-up shirt and dark jeans. Again, something tugged tightly below Madi's stomach, and she was so grateful this gorgeous man couldn't read her thoughts.

He licked his lower lip and bit it, which only made the longing flare inside Madi.

"You look like a Madi to me." Then he adddded, "Mariela and Audri were here with some friends. Audri said you were coming but when you didn't show up, they decided to head down to la Plazoleta for some food truck snacks. I was about to join them." He shrugged and flashed the kind of crooked smile that Madi had seen in heroes of her favorite movies but had never encountered in real life. Until now.

"Thanks for helping me," she said, looking down to the floor, suddenly ensorcelled by him.

She wanted to slap herself. Where was her determination not to instantly fall in love—in lust—with someone just because they were nice, good-looking, and had the right initials?

His eyes were intense and probing, but she looked up. She shifted her weight and lost her balance.

"My heel is broken!" she said, dismayed that she had destroyed her favorite shoe on her first night out, and mortified at the wail that had left her mouth.

In a swift move, he knelt in front of her and with fingers delicate and tremulous like butterfly wings unclasped the sandal.

She was way less dressed than usual, but the intimate gesture made her feel like she was catching on fire. The music swallowed her intake of breath when his skin brushed hers.

"You don't need to—" she started saying, but he was already on his feet, the precious but useless sandal in his hand.

"Running, high heels on strappy shoes, and cobblestones don't mix," he said.

"Did your girlfriend teach you that?" Madi said, taking the shoe back from him. She was determined to find out if he was in a relationship before she did something stupid.

"Being a tour guide, I've seen my fair share of shoe mishaps." He smiled. "And no girlfriend."

"Good," Madi said. Aloud.

To deflect her embarrassment, she examined her shoe.

There was no way she could try to walk on her ruined heels. She had a phobia about stepping on public floors. No sense in finding Audri and Mariela at the beach now. The only option was to go back to the hotel.

While these thoughts whirled in her mind, he looked at her with a shrewd expression on his face.

Madi couldn't resist it. She felt so oddly familiar with him, she was a little embarrassed but couldn't help playfully slapping his arm. "What?"

Back in the bar, the music switched to a tune the people seemed to love because those around them shuffled back inside as if they didn't want to miss this song, leaving them alone at the entrance.

"You can't walk like this on the beautiful but germ-ridden streets of Old San Juan, and I do happen to be prepared."

"How so?"

"I have something in my car that might help."

She got goose bumps on her arms, and she must have made a face because he shook his head and looked totally dismayed. "No. I'm not asking you to join a stranger in his car. I really have something that can help. Wait for me here."

He rushed out of the bar and left her standing, embarrassed to realize that she would've followed him to his car. What was she thinking? Had she left her brain back on her pillow? Had the flowers around her made her drunk?

She'd never acted so cluelessly or carelessly. She needed to ground herself.

After a couple of deep breaths, she sat on one of the empty settees and wondered if she should make a run for it and disappear before she embarrassed herself even more in front of this beautiful stranger of the sexy arms. Because he was beautiful. Those brown, soulful eyes . . . where was he from? He didn't look like most Puerto Ricans, even though she'd read there was a large Asian community in Puerto Rico, but Asian from where? And his mouth? Would it be as soft as his fingers?

She shivered and decided to bolt before she made a grave mistake. Yes. She must have been drunk or incapacitated by something. But right when she was trying to stand on one heeled sandal, he walked back inside carrying a package in his hands.

When their eyes met, he smiled so radiantly, she couldn't help but smile back.

Her mind blared a NO in large red neon letters and a firefighter alarm siren, but her body was stupidly willing and out of control.

"Hey," she said in a small voice, and then pointed at the package. "What do you have there?" She usually wasn't a prier, but in this case, prying was better than gawking, and she couldn't stop looking at him.

"So many of my clients come to the walking tour with the

wrong kind of shoe, so now I have an emergency stash with supplies just in case someone goes all Cinderella on me."

Clients.

With a shy smile, he knelt in front of her and said, "What can I say? I like being prepared."

His voice was flirty and fun, but a surge of jealousy that he'd helped other women in her situation rose inside Madi. She literally saw green, or it could've been the flashing lights from the dance floor in the back of the bar. She didn't understand what had taken over her.

He knelt in front of her and thankfully didn't seem to notice her reaction.

"Seriously? What do tour guides have in their magic stash?" As soon as the words were out of her mouth, she bit her lip wishing she could bring the words back. Her voice sounded husky for the lack of sleep and the AC blasting on her while she slept naked and wet, but she didn't want to give this guy the wrong impression.

It might be too late for that.

His sharp cheeks were flushed. He took out a few pairs of thin, cheap flip-flops wrapped in cellophane paper and waved them in front of her. "Pink, yellow, or green. The green ones have jewels, so choose wisely."

She smiled at his effort to make her feel at ease. "Which ones is your favorite?"

He held his gaze and his Adam's apple bobbed up and down. His eyes dropped to her crossed legs, and it was such an intimate gesture she felt he was caressing the naked skin of her legs and had to suppress a shiver.

"The pink will match your . . ." He swallowed. "Earrings?"

She knew he'd caught a peek of her lacy underwear but was too much of a gentleman to say anything. But relishing the power she held over him, this stranger who felt like someone she'd known forever, she grabbed the packet with the pink flip-flops.

"Pink it is then," she said, trying to control her breath.

He smiled and unwrapped the flip-flops and tenderly placed one on her naked foot. And then proceeded to undo the clasp of the remaining sandal. His touch was so delicate, she felt he was undressing her. He lifted his eyes just as she leaned in. They were impossibly close to each other. If she leaned forward just a little bit more, she could kiss that soft-looking mouth.

"We better go and join Mariela and Audri," he said.

Once outside the bar, he put the rest of his things in the back of a fancy black car, and she added, "I tried to text and call, but I didn't have a signal. Does your phone work?"

He checked his phone and shook his head. "This happens on the island all the time. Nothing to be alarmed over."

Her foot slipped from the sandal, but he caught her hand. "Are you okay?"

"You're going to think I'm the clumsiest person in the world," she said, rolling her eyes at herself, but didn't shake off his hand. His skin was rough and weathered, which she was pleasantly surprised to discover that she liked. Very much. This was a man who didn't spend all day scrolling on apps.

They walked side by side, the ocean beckoning them. Madi tried to pretend she was in full control of her actions, but this whole thing felt like a continuation of the dream she'd had with Abuela telling her to trust the signs. But her mind seemed to be shortcutting, like the communications system on the island.

But of one thing she was certain: Noche de San Juan or not, she was determined not to fall for anyone, no matter how handsome or kind, or what his initials were. Hadn't she learned she needed more than that shallowness?

But she relished in the feeling of holding this man's hand. A man who was a stranger, but who she felt like she'd known for eons and eons.

Chapter 8

They followed the music. Madi tried to fight the magnetic charge between them. She hadn't come to Puerto Rico for a fling.

She should clarify that she usually didn't do this, walk out of a bar with a stranger, holding hands like she was claiming him. She cleared her throat, but before she could say anything, her stomach growled so loudly it echoed against the cobblestone streets and the painted houses, bright and cheerful even in the night.

"I didn't catch that very well, but I got the overall message," he said. "You're hungry and you need food right away or else."

She groaned and peeked at him through narrowed eyes. It was kind of hard since she was so much shorter than him. But then, she was practically barefoot.

The moon bathed his face and cast it in an ethereal glow. He had a beautiful profile. She turned her gaze ahead.

"I'm legit famished!" she said. "I've only had a salad and a piragua since I landed at noon."

"A piragua?" he asked. "That's priorities. You must get a limber next to, you know, get all the Puerto Rican nutritional requirements during your stay."

She smiled when he said *limber* the Puerto Rican way, with that *R* sounding almost like an *L*, but not quite.

"A limber!" Madi held on to his arm as if she were about to faint with wanting and moaned, savoring the memory of a frozen popsicle served in a cup, without the popsicle stick, on her tongue. The treat was named after the pilot Charles Lindbergh, who landed on the island in 1928. "I haven't tasted one in so long I could cry!"

He laughed. "You'll have plenty of time to taste a limber this week."

Madi sighed, back to holding his hand. To keep her balance. "It seems like I've been here for days but all I did was go down to Paseo la Princesa for a walk and then nap all day. I'm mad I wasted my first day on the island sleeping."

"Sleeping is never a waste," he said.

"Not when I feel like I woke up in the wrong dimension." She lifted their clasped hands to show him what she meant. "When I went down for a nap, I wasn't planning on ending the evening holding hands with a stranger."

He let go of her hand at once. "Sorry. I hadn't noticed." He sounded appalled.

Before she explained that it hadn't bothered her, she considered her words for a second, not only for his benefit, but also hers. She had to establish some ground rules, especially since they were going to spend a lot of time together this week.

She shouldn't lead him on. She wasn't looking to replace Jayden now, or ever. But this man felt so familiar and his magnetism was irresistible, which made him dangerous.

Was her bar so low that she clung to anyone who made her feel safe?

"For the record, it didn't bother me," she said. "Thanks for the sandals and catching me before I fell."

He smiled. "You'd have done the same thing for me, right?"

"Considering you're taller and heavier than me, I don't know how much help I'd be, but I'd have helped you if you needed anything. You're a friend of Mariela's, and after all, a friend of a friend is a friend of mine."

"Just a few hours on the island and you've gone full Puerto Rican, making friends after a chance meeting?"

She laughed but he was right. What was it with Puerto Ricans acting like best friends when they heard each other's accent in the wild? For all her teachings and warnings about stranger danger and all that, her mom never hesitated to exchange numbers if she crossed paths with other Puerto Ricans at the grocery store or the slot machines in Las Vegas.

"I hope I'm not wrong, but you feel like a friend already," she said.

She couldn't remember the last time she'd been so at ease with someone she had just met. Someone whose company she enjoyed and who looked like he enjoyed hers too. With Jayden, she'd always had to try to tamp down her exuberance. She wanted to prove she learned from her mistakes. Nothing in his attitude changed when she'd friend-zoned him so drastically, and that was a good sign.

These last few days Madi hadn't smiled that much. The breakup with Jayden had hit her harder than the end of any other relationship. But now her face ached for the lack of practice. But she had to be careful. If she acted like her real self with this guy and he kept liking it, she'd soon start missing and craving his attention like a drug.

After all, what was she? Fifteen years old? Hadn't she learned that nothing good came of stripping all her defenses down?

But she liked this man, his infectious smile, and oddly, his protectiveness.

Protectiveness?

She didn't even know him, but she felt safe beside him, and feeling safe was as dangerous as feeling "lusted after."

These thoughts swirled in Madi's mind as they headed down to la Plazoleta, lured by the music and the scent of delicious fried food and flowers. Her foot kept sliding on the rubbery sandal. A couple of times he had the reflex to grab her hand again, but then he shoved both fists in his pockets, as if trying to stop himself. She kind of wished she hadn't let go of it to start with.

"I promise I'm not drunk," she said. "In fact, I haven't had anything to drink for hours! I'm parched."

"In that case, Parched and Famished, I know just the cure," he said, pointing ahead. "Perfect timing."

He beelined toward one of the stands that lined El Paseo de la Princesa. A man peeled oranges. He looked to be in his seventies or older, his dark skin wrinkled from the sun.

A sign next to him advertised china nativa cocktails.

China is what Puerto Ricans call oranges. Abuela Lina had told Madi it was because that's where oranges came from originally and the name had stuck.

"There's Tego," he said. "He and his sister Andrea have a finca in San Sebastián. They're my favorite Boricuas."

He said Boricuas like he wasn't one.

Now that she was paying attention, Madi realized that besides the way he'd pronounced *limber*, he didn't really sound like a Boricua. She couldn't place his accent but something in his voice and looks reminded her of Stevie. She was about to ask him about it, when Tego looked up and saw him. His face broke in a giant smile.

"Como anda', compai!" He stood from his stool and hugged Madi's companion, patting him hard on the back a couple of times. And then, he noticed Madi and did a double take. "You finally found yourself a girlfriend?"

The blush on his tanned skin was noticeable even in the semidarkness. The tarp of a tent blocked the glare from the lampposts stationed every few feet on the pedestrian section in front of the ocean.

"Tego, easy. She's a friend," he said, and turned to Madi, whose body was flooding with warmth at his sudden bashfulness.

"My pleasure, beautiful lady! And forgive my mistake." He shook Madi's hand. "My sister and I want to keep him on the island forever. Andrea is determined to find him a girlfriend before he goes back to the States. I was glad when I thought he'd finally found one himself! It seems I was mistaken."

"Ay . . ." He sent her an embarrassed look.

A dozen questions had popped in her mind with Tego's words. Just as she'd guessed, he wasn't from Puerto Rico or at least, he didn't live here permanently. But what was he doing here? And why did Tego and his sister want to keep him on the island forever?

But this wasn't the moment to ask, at least not in front of the orange vendor.

She imagined what it must have looked like for Tego. They didn't hold hands anymore, but they walked so close to each other like they were magnets, unable to pull away.

But stranger or not, he had rescued her from the drunk guy and her own clumsiness. Not that he'd asked for anything in return, but a favor for a favor was fair, right?

"He rescued me from a scary situation tonight and now he's helping me find my friend."

It sounded like a lie although it was exactly what had happened, and Tego laughed, a thunderous, happy sound. A couple of people in the nearby booths turned around to look at them.

"One night in San Juan and you're already a hero?"

He pushed his hands down in his pockets like a boy hiding something he'd stolen. "When you say it like that you make me sound like I'm *your friendly neighborhood Spider-Man*."

"When did you two meet?" Tego asked.

JR made a show of looking at the clock in the middle of the esplanade filled with people. "Half an hour ago."

Tego laughed and patted him on the back again. "Fuckin' superhero, I tell you!" But when he locked eyes with him, he winced. "Oh, shit. Pardon my French, señorita."

If this poor man ever heard the words that came out of her mouth when she watched a fútbol game with her stepdad, he'd be shocked. Not that she swore like Stevie, but she wasn't Nadia either, who still choked when she whispered "shit."

"Nothing to pardon," she said. "But I was promised something delicious to drink, and the scent of oranges is killing me. In a good way," she rushed to add in case Tego misconstrued her words. "Tell me, what do you have here?"

Tego's face lit up.

"Now we're in for it!" JR exclaimed, grabbing Madi's hand and making as if they were going to run.

"I'm thirsty," she exclaimed, stomping her foot. The gesture wasn't very effective in the foam sandals, and when Madi caught JR's eye, they both laughed.

"I don't want to detain you, but you'd be missing out if you don't try at least one of my chinas. Not to speak about my mimosa version with china nativa," Tego said with a wink.

"Mimosa, you say?" Madi said, narrowing her eyes. Up till now, mimosas had been a brunch-only drink, but she was tempted.

"With local oranges!"

JR shook his head and threw his hands in the air.

"I warned you," he muttered through the corner of his mouth.

But Madi was enchanted with Tego's enthusiasm as he described the different orange variations he and his sister grew on their farm, how Hurricane Irma took almost every fruit waiting to be harvested, and then Hurricane Maria had swept by to finish the job of destruction. "Here, try this one. It's a Valencia. My great-great-great-grandfather brought seeds from his natal Valencia, and we keep a patch of them in the most special part of the finca." He grabbed the knife from the little sheath in his belt, and in a swift movement, he cut a section of orange and handed it to Madi. Without hesitation, she bit a half of the orange segment. Her taste buds exploded and she could swear a chorus started chanting hallelujah nearby. She had a vision of sunlight and that hue of red you see when you close your eyes as you look up and the sun hits your face.

"Oh my god," she said, half-embarrassed for the soft moan that escaped her mouth. Impulsively, she put the other half of the orange segment to her new friend's mouth. "Try it!"

"I have, many, many times before," he said, but didn't stop her. He took the piece of fruit, but before Madi could withdraw her hand from his mouth, he licked his lips and brushed her finger in the process.

It was a good thing his eyes were closed because the brief contact of lips and fingers made Madi's body warm like one of the bonfires dotting the beach behind her.

"Ambrosia from the gods, right?" she said.

He opened his eyes. A corner of his mouth twitched in the ghost of a smile but there was a strange intensity when he said, "Right."

She would swear they were still talking about oranges, but she wasn't quite sure.

"Exactly," Tego said, seemingly unaware about the shift in energy between Madi and JR. He fed a few oranges to the peeler. Orange ribbons danced and finally fell into an enormous barrel to join the mountain of fragrant rinds.

"I'll make you a mimosa with chilled juice from this Valencia and a local sparkling wine," Tego said. Then he glanced at JR. "I finally got the license."

"Just in time for Noche de San Juan!"

"'Acho! It was a much-needed break." He prepared the drink lovingly.

"I didn't know there was local wine. I thought the island only produced rum," Madi said. "I'd love to see this vineyard!"

JR nodded. "I know the owners. I could hook you up."

"Good people," Tego said.

A line of curious, and thirsty, mainland-looking tourists had formed around and behind Madi and JR.

Tego noticed the line too, and looking at JR said, "She brought me good luck. Never let this 'friend' go!"

JR grabbed a cup from the table and knocked it back while a gleeful Tego handed Madi a transparent plastic cup. But she was already grabbing money from her small crossbody purse. She'd gotten cash at the hotel ATM just for the vendors.

"Don't even think about it." Tego's tone was sharp and dry and left no room for argument. "It's on the house. It was a slow night in spite of the crowds, and you brought me light and good fortune. Now, try it!"

Madi sighed, but she accepted the gift. She took a sip and her body flooded with sweet, bubbly freshness.

"Delicious!" she said, after she'd gulped down to the last drop. "I'll have another one, but I'll pay for this one."

Tego shook his head, but served her another drink while Madi placed a twenty-dollar bill in a jar on the table.

"Did you love it?" a blond woman asked Madi. When she turned to reply, she saw that Tego had playfully grabbed JR by the shirt to whisper something in his ear.

Madi didn't get to hear what they were talking about, but Tego laughed.

JR whispered in Spanish something that sounded like "I'm going to kill you."

She was about to demand they speak louder, but the woman was still waiting for her answer.

"This is the best drink I've had in a long time," she said, and sipped the rest of her cocktail, careful not to spill a drop since he had gently taken her elbow to lead her away from the orange stand.

"Bye, Tego!" Madi said, calling over her shoulder.

Tego replied, "You two go and have a great time! Don't be shy!"

JR laughed but his cheeks were flushed.

They hadn't walked very far when a woman walking in their direction called, "Nene!" Her arms were wide open and her gaze zeroed in on Madi and her new friend.

"Jaimelet," he said after they'd hugged. "I thought you'd left for Boston last month. Weren't you teaching?"

For not being from the island, he was more popular than the mayor, while the woman might have fit in a circus a century ago with her red dress and bangles and bracelets. Her skin was white, and she had green eyes, but she had a pale gold afro and a generous mouth and beautiful features that proclaimed her African heritage.

Madi never ceased to be surprised by the racial diversity of this tiny island.

"There was a little revolú in the department and in my life," Jaimelet said in the trademark Puerto Rican Spanglish. "I extended my leave of absence. I'll be back for Winter term. Will I see you there?"

He? At the university? He was full of secrets, and Madi was so curious.

He just shrugged and replied in English, "I'll be in Idaho this winter."

In the brief conversation, his accent had turned one hundred percent Western American.

At the mention of Idaho, Jaimelet winced, and he laughed.

"I know, I know," he said. "I'm doing things the opposite way rational people might go about it, but I have to take care of a few things there. If things go well, in the spring, I'd love to come back here."

Idaho in the winter? Even with snowed-in roads it wasn't that far from her small town in Utah.

But what was she thinking? She had no plans of ever seeing

him in Utah, Idaho, or Puerto Rico for that matter. She'd just met him, and she was never doing the love-at-first-sight thing ever again.

"Then I'll see you when you hopefully return," Jaimelet said, disappointed. "Need a palm reading that will help you decide?" she asked, and although she smiled, JR shook his head and rolled his eyes. "Never."

"I know you don't believe in that kind of stuff, but I had to try!" Jaimelet turned toward Madi and said, "How rude of me not to introduce myself. I'm an old friend of this guy here. Would you like a palm reading?" Jaimelet asked her, switching to Spanish.

Madi was delighted that she passed as a local *and* that she'd been offered a palm reading. Shockingly, other than one in New Orleans right after high school, she'd never had one before.

"Does the lit-up face like a child in a carousel mean yes?" Jaimelet said.

But he was shaking his head. "I don't recommend palm readings by this lady or any," he said, taking Madi's hand in his.

"Why not?" she asked, narrowing her eyes at him.

"I don't believe in fate or destiny," he said, and although Madi had been determined to bury her dreams of finding her soul mate, his words made her insides twist with disappointment.

He must have thought his words sounded a little harsh, because he added, "If you want one, you can do it, you know. But palm reading, divination, gambling, it's all the same in my opinion." His voice sounded amused but underneath his laughter, Madi felt fear. His.

That's why she decided to decline the offer. Not that she needed his permission or anyone's, but she wasn't going to get her hand read with him listening. She was self-conscious.

Jaimelet's light laugh lifted the sudden tension from them. "For all he wants to appear skeptical, he's more of a gambler and reader of signs that anyone I know."

"How so?" Madi asked.

The woman shrugged. "He's a farmer. Planting is a little like throwing caution to the wind and tempting fate. A storm could come and take everything away. Dust from the Sahara might blow and suffocate the harvest, an unknown pest or fungus might infect his crops, but he keeps going. He trusts even if the results don't all depend on his two strong hands."

She said the last thing while grabbing his hands.

He made a show of freeing himself from her grasp.

Jaimelet shook her head like he was a lost cause. "Don't be so skittish! The lines in your hands mark a map that can direct your path. It's not set in stone. It's set in your blood."

Madi's heart beat strongly. Her mind also felt bubbly. Effect of the two drinks she'd had without food in her stomach. Uh-oh! She was in trouble now.

"How is that not worse?" he asked Jaimelet. "At least you can smash stones and turn them to dust. On the other hand, you can bleed yourself dry to shed whatever destiny was passed down on you and never succeed."

"How can having a path charted for you be the worst that you can imagine? To me, the worst is walking in the dark, only because you're stubborn enough not to turn the lights on. Now that's silly. Won't you agree, mama?" Jaimelet said to Madi.

Madi was about to take Jaimelet's side of the argument when her phone rang, startling all of them as if phones were a thing that didn't belong in the magic of this night.

"Excuse me," Madi said in English when she saw the screen, and then she answered. "Audri!"

Audri said something, but Madi could hardly hear a thing with the crowd dancing along a line of tables where old men played dominos and a dog barked at the beat of the drumming music.

"I can't see you." Madi stood in the middle of the esplanade and rose to her tiptoes, which didn't help at all. She hadn't risen more than one inch. As if that would allow her to see above the line of freakishly tall European tourists trying their steps at bomba and plena. But then she caught a glimpse of her friend. "There you are! Wait for us!"

She turned to look at JR. He and his friend were still playfully arguing.

"¡Payaso!" Jaimelet slapped his shoulder.

"I found them," Madi said, still wondering why Jaimelet had called him a clown. His lips were soft with a smile, but there was a seriousness to his expression.

Although it seemed like he was just like Jayden, who didn't believe in fate or destiny, he'd been wonderful with her so far. He and his friend kissed goodbye on the cheek, and he walked toward Madi, who'd wandered to the curb trying to find Audri and Mariela. Without a word, they both crossed the street, weaving through the tourists from the cruise ships that docked overnight so the passengers could enjoy the most magical hours on the most magical night in San Juan.

"There you are!" Audri said to Madi, and hugged her tight. Then she looked up at him and said, "Thanks for bringing her back safe and sound."

He brushed his hair back, ducking as if embarrassed, and smiled. Mariela patted him on the shoulder. "I'm glad you made it down here. I was worried you'd found her and you two decided to head a different way."

"'Tas loca?" he said, making a terrified face.

Madi narrowed her eyes at him.

It wasn't that she was interested in him in a romantic way. After all, she'd friend-zoned him pretty soon after meeting, but what was she? A monster so hideous that the possibility of ditching his friend for her seemed like craziness?

Madi looked away to hide the warring feelings inside her from the group, mainly Audri, who might guess her thoughts.

Right then, she saw a group of women around her age standing on the corner, conferring with each other. A skinny one in a red dress peeled off from the group. Laughing and squealing, one of them hollered at her to stop whatever she was thinking of doing, but Red Dress took off toward JR, who seemed oblivious to them.

"Here," Red Dress said, handing him a piece of paper, her gaze resolute and unflinching. "My friend thinks you're the most gorgeous man she's ever seen. She might be a little drunk, but like the saying goes: Children and drunks always tell the truth."

"Oh my god!" he muttered, blushing to the roots of his hair.

"What do we say, handsome?" Mariela told him in a teasing voice. "Have you been away from civilization for so long that you don't even know how to take a compliment anymore?"

Audri and Madi exchanged an amused look.

"Thanks?" he said, and he pocketed the number. "I'm flattered. Have a great night."

"Great night is what you can have if you call my friend!" The woman winked at him and returned to her friends.

"Mira pa'llá!" Mariela said. "Breaking hearts left and right."

Unwillingly, his eyes flickered to Madi, but she averted her gaze from his. He was a handsome man, perhaps the most handsome guy she'd met in a long time. Why wasn't he taken if women pretty much threw themselves at him? Madi didn't long to be another one, but it was hard to pull away from him.

She was definitely feeling the effects of the two drinks she'd gulped.

"I really need some food," she said, already feeling like she was floating. She wasn't a lightweight when it came to alcohol, but she was jet-lagged and had had no food in more hours than she could count. She'd been so unlike herself today.

Or really, she'd been more like her true self, the part that she tried to hide from everyone, even herself.

"We just ate," Audri told her.

JR and Mariela walked closer to Madi and Audri.

"I'm going to get something from the food trucks," he said. "Do you want me to bring you anything?"

A delicious smell of something frying in ancient oil (the best smell in the world) lured her like in the cartoons she'd loved watching in bed as a child. She wanted to see what the options were, but at the same time, she was hesitant to spend more time alone with him.

"Go with him," Audri said, gently shoving Madi away. She had the suspicion that she wanted more time alone with Mariela, who seemed to share Audri's thoughts. Madi wasn't keen on being a third wheel.

"I'll come along," she said. "Lead the way."

They headed toward the line of food trucks in a strange silence. He hadn't been like this on their walk down to la Plazoleta. Maybe he'd like the space to call the number in his pocket?

He seemed to sense the sudden chill between them because he asked, "Everything okay? You're too quiet."

She shrugged one shoulder. "What do you usually get here? Empanadillas? Which ones do you prefer?"

"Empanadillas all the way. The pizza one is my favorite, but make sure you leave room for a jueyes one."

She wrinkled her nose. She didn't remember what jueyes was.

"Crab," he said, guessing her question.

"Of course," she replied, and then, half-embarrassed, half-concerned, she whispered, "Is it safe to eat crab from a food truck at this time of night? By the way, what time is it?"

He glanced at his watch. "Ten thirty. And don't worry, I think the hot oil kills any germs."

She laughed, and when it was her turn in line, she ordered two empanadillas, one each of pizza and jueyes.

When she was done, she looked at him. He hesitated, and then said, "I'll actually have a tripleta."

"Good choice!" the woman in the food truck exclaimed with a smile in her voice.

"A tripleta?" Madi asked. Like with jueyes, she didn't remember about them. "What is it?"

"It's basically a club sandwich," he finally said.

A teenage boy behind them scoffed, and JR turned around and looked at him questioningly. "What?"

The pimply, gangly, pasty-skinned boy rolled his eyes and, looking at Madi, said, "Yes, basically it is a club, and the key word here is 'basically.' Because it's a sandwich, but it tastes nothing like any other sandwich you'll eat anywhere else in the world. It's the bread. The sauce. And even the hand of the person preparing the sandwich."

The food truck woman said, "After such excellent recommendation, I need to give you discount!"

"I have a more glowing recommendation than that," JR said. "I don't usually eat cold meats, but I would have a tripleta from this truck every day of my life."

"What? Are you a vegetarian?" the woman asked, like being a vegetarian was a crime.

He laughed and shook his head. "It's just that I work in the food industry. I know too much!"

"Man, you look like a vegetarian," the boy said, shaking his head. "You have less game than a kindergartener. You brought her here and maybe she wanted a salad, by the looks of her."

There was a brief, painful silence. He took a deep breath, not the kind when you want to meditate, but the one before you slash someone to the point they can't recover.

Madi must have been tipsy, there was no other explanation, but the boy was plain rude, and she had to rescue JR from playing the superhero again. Apparently, this was a thing with him. She hooked her arm in his and, leveling the boy with her gaze, said, "The way to my heart is through my stomach. I appreciate a man who respects women's eating preferences without shaming them. You should learn that. The world is changing, nene."

The boy, chastised, ducked his head and smiled sheepishly.

While JR was distracted, Madi paid.

"What? No!" he said while the teenager mumbled, "No game, dude."

"I'm all for women's equality and all that, but—"

"No buts," Madi said, cutting him with a raised hand. "The world is changing, I said."

Before he could object, she grabbed his hand and led him away from the food trucks and toward the party at the beach.

Chapter 9

Madi expected that with the effect of the empanadilla, the bubbles in her head would settle a bit. But if anything, the more time she spent with JR, the bubblier she felt.

Effervescent, ebullient.

It could also be the effect of the party around them. The energy was so vibrant that it was impossible not to feel intoxicated by the joy around her. A true extrovert, she was a human emotions sponge. The vibes she got from him told her he was attracted to her.

Truth be told, she was so attracted to him, especially his luscious lips she couldn't stop staring at. Not wanting to seem too obvious, she trained her gaze to his hand, and hence, the sandwich.

And maybe because a part of him had taken the notion that the way to her heart was through her stomach, he offered her the last half of his tripleta, which, by the way, was indeed way more than a club sandwich.

"Do you want it?"

With Jayden, she'd have never said yes. Not in a million years because then he'd "joke" about her appetite for weeks until she felt self-conscious to eat in front of him again. But after this week, she'd never see JR again. Besides, he didn't seem like that type of guy . . .

Ugh! She hated when men told her "You're not like the other girls I've dated," because it was always a cop-out. She was just like every other woman she knew who wanted to be loved and accepted just the way she was. Each time she started acting like herself, the guys had been disappointed and left.

But JR felt nothing like the other guys she'd ever met. Well, maybe Marcos, her friend Nadia's fiancé, was kind of like him: respectful, kind, considerate. But Madi had only ever thought of him as that, Nadia's Marcos, almost a brother. She had already friend-zoned JR, and she hoped that when she met the love of her lives, hanging out with him would be at least a little like hanging out with JR. She'd never felt so vulnerable and yet safe with a guy like she did with him.

She took the sandwich he offered and finished it off in a couple of bites.

"We can get more food if you want," he said, nodding approvingly.

Madi laughed. A part of her, the one that wasn't drunk and that only kept guard, told her to watch her reactions. She was being a little too intense, too loud. But she couldn't help it.

"Maybe later," she said, motioning toward the bonfires on the beach.

Several groups danced around the fire to the rhythm of the typical Puerto Rican sounds of salsa, merengue, and reggaeton. The sight of Mariela and Audri dancing together, absorbed with each other as if no one else existed in the world, captivated Madi.

"Want to dance?" She extended her hand out.

He hesitated for just a second, and Madi tried not to take the pause personally. "I can teach you if you don't know how."

He laughed, throwing his head back as if she'd said the most extravagant thing in the world. "In her attempts to keep me on the island, Tego's sister made sure I learned how to dance. Not to be ridiculous at least, so, no. It's not that I don't know how to dance."

Tego's sister kept coming up in their conversation. Maybe she was in love with JR and that's why she wanted to keep him on the island? He was sure much sought after.

"But if it's not that, then why won't you dance with me?"

He gazed into her eyes for a few seconds. Good thing it was dark so maybe he couldn't see that she was blushing violently as she tried to guess what he was thinking.

"I won't step on you. I promise," she said.

He offered his hand, and she took it. Together, they headed toward one of the groups but stayed in the edges.

They waited a beat until they could join the rhythm of the salsa song. Around them, couples twirled and circled in feats of athleticism. Old and young, gringos and Latines, tourists and locals. Even if most of them would never be competing for the crown in *Dancing with the Stars*, they still moved like constellations in the sky, circling the fire like it was the sun.

The night of San Juan had a special magic that helped people forget about their woes at least for the length of a song. He started confidently and slowly, and Madi followed his lead, at ease in her own skin. He placed a hand on her waist to lead her to a turn. The warmth of his hand on her skin seared through the flimsy fabric. His gaze was glued on her face, and she returned it, unabashedly.

Men sometimes stared at her in a way that made her feel naked, vulnerable, and unsafe. But he looked at her like she was a treasure he'd lost and found after the longest quest.

His smooth, brown skin glowed under the moonlight, and when he pressed her close to him, she took in the scent of his skin and a faint cologne that smelled like grass and the ocean. The one from the elevator! She was almost swooning.

They followed each other's movements like they'd danced this way forever. Even their breathing was in sync.

She wanted to know all about him, like where his looks and accent came from, but didn't want to ask so bluntly. She hated when people asked her. So for now, they danced.

The song ended, and a charged silence thundered between them before the next song started. Madi brushed the hair from her face. He lifted the strap of her dress that kept falling down her shoulder.

Suddenly, the tension between them grew to an impossible level.

He held her gaze, his breath, and leaned in. In that moment, an alarm went off from a phone nearby, and soon, others joined.

"It's midnight!" a woman called from one of the bonfires.

Madi blinked as if she were coming out of a spell, her chest heaving with the exertion of the dance and the anticipation of a kiss she could almost taste. She felt so guilty. She didn't want him to be a one-night stand.

She told herself she was attracted to him because she was still a little drunk, and the ambiance around them was so suggestive.

As if to confirm her thoughts, the crowd headed to the ocean all at once. Couples, friend groups, even families with children.

Madi looked around but she couldn't find Audri and Mariela.

He caught her eye, and once again, offered his hand.

She took it and they headed to the edge of the water. Usually in this section of Old San Juan, people didn't get to bathe in the sea. It wasn't a beach per se, but there was a crescent of sand, and the ocean was calm and shallow. The police officers on duty didn't bar anyone's march to the water.

Ahead of her, people were falling into the water on their backs, the friends around them counting and laughing and clapping.

The sand still held some heat from the day's scorching sun. She held her breath as a small wave reached to her. When the warm sea-foam touched her, she gasped.

"Is it cold?" he asked, smiling, as he braced himself to step into the water.

"Not at all," she said, and walked on. "It surprised me, that's all."

She was just full of emotion at being in the sea again. She'd longed to be in the water as if she were a mermaid, like she had pretended when she was little and swam with her abuela and her cousins. Her body broke in goose bumps as the water kissed her skin, but it wasn't because she was cold. She was excited. Her nerve endings were tingling.

"Ready for your wishes?" he asked, his wet button-up shirt clinging to his muscles.

She looked down at her dress and realized that her outfit wasn't the most modest for this occasion.

"Pretend you're wearing a bikini underneath," he said, shrugging as if he'd seen it all and nothing could faze him anymore.

She laughed.

"Should we take turns or go together?"

He considered for a second. "Together."

It was better this way so he wasn't staring at her and vice versa. What if she had a wardrobe malfunction?

Holding her hands, he said, "At the count of three."

"Wait," she said. "How many times?"

"Seven's a good number."

"The best number."

Her birthday was February seventh. As a true Aquarius, she was dreamy and airy. *Airhead,* one of her boyfriends had called her once. She had laughed it off, but years after they'd broken up, it still bothered her. She hoped that along with taking her wish, the water would wash away the hurts that she'd accumulated over the years.

"Okay, ready?" he asked.

"Ready."

"One, two, three," they said in unison.

They went under the water at the same time. Seven times. Later, when Madi revisited this moment, she'd have flashes of the stars, the Morro Castle in the background, the fire on the beach, his incandescent smile. She wanted to remember the moment forever.

She had lost count of how many times they'd gone under, and she hadn't thought of a wish yet. She had to do it quickly.

"Help me find him," she whispered, her heart pounding because maybe she already had. Would it be possible that she'd have a strong connection and attraction like this if JR wasn't the man she was supposed to spend all eternity with?

She didn't know what to think.

"Are we done?" he asked.

Gasping for air after diving under the surface for the seventh time, she stopped to look up at him.

She shouldn't have done that.

He was Mariela's cousin. He was their tour guide. Madi should just make friends first. She didn't want a fling. She'd been so involved in her relationship with Jayden, that she'd forgotten who she was. She'd promised she'd give herself time before she was ready for another relationship. This was against all her plans.

But Madi was gonna Madi.

Since when did she follow strict plans? She always decided with her heart, like a feather tossed by the wind.

And right now, she was a feather tossed by the ocean waves, the magic of the night, and his magnetic gaze.

"Did you make your wish?" she asked.

He stared into her eyes and his eyes flickered to her lips. He nodded.

As if telling them to stop the games, a wave, much bigger and stronger than the rest, pushed her against him. He caught her in his arms.

"I got you," he whispered to her ear.

Lift your head and kiss him, a part of her demanded.

Don't you dare! said another.

She didn't even know who to obey. She was too scared to really know what she wanted. Or to accept it.

This was her first night in San Juan and she was already making a mess of everything. She was here for business. If she wanted her career to be treated seriously, she had to be the first one to act like a professional.

But she couldn't help it.

It wasn't only the physical beauty. What could she say? She liked beautiful people, and she wouldn't apologize for it. But even though they'd only known each other for a measly couple of hours, she could tell he was also beautiful on the inside. She couldn't see auras or anything like that. But she sensed he had a bluish glow, that of pure, healthy light.

The kind that attracts mosquitos and other insects.

What did that make her? A fly?

A light breeze blew from the open sea. She shuddered and crossed her arms, which were covered with goose bumps. She did it more to shield her from doing something she'd regret than to protect her from him.

Beyond the castle, the waves broke in magical white foam. She was so conflicted that she got a little dizzy. Or maybe she was still much drunker than she'd imagined. She stepped closer to him, and buoyed by the water, she found her mouth wasn't that far from his.

"Javier," she whispered, tasting how his name sounded on her lips. She closed her eyes and lifted her face, her lips parted.

But . . . he didn't kiss her.

She cracked her eyes open and saw him staring into her face. His expression had changed. He didn't look like he was going to kiss her anymore. He looked confused and . . . angry?

Alarms went on in her mind.

"What happened?" she asked, disappointed that the magic between them had dissolved like sea-foam.

"What did you call me?" he asked instead of answering her question.

She stepped back, but since they were much deeper in the water than she'd anticipated, she still had to hold on to him.

"What?" she said. "I just whispered your name."

"What name though?"

He wasn't making any sense.

"Javier. Which other name would I say?"

He scoffed. "That's not my name. I'm Peter."

A niggling suspicion fell on her.

"No," she said, stubbornly. "You're our tour guide, Javier Rodriguez. JR, right?"

But he'd never told her his name. She'd assumed. She knew their tour guide was Javier, JR, and when this guy had introduced himself as the tour guide, she'd made the connection. The wrong connection.

"Javier had to fly to Miami this morning. It's his daughter's birthday in a couple of days, and he had to figure out a few things with the mother. He asked me to cover for him." Not-JR narrowed his eyes at her. "Although I never thought you were part of the deal."

Madi let go of him as if his skin burned. A wave slapped her, and it took her a couple of seconds to catch her breath.

A bout of nausea rose inside her.

"Did you and Javier have an . . . understanding online or something that I didn't know about? Sometimes people say we look alike at first glance, but . . ."

"Oh my gosh," she said, understanding all the assumptions he was making in his mind. All the wrong assumptions. "It's nothing like that. It's just that . . ."

She didn't know how to explain that she had weaved a complete fiction in her mind and now she was too embarrassed to tell him she'd been willing to be swept away by his looks and his charms because she'd thought he had the right initials.

Now that she saw things from this clear perspective, it all sounded so ridiculous.

She wanted to cry. The nausea crested like a wave, but she

didn't want to throw up in the ocean. If she threw up now, there would be no recovery from the trauma and humiliation.

She looked at JR—no, at Peter, with alarm, and he, probably sensing her distress, took a step in her direction.

"No," she managed to say, pressing one hand to her mouth, and raising the other as if to stop him. Without another thought, she dashed back to the beach, and beelined straight to a single palm tree that stood next to one of the now empty bonfires. She braced herself against the coarse tree trunk with her hands and breathed deeply until the nausea passed.

She wanted to disappear. She wanted to wake up from this nightmare.

She'd made a fool of herself.

Chapter 10

In a perfect world, Madi would have had the presence of mind to explain to him why she'd called him Javier. Maybe they would have laughed about the whole misunderstanding. It would make for a sweet meet-cute story in the future.

But she had to run away and act like he made her sick.

By the time Peter found her by the palm tree, she was shivering with cold, and embarrassment. Like a gentleman, he grabbed their phones from under some rocks where he had suggested they hide them. Up until he'd mentioned it, Madi hadn't even considered how she'd go in the water and not ruin her phone for the rest of her trip. She could slap herself.

Without a word, he draped a jacket over her shoulders. The scent of his woodsy cologne never failed to tickle her stomach. Why didn't her body get the message that nothing would happen between this man and her now she'd made a complete fool of herself?

"Thanks," she whispered.

"You're at Casa Grande Hotel, right? I'm staying there too."

His voice was still kind, but the light had gone out of him. The magnetic connection between them was gone.

Madi couldn't stand it, but she didn't know how to explain what had happened without sounding like an idiot. Or a worse idiot. Who falls in love with someone only because they might have the initials she saw in a childhood dream? Peter had told his friend Jaimelet he didn't believe in fate or destiny. He'd think she was unhinged.

"I'm there, but what about Audri?" Madi asked. Her phone still didn't have a signal.

"I'm pretty sure she'll guess you headed back," Peter said.

"And your car? It's by La Sirena."

"I'll get it tomorrow. There's no rush."

She was too humiliated and emotionally exhausted to argue. She didn't feel like a sexy goddess or even Cinderella anymore. She felt like a wet goose. She felt like Cinderella's pumpkin the morning after the ball. She felt like a rubber flip-flop left out under the sun on a scorching summer day.

Whatever the waves had taken from her, she hoped they'd left a little bit of dignity for the rest of her stay on the island.

Madi was harsher with herself than anyone else could ever be. She was so disappointed in her behavior. The squelching sounds of her rubber sandals as she trudged uphill made her wince. The silence between them was suffocating but she didn't even have the strength to take a deep breath to clear her mind. At this point, the only thing that would help her was falling asleep to reset.

Finally, they arrived at Casa Grande Hotel. The receptionist flashed them a radiant smile. Well, not them. Him.

"Hi, Peter," she said in a breathy voice. Her name tag read ADA.

Her expression was proof that it hadn't been Madi's fault that she'd fallen for this gorgeousness of a man. Every woman melted at the sight of his perfectly chiseled face. Every woman felt captive to the seductive way he didn't seem to know how hot a kind, unassuming guy was. Even a flitting glimpse of his strong forearms hugged by his rolled-up shirt made Madi's tummy tickle again. But she sighed, hoping tomorrow morning her head would be clearer.

Peter not only reciprocated the blond beauty's smile but breached the imaginary barrier of her desk and kissed her on the cheek.

"Almost done for the night?" he asked.

"Almost," she said.

A few people lingered by the bubbling fountain in the hotel's internal patio.

Ada, the picture of professionalism, turned to Madi and asked, "Anything I can help you with, Miss Ramírez?"

"No, thanks," Madi replied, then she turned to Peter. "You didn't have to walk me but thank you. And thanks for the sandals."

"My pleasure," he said, but she was too embarrassed to look him in the face.

"Bye," she said, and headed to her room half in relief and half in agony that she wouldn't see him again until the next day.

"Bye," Peter replied, but she didn't turn to see if he was looking at her. There was no need—he and Ada were entertained with each other.

All night long, Madi tossed and turned in bed as she relived the night. Everything had been magical. That is, until she whispered the wrong name. It was so cringey! What must JR—Peter—think of her?

Everything had been perfect. He had been perfect. What did it matter that his name wasn't what she thought? It wasn't like he had deceived her! But hers had been an honest mistake. If only she'd explained it to him instead of running away . . .

Now he had the completely wrong idea. Her stepdad, Santiago, always said there was only one chance to make a great first impression.

But she had no one else to blame but herself.

For all her determination not to let herself be tossed by instalove—like always—she had thrown caution to the wind and acted like a fool.

When she was almost asleep, her phone chimed with a notification. It was Audri.

Are you in your room? Everything all right?

Madi didn't know what to say. Nothing was all right. She was so embarrassed, so she replied, **In my room. See you tomorrow.**
She hoped the tone of her text wasn't too cutting, so she added, **And you?**

If the three dots dancing on the screen were an indication, Audri's night seemed to have gone much better than Madi's.

It was amazing. I'll tell you later in the lobby. 8 am sharp, sounds good? The tour meets at 9.

The clock on the nightstand flashed two a.m. Madi groaned as she covered her face with a pillow in case the people next door were paying attention to what was happening in her room and got the wrong impression.

How was she going to face Peter in just a few hours?

Maybe if she made a run for it, she might be able to catch a flight to somewhere no one knew her, and she could start all over. But she would die of loneliness and boredom.

The only way out is through.

Another one of Santiago's sayings. The easiest way was for her to face the mess that she'd made.

Now all she wanted was the sweet relief of oblivion.

Of course, oblivion wouldn't come.

Her body was too tight, and not even a quick yoga flow helped soothe her clenched muscles. She meditated, prayed, listened to affirmations, counted sheep.

But all she saw was his hurt face when she'd called him Javier and the cycle would start all over again. She was even scared of revisiting the whole night in her dreams, or worse, seeing another one of those in which she had found her soul mate only to wake up and realize it had all been a trick of her overactive imagination.

Finally, when the birds were already waking up and chirping out her window, she dozed off.

With a sliver of consciousness, she clung to sleepiness like she taught during her yoga nidra classes. She was eager to escape the endless, dark loop of humiliation in which she remembered not only the events of the night but also every embarrassing thing she'd done throughout her life. The list was long, to say the least, but she was exhausted.

Eventually, her mind and body sank deeper and deeper into unconsciousness.

Sleep claimed her, and she dreamed.

She was in the ocean. She was a fish in a swarm of sentient red koi, their fins silky and long like ribbons. At the front their pod, their leader—mother?—advised them to swim ahead. A little distance away in the ocean, a similar pod swam up to meet their mates in Madi's pod.

Madi the fish swam with ease and confidence.

With a certainty she couldn't explain, she knew that soon, she'd see someone who would change the course of her life. She never got a sign from the mother/leader, but she felt something propel her ahead to her destiny. When the two pods met, she saw a crimson fish that stood out against the rest, and she followed it. He was identical to the others, and yet, uniquely beautiful and attractive. She was mesmerized by his glamour. The fish flickered a fin, and she knew he felt exactly as she did.

Her fins flickered too.

One by one, her companions paired up, and as one, rose to the surface.

Madi waited for her mate, her companion, and together, they swam up, up, up to the unknown.

When her head broke through the surface, strange constellations danced in a purple and red sky. A ringed planet like Saturn emitted a milky light that softly bathed the whole firmament and ocean. Next to her was *her* ribbon koi fish, the soul that called her from life to life. He was the complement of her soul.

The same but, oh, so different.

Just when they were about to touch heads like it was the custom in their species, Madi woke up. Her alarm was blaring.

Outside the window, the sky had a purplish hue that reminded her of the ocean of her dreams. She plopped back on the pillow, her heart pounding with urgency, longing, and a tinge of sadness.

A tug in the center of her solar plexus urged her to find her person. But what if she'd already found him?

Peter's face flashed in her mind, and for all she tried, she couldn't shake it away.

She had to stop these dreams. They were making her life miserable with longing.

Last night with him had been so strange and magical that it seemed more distant and improbable than the dream with the ribbon koi fish. Saltwater koi fish at that.

Maybe he'd feel the same way and ignore her blunder.

She found her phone in the tangled covers, and texted Audri to let her know she'd meet her at the fountain in the hotel's internal patio. Today they were heading west, to the Caves of Camuy, which she'd wanted to visit since she was a kid.

The observatory in Arecibo had collapsed for lack of maintenance, but there was still a visitors' area.

When she was little, she and Abuela Lina had watched the movie *Contact* countless times. Abuela had promised her that one day they'd see the observatory together. The telescope might not work anymore, but Madi still wanted to take a look at it at least.

Although her mind was still full of cotton, she set out her clothes for the day and repacked her bags in case the day went horrible and she decided to check out and go back home.

But just as she wanted to explore the island, she also wanted to explore the hotel that once upon a time had been a home for nuns. Although the room was comfortable, it still had a flair of the colonial area. The hallways were dark and moody, the perfect setting for a romantic story—or a horror one.

But there was no horror like the prospect of seeing Peter in the daytime. Every time she thought about it, her heart galloped in double step. No breathing exercise or meditation slowed it down. In these moments, the only way to vanquish the anxiety was to get things done.

The shower was luxurious and hot, and once she opened the bathroom door, the steam fogged up the whole room. She got dressed and checked her phone. She almost dropped it. She had a long text from Jayden.

Last night, I had a dream about you. Several, actually, the kind that I haven't had since I was a teen. I don't know what is happening, but I miss you and I needed to tell you.

Her first reaction was curiosity. It was four in the morning in California, his first stop in his endless summer business trips. Had he had the same dream about the saltwater koi fish? Her fingertips were itching to type the question. But mercifully, reason took over. Why was she excited he had a dream about her and thought it was a good idea to tell her?

Jayden probably thought she should be flattered that he'd dreamed about her, and that kind of dream to boot. But she felt offended actually that his first reaction was to say he didn't know what was happening. They'd been talking about getting married. She had proposed to him and he couldn't even acknowledge that he loved her? And most importantly, couldn't he show her he missed her without implying that it was only because he missed the sex?

All heated up because of the humidity and her racing heart, she took a last glance at herself in the mirror. Her black leggings and flowy top covered what needed to be covered. No one could ever accuse her of trying to seduce anyone. She pulled her hair up in a demure knot on the top of her head and reapplied her lip gloss.

She wanted to look respectable, someone to take seriously, but she wasn't sure she was pulling it off. She'd be happy to settle for basic tourist.

There was only one way to tell.

She made sure she had all her money, her hotel key, and an extra phone battery in her backpack, and left the room. Her footsteps echoed loudly against the hallway walls. The elevator arrived promptly, and she tapped each of her fingers against her thumbs as she repeated the mantra of the Kirtan Kriya to calm herself down.

Sa Ta Na Ma, she repeated softly. Sa Ta Na Ma.

It wasn't working. Her heart was still racing.

Luckily, she didn't cross paths with anyone. She needed a coffee and checking in with Audri before she could face the day. The gurgling music of the fountain in the courtyard grounded her. It must be her Sagittarius moon that longed for the coolness of water to quench her spirit.

Sometimes she wondered if she was the only unmoored and unattached person in the world. Maybe that's why she gravitated to men like Jayden. Men that reminded her of life's everyday concerns. But she always forgot her real purpose in life and ended up letting herself down.

"Breakfast for one?" the restaurant's hostess asked with a pleasant smile as Madi approached her podium.

Madi smiled back. She scanned the tables in case Audri was already there, but she didn't see her friend. "Table for two, please. My friend will join me shortly."

"Follow me," the hostess said, and led her to a quaint table behind the fountain. Perfect spot for gossiping and catching up without being overheard. When Madi sat down, a waiter fluttered gracefully to her side and poured juice in her glass.

"Fresh jugo de parcha on the house," he said.

Madi's taste buds prickled in anticipation of the sweet and tangy fruit she loved. She took a sip and wasn't disappointed. Calmness flooded her as the natural sugar hit her just right.

They used to have a parcha plant in Utah, but although it flowered once, it never gave fruit. Santiago called it mburucuyá. The lilac and indigo flowers had raised filaments that crisscrossed on the top of the corolla and formed a yellow cross, fat with pollen. The conquistadores, trying to see any justifications for the massacre taking place in the name of religion and their queen, when it was only their egos and greed leading them, had named the plant and its flower Pasionaria, for the passion of Christ. Way to add guilt and shame on everything. To her, it looked like a vulva. Pasionaria. Yes, full of passion.

"There you are!" Audri said, kissing her on the cheek and then sitting across from her.

Madi exhaled, both relieved and nervous. She had to tell someone what had happened the night before, but she was also worried Audri's opinion of her would change.

"Are you okay?" Audri asked, her forehead furrowed.

"Ah! I wanted to talk with you before the tour." She pressed her friend's hand for emphasis.

The waiter poured juice in Audri's glass and said, "Take a look at the menu and I'll be around shortly to take your order."

"Thanks," they said in unison.

Although the internal patio had an open ceiling, it was shady under the luscious foliage of so many plants. But Audri kept her sunglasses on. She looked like a reggaeton artist.

"Sorry I'm a little late. It was hard to get up this morning," she said.

"Understatement of the year," Madi said. "I feel like Midsummer Night ran me over like a truck."

Audri sipped from her glass and exhaled loudly. "This is delish. Good thing I don't live here, or I'd never stop eating and drinking. How is everything more delicious here?"

Madi was mid-swallow when she saw Peter walking into the restaurant by himself. She almost choked. She'd been wrong. Seeing him this morning was worse than a nightmare.

How was she going to go through a whole week of mortification?

Audri craned her neck to see what had affected Madi so much, and when she saw Peter, she nodded as if now everything made complete and total sense.

"And how can everyone be so much better looking in tropical weather? That man is just unfairly beautiful."

Madi still couldn't speak and Audri continued. "Mariela told me he's Japanese Peruvian on his mom's side and Puerto Rican on the dad's. I tell you, the people of this island are the most beautiful I've seen in my life."

After a sip of passion fruit juice, Madi had regained her speech. "I have to tell you something I did last night. You're going to think I'm a klutz, but I can't stand it anymore."

But before she bore her soul to her friend, they gave the waiter their robust breakfast order. Mallorcas, eggs, and a fruit and cheese platter, and coffee del país con leche. It was their first morning, but they wanted to try it all.

"It sounds just like grits," Audri said after the waiter had patiently gone over the most popular items on their menu and convinced them to try the cream de maíz.

Once he left, Madi leaned on her elbows and lowered her head to confess to her friend.

"Audri, I messed up our whole week," she said. "I'm so sorry."

Audri patted Madi's hand. "You slept with him." It wasn't even a question. It was a statement that left Madi speechless.

Audri continued. "Was he terrible, then? It wouldn't be the first or the last time that a guy with those looks can't match the expectations in bed, but what a shame. It'll be awkward only if he's being a jerk about it, but, love, you have no obligation to even talk to him again."

Audri thought she and Peter had slept together? Madi was so mortified. "What? No! I didn't sleep with him!"

"What happened then?" Audri's face transformed from compassion and understanding to sudden rage. "He was a jerk?" She looked over her shoulder as if she was determined to go strangle Peter with her bare hands.

Madi's eyes darted beyond the fountain, but she couldn't see where Peter had sat. Hopefully, he'd taken his breakfast to go. She couldn't add one more blunder to her long list of humiliations.

"Audri, please, let me talk. It was nothing like that!"

"Tell me then before I do something stupid!"

Madi sighed and hid her face in her hands. "When we were about to kiss, I called him the wrong name."

"Jayden's?"

"No," Madi said, her voice a whisper. "I called him Javier."

Audri made a head roll like she was dizzy. Putting a hand up, she demanded to know. "Wait. Javier? Why would you call him Javier? Our tour guide? How do you know him? And why was Peter upset?"

Madi swallowed the knot in her throat. If she wanted Audri to understand how dire her situation was, she'd have to start at the beginning.

"For you to understand, I have to tell you a little side story first. From a vision I had when I was thirteen."

Audri blew air from her puckered lips like she was teaching a hot yoga class and had to cool her body somehow. Like Madi, she too was a yoga instructor. But unlike Madi, Audri wasn't into the spiritual aspects of it. She professed no religion, but she was tolerant of Madi's and Reyna's esoteric and Christian/Buddhist/pagan inclinations.

The waiter brought the food just as Madi was gathering steam to confess the worst part. Audri ate a little of everything while listening attentively.

"And right after we bathed in the sea, we looked at each other and I felt this connection, like I knew him forever, you know?" Madi felt pure light coming out of her whole being as she recalled the feelings from the night before. "But the whole time, I thought he was Javier, JR, and right before we kissed, like, I could almost taste him, I called him *Javier*."

"Did he freak out then?" Audri asked.

Madi thought. "No. Not really. I think he would've laughed it off if I had played it cool. *I* was the one who freaked out and ran from him like he had turned into the prince from *Beauty and the Beast*."

Audri grimaced. "Not *that* prince! Ew!"

"Exactly," Madi said, slapping her hand on the table. Her café con leche sloshed from the teacup, and she dabbed at the table with one of the extra napkins. "I looked at him like I had woken up. In a way, it's true. I came to my senses. I understood how close I'd come to kissing someone I thought was someone else. It took me a minute or two to process that I wanted to kiss Peter no matter what, even if he had different initials. What I felt was real. I know he felt it too, but I had to go and put my foot in my mouth, like always. Now I'm too embarrassed to explain."

"I know he felt the same way," Audri said, pulling her phone out of her black fanny pack. Madi thought she was going to show her an incriminating text or email Peter had sent Audri, but it was a picture.

A selfie, more precisely. Audri and Mariela smiled right in the foreground, but the interesting image was in the background.

Madi's blood drained from her face.

"Ay, bendito!" she exclaimed, and grabbed the phone to squint at it better.

"Here," Audri said, and zoomed in with a pinch.

Blown up, the image both validated Madi's feelings that Peter had been totally into her as well. It also embarrassed her to no end.

She and Peter were dancing like it was just the two of them in *Dirty Dancing: San Juan Edition*.

Peter's face pressing down on her neck with her thrown-back hair caught in a frozen frame of an arch like spilled ink against the horizon glittering with stars. The people around them clapped while others watched in admiration and surprise. She caught a peek of the pink rubber flip-flops discarded by the bonfire and she cringed.

People had clapped at them? Some had even taken pictures? How many shots from different angles were circulating online by now? Had she been made into a TikTok?

So much for professionalism and dignity.

"Oh my stars," she muttered, and covered her face.

She imagined she was the living representation of the face-palm emoji.

"It's not that bad," Audri said.

"It's worse than bad, Aud. What must he think of me?"

"What do *you* think of him?" Audri shot back. The tone in her voice pulled Madi from her own private pity party. "From what Mariela said, Peter has a reputation for being untouchable. I mean, women *and* men throw themselves at him. You saw it with your own eyes. He, however, has never ever fallen for anyone. Mariela said she thought he was ace or aro—" Audri must have guessed the questions on Madi's face because she quickly added, "Asexual or aromantic. You know, someone who either doesn't feel physical sexual attraction or isn't interested in a romantic relationship."

"I don't know . . . He seemed pretty . . . physically, sexually attracted to me last night, like, I could feel it when we were dancing, and I'm not talking about a metaphor or anything abstract like that. He was . . . into me, you know what I mean?"

"Exactly," Audri said, widening her eyes and fanning her face. "Oof, yes. That's what Mariela found out from Javier once when she made that comment to him."

"And how does this guy Javier know that Peter isn't ace or aro?"

"Javier and Peter go way back. They were roommates freshmen year and have been friends ever since. They went on to get agronomy master's somewhere in Texas, but Javier set up a tourist company. Sometimes Peter helps him run things, but he works at a potato farm nearby."

"Potatoes?" Madi knew Idaho was known for its potatoes but she'd never met anyone who'd been involved with them at all.

"Anyway," Audri said, "apparently, Peter dated this woman all through college and graduate school until they had a terrible breakup last year. He hasn't had a girlfriend ever since. No one knows for sure, but it's like after his ex, he renounced relationships and love."

"So he's available," said Madi, trying not to get her hopes up. She thought she'd tamped down her enthusiasm, but she had obviously failed.

Audri cracked up, laughing.

"Oh my gosh! I love that you're so optimistic!"

"Optimistic? I'm such a fool!" Madi held her head with her hands as if it was too heavy with depressing thoughts. She was flattered Peter had been so into her, but she couldn't get over the fact that she'd messed things up so completely.

Madi sipped from her coffee and grimaced. It was lukewarm, but she drank to the last drop. She needed all the caffeine she could get since she hadn't meditated this morning and had only done a short yoga flow to recharge and recenter herself.

"What am I going to do now?" she said. "I may have ruined something beautiful and now it won't even have the chance to grow."

Audri drank the last of the passion fruit juice before she chimed, "Actually, and like always, I think applying the yoga themes is the best course of action."

This was what Madi wanted. What she needed. Someone to tell her exactly what to do.

"Surrender to the flow," Audri said, enumerating the themes as she counted with her fingers. "Let go of your ego to grow. Accept What Is. Embrace Non-Attachment. Find Stillness. Find Peace."

"Find Peace," Madi added, visualizing the giant poster they had at the studio.

The words reverberated around her. She knew these tenets by heart if not by practice. The first one, going with the flow, was the hardest.

In the past, she'd thought she was surrendering to the flow, but she was really waiting for things to happen to her. Her ego was pretty much in shambles, so letting go of the leftovers shouldn't be so hard for her. But embracing non-attachment to the idea of soul mates? And how was she going to find stillness if her mind never stopped chattering?

"More than find peace I want to find love, Aud. Isn't love the guiding force of the universe?"

"It is," Audri reassured her.

"If I can't find the love of my lives, maybe I can just find a little house by the beach to spend the rest of my life like a recluse," she said, knowing she sounded pathetic.

"I think that first, you need to fall in love with yourself again, Madi," Audri said in a patient voice. "Self-love is very underrated, but it's the driving force of the universe. And I'm not talking about the influencer version of self-love, but the real one. Then you'll have peace and be ready to find the love of a companion. At least that's what I think."

Madi wasn't too thrilled about the idea of falling in love with herself first, but she couldn't argue that forcing love or romance with someone else hadn't exactly worked for her.

What could she lose if she just tried to find inner peace?

Audri's watch chirped with an alarm. They paid their bill and headed to the lobby to join the rest of the tour group, and Peter.

Chapter 11

For all her determination to go with the flow and choose non-attachment, as soon as Madi saw Peter in the middle of a small group of people, every nerve ending in her body seemed to burst into fire. Perhaps he was experiencing a similar thing because when she approached the group, his eyes flickered in her direction.

It wasn't Madi's imagination. Their bodies were attuned to each other even if consciously they wanted to keep a distance.

To Madi's disappointment and relief though, when he was done talking with a woman who had a baby in a stroller, Peter walked out of the lobby into the street.

"He's going to check that the shuttle is here," the woman said to Madi. She must have misunderstood the look on her face.

"That means Mariela is here!" Audri exclaimed. "I'm going to say hi to her. Do you want to come?"

Madi would've followed her friend, but she felt too self-conscious to walk out too. She shook her head. "If you board first, save me a seat by the window."

Audri gave her a thumbs-up and headed outside. Madi felt bad she hadn't asked her friend anything about how things had gone with Mariela. It was undeniable that they had hit it off. The selfie of the two of them was adorable, but Madi had been so immersed in her own drama that she'd failed to notice her friend wanted to share something special with her. It was too late to turn back time, but she was determined to do better. Not only with Audri, but with the rest of the people in the tour.

They had ended up together for a reason, after all.

"Are you in the tour with El Isleño?" she asked the woman.

The woman brushed her reddish curls from her forehead and nodded. "I hope the ride isn't too harsh for my baby."

Madi peeked into the stroller. Madi didn't have a lot of experience with babies, but the child in the stroller looked around two or three years old. It was a girl and looked just like a mini replica of her mom, down to the matching striped shorts, leather sandals, and short reddish hair that curled just so and made them look cherubic.

"What's her name?" Madi asked.

The mom's face lit up in that way mothers' do when someone notices their child. "Her name's Rita. She didn't really sleep last night and as soon as I put her in the stroller, she fell asleep. I hope she stays asleep the rest of the way."

According to the map Madi had looked at back home in Utah, the drive to the caves wasn't extremely long, just above an hour.

"She'll be just fine," Madi reassured the mom. "I'm Madi, by the way. What's your name?"

"I'm Mariah," the woman said. "Nice to meet you. Are you local?"

Madi replied she lived in Utah, and promptly turned the conversation back to Mariah. She and her husband, Paul, were from Montana and were visiting the island for the first time since their honeymoon, when Rita had been conceived, Mariah added with an expression that was part grimace, part amusement.

"Some things—and some people—are meant to be," she said, caressing her sleeping daughter with her gaze.

Madi liked her immediately.

They talked for a few minutes until Peter walked into the lobby again. His and Madi's eyes locked. The electricity between them made Madi's cheeks warm. He gave her a small smile and then turned to the rest of their group. Without him saying a word, everyone gathered around him, waiting for instructions.

"Ready for our first adventure?" he asked in English, clapping once with enthusiasm.

"Ready!" some people from the group replied. There were about ten other people in their tour.

"Friends, we're about to set out to las Cavernas de Camuy. It's an hour drive to the west side of the island, maybe a little more. Hopefully, we won't have to make any stops on the way so we can arrive on time for our appointment. I advise you all to visit the facilities before we leave, but of course, if there's an emergency, we can make accommodations. We'll do the caves, go on a quick swim in the internal volcanic lake, and then have lunch. After, we'll head to Arecibo and the old observatory. The drive is long, but the views are beautiful. I will have snacks in the van to trick our stomachs, but the restaurant we'll visit for lunch is world-renowned so, channeling my mother, I'd say don't ruin your appetite. We'll spend about two hours in Arecibo, and then it will be a couple of hours at the beach before we head back to San Juan. You can nap on the way back to regain energy for another night in the old city."

His eyes glanced toward Madi.

Again, fire flared from the bottom of her soles to the crown of her head. She smiled at him, and he smiled back, and stupidly, a knot lodged in her throat. It was like he'd said everything was okay between them. He had no hard feelings, but still, Madi had to proceed with caution.

There wouldn't be another chance for a first impression.

Peter was dressed in an impeccable getup of khaki pants and

a linen guayabera with a Mao collar and that little button done, like a closed door. A gold chain glinted under the fabric. He wore no rings or other jewelry besides two thin leather bracelets clasped around his right wrist. Veins bulged in his biceps. Madi remembered the feel of the almost golden fuzz under her fingers when they had danced, the warmth of his fingers tracing circles on her naked back.

Before her imagination got out of control, she peeled her eyes from him, her attention snagged by two men standing next to Audri.

They seemed like they were a couple. Both were buff and muscular, with tattoos covering their meaty arms and legs. One had a pot belly, but there was an aura of strength that made him look like Ares, god of war. The other man was a little taller but had sweet blue eyes that gazed at his companion with adoration. Madi wasn't an envious person, but she had a visceral desire for someone to look at her that way.

Peter had looked at her that way last night, but now that he was done giving instructions to the group, he was obviously avoiding looking in her direction.

Trying to make things simpler for him, Madi headed to Audri's side.

Her friend smiled at her and hugged her tenderly. "This is my friend Madi," she said.

The taller man shook her hand first and said, "Hi, I'm Todd."

"And I'm Jesús," said the god-looking one. They shook hands, and she could feel the radiance of his aura. Mixed with the self-confidence that he projected, there was a little bit of hurt that he tried to cover with tattoos and muscles. People used all kinds of masks to hide their sorrows, but the aura never lied.

"Nice to meet you," she said. "First time in Puerto Rico?"

They looked at each other, and Jesús smiled widely. "Yes, and no. I was born here, but have lived in the Bay Area all my life."

"We're on our honeymoon now," Todd added. His thick beard couldn't quite hide the pinkish glow on his face.

"Congratulations," Madi said.

Things always happen for a reason, and she was relieved that she was meeting them when Jayden wasn't a part of her life anymore. No matter how open-minded Jayden declared he was, he and his stupid friends were always making homophobic jokes.

Audri was telling Todd and Jesús about their plan to start a yoga retreat in the area, and from the corner of her eye, Madi looked around to the rest of their tour group. There was another couple, middle aged. She was gorgeous with long brown hair to her waist. The man was ruddy red, like he spent a lot of time outside. Americans too. There were two older Black women who looked like sisters, and a family made up of a tired-looking father and mother and three teenagers, two boys and a girl. While their parents talked with Peter, the kids stared at their phones.

The teenage boys had Starbucks cups, and the sister a bottle of water. She was thin like a reed with shoulder-length brown hair. The boys, a couple of years younger than her, seemed to be twins.

The girl caught Madi's eye and Madi smiled at her. She looked away like a nervous little mouse, but then looked back at Madi and smiled tentatively.

Finally, Peter whistled to call everyone's attention. "Follow me," he said, holding a stick with a brownish frog on top of it.

And they all followed him to the minibus.

Chapter 12

Madi waited last in line as the group boarded the bus. She tried not to make eye contact with Peter, but every few seconds she involuntarily looked up, and without fail, found him glancing in her direction to quickly look away.

They were two third graders trying to deal with their first crush. The agony of butterflies in her stomach was the same kind of exquisite. But back when she was eight, her self-esteem had still been rock solid and she hadn't had to fight with embarrassment for her actions. Or her true feelings. At that age, she hadn't had the "dream" and hadn't let her life be led by it. She liked who she liked.

If only his initials had been the right ones! Then she wouldn't have called him the wrong name and she wouldn't be here in this position.

To distract herself, she opened the one social media app she lurked in and found Jayden's profile. He hadn't posted anything in his timeline, but there was a new story. Madi clicked on it and a second later, she wished she hadn't.

In the story, Jayden was golfing with his ex-girlfriend, who happened to work in the same industry he did.

Disturbed, she put the phone away, but the image was seared into her eyes and her heart. What more confirmation did she want to understand that no matter what his dreams were, Jayden had moved on with his life? She should move on too. She held the tears back until all she could taste was bitterness.

Soon it was her and Audri's turn to board. Her friend stepped onto the bus. Madi lifted her hand to grab the handrail, but instead grabbed Peter's hand.

He had been giving out little squares of hand sanitizer and she hadn't noticed until she felt the sharp corners bite into her hand. To his credit, he played it cool and helped her step onto the bus.

"Thanks," she whispered without looking in his direction, but she felt his intense eyes on her. The sun was bright and hot, but she knew it wasn't the reason she was burning up.

"Of course," he replied.

"Good morning, bella!" Mariela greeted her from the driver's seat. Madi couldn't help reciprocating a big smile while she wiped the sweat off her face with the back of her hand.

"Good morning!" she said as she walked to the back of the bus where Audri was saving her a window seat.

Peter had boarded right after her and started giving out packets of crackers and little bottles of water. When she grabbed hers, she made sure not to even brush his skin. She couldn't afford another embarrassing moment.

"Are you okay?" Audri asked, passing her a foldable fan that showed a typical Puerto Rican scene of a couple of jíbaros and a coquí frog with the one-star flag in the background.

Madi moved the AC vent directly to her face and fanned herself fiercely. "I'm okay. Thanks."

The bus took off, and Madi finally acknowledged that she was far from okay. Still, she flashed a smile to her friend. She felt terrible that she was lying, but she didn't want to ruin the trip.

At the front of the bus, Peter held a microphone to share the (abbreviated) history of the landmarks he pointed to. Even though her ears blared with memories from the previous night, Madi wanted to learn everything Peter was saying.

Abuela Lina had told her Puerto Rican legends and tall tales, but no real history. Not that they taught much Latin American or Caribbean history in school, but Madi had never been interested until now when she wanted to connect with the place where her roots were planted. In Utah, everything was so relatively new, dating only to the late nineteenth century, that a castle dating back to the fifteen hundreds seemed impossible.

She'd never been in Europe. Stevie, who'd traveled all over the world, had told her that standing next to the stone circle in Stonehenge had been a life-changing event. Those rocks were placed more than five thousand years ago! Not to speak of London, and France, where every stone had historical significance. In Spain, she'd felt weirdly at home, despite the issues with colonization and some locals' disdain for US-based Latin Americans and their descendants.

Madi didn't know much about Puerto Rico, but she felt at home here in a way that she'd never felt in Utah, where she'd been born and raised.

As if she needed another confirmation that her relationship with Jayden was doomed to fail, she realized that if he had accepted her proposal, she'd always live a half-life and not her full potential, always having to hide the Latina part of her personality, which was her whole self, after all.

Traffic on a Saturday morning after the night of San Juan wasn't that bad, and soon, they were out of the old city.

During a lull in the tour narration, the teenage girl, who was sitting up front with her family, asked Peter about the frogs that sang all night.

"At first I didn't realize what the sound was, but then, it seemed like it was coming from every direction."

Although she could have looked it up online, Madi wanted to know what he'd say.

"That's the national soundtrack of the island, the song of the coquí tree frog," Peter replied. "The name coquí refers to two species of tree frogs: the common coquí and the upland coquí. The male is the singer. Popular lore says that the sound *co* is to mark their territory, and the sound *kee* is to call for a female partner to mate."

The girl's brothers giggled like buffoons, like all teens, and their mother sent them a pointed look.

"Can they live elsewhere?" the girl asked. "I heard they were introduced in Florida a few times."

Peter smiled. "Although the lore says the coquí can't live elsewhere, that it dies when you take it away from the island, the truth is that it can, and it actually survives in other places. Currently there's a population in Hawaii where it's considered a pest."

"How can that be?" said Mariah, the woman with the toddler.

Peter shrugged. "They say it's a noise nuisance, and that it competes with birds and autochthonous predators for insects and other resources."

"But they're adorable!" Mariah said and some of the other passengers echoed in agreement.

"There can be too much of a good thing," Peter said. "And every time a new species is introduced in a new area—"

"Or eliminated," one of the teenage boys said.

His brother added, "Yes, or eliminated like the wolves in Yellowstone."

Peter put a hand up as if to stop himself. "But that's another topic that I can rant on forever," he said. "Going back to the coquí though in Hawaii, it's ironic that it's considered a pest there, and here in its birthplace, it's a threatened species."

"No!" Jesús exclaimed. "Not the coquís!"

"Pesticides, lack of habitat, pipelines, and invasive predators brought from the States all contribute to the decline in their population."

"How did they get to Hawaii?" asked Audri.

Peter's eyes flew to Madi, and she looked away.

"It's believed they arrived in nursery plants. Interesting, huh?"

"Wow," Audri murmured.

The view flashed past her window, and with the combination of tiredness from partying into the night (or tending young children) and the drone of the AC, several of the passengers fell asleep.

Madi wanted to ask Audri about her night. It seemed to have gone well with Mariela, considering the driver's excellent humor. But she didn't want to risk their whispers traveling to the wrong ears. Besides, Audri too had closed her eyes and was breathing like she was asleep.

She might be meditating too, which Madi should do.

She hadn't done any exercise more strenuous than a quick flow the day before or this morning, and she felt incomplete and stiff. For all her determination to keep up her practice on the road, she wasn't doing so well. No wonder she felt ungrounded and confused.

She was too wired to sleep, but when she looked at the front of the bus, she caught Peter's eyes. Her stomach gave a violent somersault. The sparks that flew between them were so intense, she could swear she'd heard a crackle of electricity—or it might have been the wrapper of a candy bar Todd was ripping on the seat in front of her.

Not that Madi mentioned anything about the wrapper, but maybe Todd felt her attention on him because he turned around and offered her another candy bar with a friendly expression on his face. Next to him, Jesús was asleep too.

"Thank you," she said, taking the chocolate. Her wrapper tore soundlessly.

"You're a pro at surreptitiously eating."

"It's one of my most underrated skills. I'm glad you noticed."

He gestured as if to turn around, but he changed his mind and positioned his back against the window to see her better while they chatted.

"I love these tours, but I always get anxious I'm going to get carsick. It sounds counterproductive to eat something, but the sugar actually settles my stomach."

Honestly, Madi's stomach had settled too after the first bite. "I feel you. This route is much better, but I remember back in the day, when I was little, I always used to get carsick when my family traveled to San Sebastián."

"Is that where your family is from?"

"Part of it. My mom's side actually."

"I've never been to San Sebastián here, but I've been to the one in Spain."

"For the festival?"

Todd smiled and nodded, pleasantly surprised she was familiar with the film festival that took place every year.

"Do you make movies?" she asked.

"Documentaries," he said.

"I love documentaries. I actually wanted to make one once upon a time," she said, loving how Todd's eyes lit up. She knew she sounded just like people who asked her spiritual questions when they found out she was a yoga teacher.

But Todd was a gentleman and he looked encouraging.

She loved this moment of connecting with another person who at first glance seemed like they could have nothing in common with her. "I'm mainly a watcher though. I get a yearly pass for the Sundance festival and, sometimes, I drag my friends and fiancé, I mean, ex-fiancé, boyfriend . . . whatever." She looked down, wishing she could take the words back. She'd been so at ease with Todd, that the words spilled out of her.

"It's a long story. You don't want to know," she said.

Todd's face softened as if he too knew how complicated relationships could be. "Don't worry about me, I didn't hear a thing. Now, tell me, what did you want to make the documentary about?"

She knew exactly what she would've made a documentary on had she had the chance, skills, and stamina. Todd listed attentively to her story.

When she was in middle school, she'd wanted to remake *Gone with the Wind*, which she loathed for the misrepresentation. For weeks, she'd researched all the issues the movie had gotten wrong—mainly the romanticization of slavery and plantations.

But halfway through writing the script, her doubts attacked. Some of her Black ancestors had been brought to Puerto Rico through the slave trade. Because of her dad's Italian genes, she didn't look it much, but Madi had Black ancestry. All her life, though, especially after she'd started highlighting her hair blond, she could pass as white. Was she allowed to write about these issues? Was she overstepping even if it mattered to her?

In the end, she gave in to her doubts and decided it would be a better idea to do a different project. She'd done one about immigration with Stevie and Nadia, which the teacher expected from them, being the only three Latinas in their class.

But to Todd she only said, "I didn't think I had the chops."

"The chops?"

"I didn't think I was skilled enough to do my argument justice, so I self-rejected before the critics broke my heart. Maybe it was just that I wasn't meant to do it after all."

There was a small pause, and then he said, "That happens to me sometimes. I self-reject, although that always feels worse than anyone else's criticism." He swallowed. "But, the best course of action is to keep pushing for a breakthrough. It's good to know when to keep ramming against a wall and when to change course and pursue something else instead. Sometimes it's not either or, but the opportunities that open and we hadn't seen coming."

Madi's skin tingled. She got this feeling when she was having a conversation with a stranger, and it turned out to be a
message from her guides, her angels, her higher self, speaking
through someone else's mouth.

His words sank in slowly. The wise advice could apply to her
love life.

For a long time, finding the love of her lives had been her
particular Ashley Wilkes, something (or someone) who doesn't
fit your dreams anymore, but you stubbornly pursue even at the
risk of unhappiness.

Once again, she realized that she'd been so determined to
make Jayden fit into her fantasy, that she'd still tried to make
things work in spite of all the red flags telling her to run away
from him. Not because he wasn't a good guy, but because he
wasn't what she'd been looking for. It had been like jamming a
square peg into a round spot. Her life didn't have to be settling
for less with Jayden or being alone forever. It could be alone for
now, until she was finally ready to recognize the love she longed
for.

She shook her head slightly and asked him, "What are you
working on now? I mean, not now, seeing as how this is your
honeymoon."

He winced and blushed to the tips of his ears. "Yikes. You
found me out. This is our honeymoon, but I have wanted to
come to Puerto Rico so I could also do some research."

"What kind of research?"

"Micro-farms."

Madi wasn't familiar with the term and her face must have
shown it because Todd explained, "Small-scale, specialized
family farms that are trying to revitalize native crops, and in
some cases, nonnative crops as well." He glanced up at the front
of the bus, and added, "For example, Peter manages a potato
farm in Cayey."

"Cayey?" Madi asked although this was the wrong question. She wanted to know about Peter and why potatoes, but she didn't want him to think she was overly curious about him.

Todd didn't seem to notice her interest in their tour guide though. "Cayey is one of the mountainous towns that's the perfect climate for potatoes and reggaeton artists, it seems."

Madi laughed, and then covered her mouth when Audri stirred in her seat. "Yikes! I don't want to wake her. But I know who you're talking about. Wisin and . . . what's his name?"

"Yandel," Todd said. "Los Extraterrestres," he added in a robotic voice.

Madi covered her mouth so she wouldn't laugh loudly again and wake anyone up, especially the baby.

"My stepdad is from Argentina, but even he loves classic reggaeton. I used to play Wisin and Yandel all the time when I was little." She sang, "No puedo olvidar tus besos mojados . . ."

The lyrics about wet kisses and long nights of passion under the moon had been so inappropriate for a kid to sing!

Todd laughed silently, and then motioned with his head toward Jesús and said, "We went to their concert in El Paso, Texas. It was unreal!"

"They put Cayey on the map," she said.

"They're more famous than the Coca-Cola plant there too. Now Peter is trying to make them the potato capital of the Caribbean."

Madi glanced at the front of the bus. Peter and Mariela were chatting, but she had the impression that he knew they were talking about him.

"That's interesting," she said.

"You should ask him about it. He's passionate about farming and planting in general," Todd replied, finishing his candy bar with one last bite.

"Will do," she said. "Thanks for helping me fight the carsickness by talking with me."

"Thank you," he said. "I'd been fighting the temptation

to distract myself with my phone, which would have made it worse."

Jesús snored, and Todd smiled, tenderly. "His carsickness is worse than mine. This is his coping mechanism."

"Not yours?"

"I can't fall asleep when I'm riding a car as a passenger or even an airplane."

"You like being in control of the situation," she said.

He nodded as if he hadn't considered this before. "I'm afraid of not waking up again until I'm in heaven, and then I realize I'm in the bad place for eternity with a tourist's outfit . . ."

She laughed. "I think we can trust our driver, though."

"Thanks for the vote of confidence," Mariela called out from the driver's seat, proving that Madi's and Todd's hushed voices carried all the way. "I'm not going to say that I have a clean record and tempt the Fates, but statistically speaking, you're in good hands."

"Oooh!" Todd exclaimed. "I love the mixture of superstition and numbers all thrown in together."

"It's incredible how this road healed after the storm," Mariah said from the seat across from Todd's. "I saw pictures after the hurricane, and it's amazing to see how resilient nature is."

"It takes longer for the infrastructure and people to keep going with their lives," Todd said.

"Some lives will never be the same," Peter said, and again, Madi was dying to hear why his voice carried so much sorrow.

"Which is why I'm fascinated with the micro-farming revolution," Todd said, bringing her conversation back full circle.

Their bus slowed down and one by one, the sleeping passengers yawned and stirred.

Audri opened her eyes and looked at Madi like she didn't know where they were.

"Good morning, sleepyhead," Madi said, winking at her.

There were rustling sounds from the front rows. Rita the toddler's bright voice chimed, "Look, Daddy! The forest!"

There was so much joy and wonder in her voice. Everyone looked out the windows to appreciate the scenery.

"It is a forest," Audri said. "I mean, I knew intellectually but I can't get over how beautiful and green everything is."

Madi had experienced the wonder of this sight plenty of times in her visits to the island, but it never got old. Even Peter wasn't immune to the beauty around them.

How hard it must have been for her mother and grandma to leave the island. No one left this paradise on earth lightly. No one stayed behind without weighing the consequences of that decision either.

A couple of rows ahead of Madi, Heather, the teenagers' mom, and Mariah were chatting. "For the first time in my life I saw an ocean so blue. I understand why Enya called her song 'Caribbean Blue,'" Heather said.

As if on cue, the two boys and the girls started humming the melody of the Enya song, and the whole bus was laughing, even their mom, whose cheeks were bright red.

"How do you kids know the new age anthem of the nineties?" Audri asked when the laughter had subsided a little.

"She's doing the yoga certification, and that's her favorite meditation song," the father, Austin, said.

Immediately, Madi turned toward them and said, "That is fantastic! I'm a yoga instructor, and so is Audri!"

Although she'd learned the hard way that yoga people came in all shapes and forms, she loved connecting with them in all their iterations; yogis and yoga enthusiasts belonged to all religions and had all kinds of ideas, even some outdated, outlandish, or even offensive ones that were incomprehensible to Madi.

How could the beliefs that were the I Am's incarnations, divinity personified, coexist with racism or misogyny in the same space? But it happened, and she'd stopped being shocked over it. Maybe that was a sign of her privilege, because Audri often pointed out that in her eagerness to include everyone, she still had glaring blind spots.

Audri had a little smile that usually boded mischief. "Madi here says she's an 'instructor,' but she's actually a yoga master."

"And so are you," Madi said, mortified to think that she hadn't practiced much since leaving Utah. What kind of master was she after all?

"But I'm not modest about it and you are. Tell me, Heather, what kind of certification are you working on?"

Finding herself the spotlight of the conversation, Heather looked like a newborn butterfly, still missing the chrysalis, and tucking her wings in. Madi hoped she could feel she and Audri were being sincerely curious. Heather's shyness broke away, and little by little she started telling them about her journey from postpartum depression to yoga certification.

"I thought that after years of attending classes, I should just take the plunge and become a teacher. Not only to teach, but to deepen my practice, you know?"

"Of course," said Audri. "Even if you're still saying things like 'should,' teaching is the best way to learn."

"We're all happy she's finally doing something for herself," Tyce, one of the twins, reassured his mom with a protective hand on her shoulder.

"I'm so happy too," Madi said. Lately, words weren't cooperating with her, but she felt the woman knew that her journey was inspiring for her too.

"If you have any questions, let us know," Audri added.

"Thank you," Heather said. "I feel like you two are kindred souls even if we just met."

Audri smiled at Madi as if telling her that she wasn't the only one with weird ideas of having met people in other lives.

The bus came to a stop.

Peter announced, "Here we are. Las Cavernas de Camuy."

One by one, the passengers got off the bus. Since Madi had been the last one on, she was the last one off. But this time, Peter wasn't there to take her hand. In fact, he was making a point of putting as much distance from her as he could.

She tried to push her disappointment down, but then, she knew she'd have to talk to him and explain if she wanted the bad vibes between them to go away.

She took a big breath. The greenness of her surroundings filled her lungs. She closed her eyes and stretched to the sky and the bright sun.

Even if there was no way something could happen between them, they could still be friends, right? She never wanted to regret turning her back on a kindred soul.

Chapter 13

Peter had obviously been to the caverns many times before, but he was patient as he led his group like a mother hen with a bunch of little chicks. Madi hated the heaviness between them, but she didn't know if she'd have the chance to clear things with Peter with so many people demanding his attention.

He handed everyone their tickets and said, "This is a self-guided tour, but with this ticket you can get a narration device that will explain what you're seeing. Of course, the guide is available in English and Spanish. Stay on the path and walk at your own leisure. We'll get together at the end to visit the Sumidero de Empalme. The park ranger just informed me that because of the heavy rains last week, we won't be able to swim in the river."

There was a chorus of disappointed voices.

"I know. I know," Peter said placatingly. "But I'd rather be safe than sorry."

In that moment, a group of men carrying scuba diving gear were heading back to their SUV, looking downcast too.

"If it's not safe for divers, I guess it's even less safe for swimmers," Heather said.

"Things happen for a reason," Madi said. "Let's go with the flow."

It was more of a reminder for herself than for the rest of the group, but it helped to lighten up the mood.

Since strollers weren't allowed and Rita refused to go into the carrier her father had strapped to his back, Peter offered to carry her. Happily, she agreed to ride on his shoulders. When they walked into the main cave, she lifted her little hands toward the stalactites which were still several feet out of her reach.

The musty smell of the cave made Madi sneeze. She half listened to the Spanish narration from her headphones, and half overheard Peter's narration to keep Rita entertained. He was patient with the toddler even though she'd grabbed his hair like reins, and when she pulled too hard, he sweetly held on to her hands instead, although it mustn't have been the most comfortable position to hold for such a long time. But Rita's parents had the chance to appreciate the tour, knowing their daughter was safe and contained.

Madi was glad she'd chosen to wear sneakers instead of sandals. When Peter mentioned bats, the teenagers pretended to be terrified while their dad said, "Imagine we find the true Batman in here."

"Actually, for one of the Batman movies—I forget which one—they used real sound footage from this cave."

"Cool," Todd and Jesús said.

Peter told them that not long ago, the community had started using guano, the manure from the bats, in their fields as fertilizer, bringing back Taíno customs from millennia ago, to save the island from the damage of pesticides and monocultures.

"It's a win-win for the tourism and the agricultural industries," Peter said.

The narration in Madi's headphones said the Rio Camuy underground system was the third largest in the world, and at first, Madi had chills thinking how she was inside the earth. But then, the thought sank in a little more and she was comforted in knowing she was surrounded by the energy of Mother Earth. The guide had instructed them not to touch the walls of the caves to preserve their nature. Still, Madi wished she could brush her fingers along the walls that had withstood eons of time and change.

After a while, Rita, tired of guiding her steed Peter, went back to her father's arms and Peter lingered around the group in case anyone had questions. There was a solemnity in the air, and everyone, even the teens, spoke in soft tones. Maybe they were scared of startling the bats, but Madi suspected it was more than that.

The water that dripped from the walls had been part of the river and then the clouds that fed the greenness of the island and nurtured the people since the beginning of time. In a way, she imagined the water inside her had traces of the same water in the caverns, and she felt at peace.

And maybe because she was vibrating at a high frequency, at the end of the trek, the marvelous sight of the Empalme Sinkhole, she found herself filled with an emotion she couldn't name at first.

Contentment. The word rang in her mind and reverberated all the way to her heart.

The silence around them was like they were in a cathedral or sacred place. The sun filtered down to the cavern through an opening four hundred feet above them. The sounds of thousands of sleeping bats and the river Camuy running below were a soothing melody.

Audri was standing right under a ray of sun like she was soaking up its energy. The families and groups gathered to gaze up to the natural window above them, or into the dark waters of the river.

And when she turned to sit on one of the benches, she found herself face-to-face with Peter. His eyes widened when he realized they were practically alone, and for a second Madi worried he'd turn around and walk away. But he exhaled like he was carrying a heavy weight on his shoulders and said, "Hey."

Her whole body seemed electrified. "Hey." She motioned to the bench and said, "Do you want to sit with me?"

He glanced toward the rest of the group. Everyone seemed entertained studying the caves around them and taking pictures of the stalactites and stalagmites. Rita was pointing to a small rainbow above one of the waterfalls where the sun hit it just right.

"Okay," he said, and followed Madi.

Her heart seemed like it was going to burst out of her chest, but it was now or never.

"I'm sorry—" they both said.

His voice still rang in her ears, when he said, "Okay, you go first."

She inhaled to gather strength. "I'm sorry I called you Javier last night. It's not like . . . I just thought you were him, but it's not like I had a thing with him at all. I don't even know him! I knew he was going to be our guide this whole week, and that's why I thought you were him. That's all."

He smiled, brushing a hand through his hair. "Javier has a daughter who lives in Orlando, and something came up. Nothing serious, but he had to be there for a medical procedure. Her name's Bianka and she just turned one a couple of weeks ago. I wasn't even supposed to be in San Juan this week, but I'm her godfather, so anything for her, you know?" He rummaged in his pocket and took out his phone. He showed her the screensaver. It was him and a little girl, younger than Rita. She looked at Peter with adoration. Pink ribbons held back the soft cloud of her curly hair.

"Javier asked me to cover for him this week. Before I started with the micro-farm, I helped him with tours, but I haven't for a while. I couldn't say no. Most of the guides have left the island, and he had no one else. Luckily, it's no big deal if I'm gone from the farm this week. Not that there's a surplus of farm workers, but I had people to cover for me. That's why I'm here. I'm sorry I didn't introduce myself last night."

She smiled at him, regretting that they had started on the wrong foot.

"I'm sorry I assumed," she said. "And I'm sorry I panicked. I'm Madison Ramírez." She offered her hand for him to shake.

"I'm Peter Tokeshi, at your service."

They shook hands firmly, and Madi was sad to let go, but she didn't want to make things awkward between them now that they were fixing it.

"That's a unique name for a Puerto Rican," she said, hoping her words didn't sound too intrusive.

He smiled like he was used to this kind of question. "I go by my mother's last name. Her name was Cristina and she passed away last year."

A shadow passed over his face. Her loss still hurt him. Madi couldn't imagine such a loss. Losing her grandma had been hard, but if anything happened to her mom, she wouldn't know how to keep going.

Impulsively, she pressed his hand.

"I'm sorry."

"So am I. It was only the two of us all my life. Her great-grandparents on her father's side were born in Japan but they settled in Lima, Peru, after World War Two."

"My friend Stevie's family is also Japanese-Peruvian," Madi said with surprise.

His face lit up. "That's so cool. My mom moved to the US when she was seventeen and met my dad soon after. He was Puerto Rican from Ponce, but he left before he even knew I was on the way. He's never been part of my life, and I've been at peace with that . . ."

Something in his voice told Madi he was far from at peace with it, but she didn't pry, and he continued. "In a strange turn of luck, my college roommate freshman year was Javier, and you know how it is sometimes, when a Boricua meets another one in the diaspora, it's like they're long-lost brothers or cousins. That's how it was with us. Even though my accent was so weird, neither Peruvian nor Puerto Rican, he adopted me into his family. When he came back to the island, he decided to switch gears and go into tourism instead of agriculture. Like I said, I help him sometimes when he's shorthanded, but my passion is the land. It calls to me."

"That's very cool," she said. "I feel the call of the land too."

She looked around at the tree roots peeking through the walls, at how they went so deep into the earth that not even the most destructive hurricane could pull them out. In a way, it was the same with Peter and her. Their Puerto Rican roots were so deep, but they were in the dark. To heal they had to help the roots see the light of the surface too. Speaking with him helped her do that a little.

"My biological dad was never part of my life either. He's from Argentina, like my stepdad."

"South Americans are irresistible to Boricuas, my mom used to joke," he said.

Madi chuckled. "That's so true! I love my Argentine heritage, but I've always been closer to my Puerto Rican side, you know? But ever since my grandma passed away when I was thirteen, I felt that connection become weaker and weaker."

"I'm sorry about your grandma," he said. "It doesn't matter if our loved ones left us recently or so long ago their memories feel like a dream. The loss still hurts."

A knot grew in Madi's throat. She'd thought she had grieved her grandma properly, the loss of connection to a part of her culture, but apparently, there were unresolved things in her soul that were bubbling to the surface. Sooner or later, she'd have to confront them.

Peter had shared something precious with her, and although he didn't ask anything in return, she felt safe opening up to him.

"I came back to find a venue where my boss and friend,

Reyna, can do yoga retreats," she said. "But I also came back to bring my abuela Lina's ashes back to the island so she can rest in peace."

"Have you already done it? Do you have a special place?"

She shook her head. "I haven't yet. She asked me to scatter them in Culebra, and that's why I'm going there at the end of the trip, although now I wonder if I should have done that first."

He smiled tenderly at her. "I think that's a good plan, to end your visit with a kept promise."

"I love looking it at it that way," she said.

Rita started crying, and her dad picked her up and started the way back to the trail. The group had their fill of the majesty of the cave, and one by one, they started heading back. Audri sent Madi a curious look, and when Madi nodded to let her know she was okay, she continued toward the bus along with Todd and Jesús.

Madi's stomach rumbled. Even if she lost track of time, her stomach always knew to remind her it was lunchtime.

Peter narrowed his eyes at her. "I think your stomach's ready for some food."

She laughed. "I can't lie to you." Then, feeling the intensity of his gaze, she added, "Friends?"

His intense eyes studied her cautiously. Peter didn't seem like the kind of guy to make the same mistake twice. He'd been so open with her the night before, but then he felt foolish, and he'd had to pull back.

Madi was grateful for the space, but she felt an attraction to him that she wanted to understand. She didn't think she'd get over his rejection.

Finally, he smiled, took her hand in his, and said, "Friends."

His reply was just what Madi had asked of him, so why did it hurt? Why did she feel that friendship was a harder barrier between them? But at least it was better than putting him out of her mind—and heart.

They headed back to the bus, her mind bursting with even more questions.

She chose one of the least intrusive ones.

"You're very good at being a guide. Like, you're so good at giving the right amount of information and space. What's your favorite part of being a tour guide?"

He considered for a second and then he said, "Maybe because I'm new to the island, I love to show newcomers those things that sometimes locals take for granted because they grew up and lived here all their lives. I love to see others discover Boriként and see it with new eyes depending on their point of view. They call this the Isla del Encanto, and it's true that it enchants everyone. I've lost count of all the times people ask me if I need an assistant or how they can buy a home here."

"I've been wondering the same thing," she said, noting how he used the Taíno name for the island, and not the westernized Borinquen. "Not wanting to become your assistant, but how much it costs to live here."

"A lot, sadly. There are tax incentives for businesses and entrepreneurs to move to the island from the continental US."

"I heard they have to live here most of the year, right?"

"Six months and one day," he said, scratching his head. "There are loopholes around it though, and things haven't panned out the way the government said they would. Perhaps it's all coming out exactly as planned, but they won't tell people that. In any case, millionaires, including crypto bros, flock to the island and with the higher demand for housing, real estate exploded. Now locals can't even afford to buy an apartment. And worse, the beaches around the island are being developed and privatized. The flora and fauna suffer, and the locals can't even access the beach, while the mainlanders come and exploit the island resources. I hesitate to say 'our' because I'm still a newcomer myself."

"But your father was Puerto Rican," she said because she felt protective of her heritage. Although she had been raised by two proud Puerto Rican women, like Peter, she hadn't been born on the island.

"It's complicated," he said. "I'm not an expat, like they call themselves. I'm not a rich entrepreneur, but I am a thirtysomething trying to find myself, minus the hedge fund."

She appreciated the touch of humor and the sincerity. He was trying to find himself, and she was trying to find the love of her life, but when she thought about it, she wasn't sure who she was or who she really wanted to be. A few weeks ago, she'd been convinced she wanted to be with Jayden forever, and now, she knew going down that path would have been a sure way to unhappiness. Alone.

For so long finding the love of her lives had been her guiding compass, and now, she felt rudderless, at the mercy of the changing winds and tides, and she didn't like the feeling.

She'd have to find peace with keeping herself company, and Madi, who'd always thought she had a great inner life, realized she was a stranger to herself because she'd stopped listening to her inner voice such a long time ago. Her intuition had become a stranger.

A stranger like Peter, and like him, someone she wanted to know more and better.

At the end of the path back to the bus, several members of the group headed to the restroom. Peter excused himself and headed there.

For her part, Madi went to the concession and ordered enough bocaditos for her, Audri, and Peter.

When he returned, he had a cup of pink juice in each hand.

He offered one to her. "This is the best jugo de acerola on the island," he said.

"I don't know if this is the best bocadito on the island, but it hit the right spot. Here's one for you."

His whole face lit up like she had just fulfilled one of his lifelong dreams.

She took a sip of the juice and she smiled at the tartness of the cherry that was an island trademark like parcha was.

"I'm still embarrassed about last night. I . . . I never had a fling with a client, and if you hadn't run off when you found out my name, I don't know what would've happened. Today would have been a thousand times more awkward and confusing."

"You did nothing wrong," she said. "Unless you're engaged or married or in a serious relationship . . ."

"Nope and nope."

She sighed, relieved. "I had a really great time last night . . ." She hoped her words didn't sound hollow and tried to channel all her sincerity. "I hope no matter what, the rest of the trip won't be awkward. We still have a few more outings booked with Javier's company."

"I know," he replied. "I promise I'll be on my best behavior."

Again, that sounded like a challenge as they headed to the bus to head to lunch and the promised visit to the Arecibo Observatory.

Chapter 14

According to Peter, in Taíno culture, a batey was the communal area where the people celebrated everything from weddings to war councils, where they exchanged news and got to know their neighbors, and where they also worshipped their gods.

When the group arrived at El Batey, a few in the group (Todd and the teenage girl, Mya) were nervous about what it looked like from the outside.

"Are you sure this is the right place?" Mya asked.

"Just like you don't judge a book by its cover, I'd advise not to judge the food by the building's façade," Mariela said.

Mya ducked, chastised but not totally convinced. Madi caught a peek of her screen as the girl frantically read reviews on Yelp.

El Batey Restaurant was sandwiched in a strip mall between a phone accessory store and a day care. The sign was bleached of color, and Madi thought that if she'd had to find it, she would've never done so. But Mariela and Peter were adamant that they were in the right place, and they were the experts.

Now that she and Peter had made their peace, Madi didn't trail at the end of the group. She was one of the first ones to go in and was relieved that the AC was on, but the temperature wasn't uncomfortably cold.

"Come to the ladies' with me," Audri said.

Madi followed her and again, was relieved that the bathroom was clean, the one sign that the place was safe. The small bathroom was decorated with fascinating Taíno-style decorations. She had believed that the indigenous culture had died with colonization, but the art was at the same time new and familiar to her. It reminded her of some Mayan sculptures she had seen in Mexico. It made sense, since both cultures grew around the Caribbean Sea.

There was a tapestry that depicted three deities, a male, a female, and one in the shape of a dog.

"This is so cool," Audri said.

She and Madi stood in front of the plaque that explained that Taínos believed in two main gods, Yucahú and Atabey, his mother and the goddess of fertility. The final of the three manifestations was a doglike deity, the overseer of the gate to the underworld and the recently dead. The culture placed significance on the communication with their dead ancestors.

"That explains a lot," Madi said, and Audri laughed, but she hadn't meant that as a joke. Maybe the Taíno traditions weren't completely forgotten by a part of Madi's subconscious.

When they went back to the restaurant, the waitress was already bringing plates laden with mofongo, rice and beans, vegetables and roots, and steaming tostones, the savory plantain fritters that Madi loved.

The waitress turned out to be the owner of the place. Her name was Alexandra.

While the group ate, she told them the restaurant's story.

"I took over in 2020. The last owner was an elderly man who had managed it after his father and grandfather. But his children moved to Florida after Maria. He held on, but after the series of earthquakes that rattled the island, he couldn't do it anymore. He wanted to live near his children and grandchildren. This restaurant was an institution, a landmark like the caverns. I remember stopping by after visiting the caverns as a little girl. My grandmother had eaten here as a little girl." The group chuckled right on the beat, and Alexandra continued, "In 2020 I had this impression that I had to return to the island. I met Mr. Manolo on my first day here, and we closed the deal a few days later."

Madi listened with admiration. Here Alexandra had followed a hunch and it had worked for her.

"It's not easy to stay afloat with the electricity going out every few days without warning, the problems with the supply chain, the rising costs, and the lack of personnel. Some people tell me I should relocate somewhere more remunerable. Do something easier, but the truth is that I feel part of a purpose. I'm helping my islita to progress even if it's two steps forward and three steps back. This is my place and I love doing what I do."

The tour group clapped for Alexandra when she was done, and she brought a round of drinks and dessert, on the house. "Feeding people the best food is how my family showed love, and that's what I like to do with everyone who steps into my restaurant. You're all my familia, and I'm glad I got to feed you."

When she was done, Todd and Jesús got her number. Todd's sister was thinking of a destination wedding in Puerto Rico, and she would love this food. Madi got her number too. She hadn't found a place where they could host the retreats yet but providing good food for the guests would be one of the main priorities.

"I'll be in touch," she told Alexandra.

The woman, who was in her fifties, kissed Peter on the cheek. "Thanks for all your help, papo," she said.

"You're welcome," he replied. "We all need to help each other. We might live on an island, but we're not isolated from each other. We can't be. We need to be connected in our net."

Bellies full and inspired, they headed to the observatory.

When they arrived, it was exactly like Madi had expected, and at the same time, it was nothing like she had dreamed of.

Since its construction in the 1960s, the radio telescope in Arecibo had been an important tool in detecting asteroids, exoplanets, and satellites. But the storms and earthquakes had wreaked so much havoc that in 2020 it too had collapsed like many buildings and structures on the island.

Their tour guide, a tall man with a strong Texan accent, told the group that there were plans to rebuild it or replace the dome, but nothing was conclusive yet.

"We're still operating with a smaller telescope, and continuing our labor, like the rest of the island," he said. Then, with a wistful smile he added, "This facility is situated in the barrio called La Esperanza. I think it's fitting because in this profession, in this location, the only thing that keeps us going is hope."

While the rest of the group went inside for a brief documentary, Madi walked to the edge of the railing and watched the ruin that once upon a time had been the literal star of one of her favorite movies, *Contact*. She heard footsteps behind her, and thinking it was Audri, she didn't turn around.

"Kind of sad, huh," Peter said next to her.

She was surprised that he'd sought her out, but she recognized in his eyes the sadness that she felt. "I can't believe they let it come to this."

"Being in a political limbo, Puerto Rico has never been a priority, you know?" he said. "But like the park ranger and

Alexandra at the restaurant said, we keep going with hope that even in this situation, our work on the island is still making a difference, that it matters."

She gazed at the fallen dome, and the sea of vegetation behind it.

Fat, cottony dark clouds crossed the bright blue sky and blotted the sun. The mysteries of what lay beyond them, far into the universe, might have been discovered from this telescope.

"If the aliens were trying to communicate through this telescope, then they might think we're not interested," she said.

"I guess they'll have to use an alternate method," he replied. "In my experience, when the universe realizes a means of communication isn't working, it finds another one. It never gives up."

"Like Puerto Rico," she said.

"Like Puerto Rico," Peter echoed. "But it's tiring, you know."

Birds cawed from the nearby trees, as if warning each other of the oncoming storm. The clouds had moved upon them surprisingly quickly, and Madi's arms broke in goose bumps when a heavy, humid breeze blew from the ocean beyond the greenness of the trees. The weather was so mercurial, like the mood of the people on the island, she'd discovered. And herself. How could she be so elated and thrilled by the beauty around her one minute, and another so despondent for the state of this place?

Maybe Peter was feeling similar things because gloominess seemed to cover him like a wet towel as he gazed down to the ruined telescope dome.

"Where did you live before you came to the island?" she asked, wrenching herself from her spiraling thoughts. If she didn't, her mood would end up shattered on the floor like the telescope.

He inhaled deeply and then said, "Idaho."

"Idaho?"

He turned toward her, his face amused and defensive at the

same time. "What's wrong with Idaho? Have you even been there before? It's called the Gem State for a reason."

She laughed at his expression. "I have nothing against Idaho, which is gorgeous. I'm very familiar with it considering how I was born and raised in Utah."

Now he was the one who laughed. "No way!" He clapped his hands just like South Americans did to show their surprise. "What? You don't look like a Utah girl."

"And what does a Utah girl look like? You don't look like a stereotypical Idaho guy, either, in case no one has mentioned that before."

He stepped closer to her and took out his phone from his pocket. He tapped at the screen and showed her a picture of a group of brown-skinned kids wearing graduation gowns and caps.

"This is my friend group from elementary, middle, and high school. There were a ton of us Latine kids in our town."

She tried not to fixate on the fact that in the picture he'd been surrounded by four girls and only one other boy. He must have been popular with the ladies. Although in person his Asian features were more striking, he looked just like the other kids in the picture.

Madi, not wanting to be undone, pulled out her own phone. She didn't have to navigate much to find pictures with her best friends, Nadia and Stevie. She had a folder with thousands and thousands of them. Nadia had made a collage with pictures from sixth grade and senior year and one of her double quinceañera party that showed how much their friendship had grown through the years, and how much they'd all glowed up. They had always been beautiful, but aging had been kind to them, one of the advantages of amazing genes. Like her mom said, Latin like satin.

She showed him the picture. "Not all Latine kids from our high school are pictured here, but I promise, there were a lot of us."

He looked at the picture and there was a sweet tenderness on his face. "Is this your friend who's also Japanese Peruvian?"

She smiled just thinking of her daredevil friend. If she were here, she'd tell Madi to grab the front of Peter's T-shirt, pull him toward her, and kiss him until even he forgot his initials weren't JR.

"That's Stevie," she said. "Pretty, huh?"

He looked at Madi and said, "Pretty."

Something in the way he said it or the way he looked at her made her insides tickle. She wouldn't be ovulating for a few more days but her body was already hard at work and clinging to every clue. She pressed her lips to stop herself from smiling. She didn't want Peter asking her what she was smiling about because she'd blurt out the truth and then he'd think she was even weirder than he already did.

"Do you love Idaho?" she asked.

He shrugged. "It's home."

"Winter though." She groaned.

He groaned too. "Yes, winter . . . But, hear me out, without the agony of winter, spring and summer wouldn't be so sweet."

She shook her head, unconvinced. "I don't know, man. Endless summer seems pretty fantastic to me."

"It is. And to be fair, although the seasons are as marked as in other places, there are seasons for everything here too. A time to plant, a time to wait, a time to harvest. It's the same rhythm but different setting."

"Plus there's the beach," she said.

"The ocean, more precisely. I could do without the sand."

She looked at him outraged. "What?"

"Are you going to revoke my Boricua card?"

"Maybe," she said.

There was a brief silence she desperately wanted to fill. She wished the documentary would never end, so she could have the excuse to spend safe time alone with Peter, getting to know him more.

"What do you plant in Idaho?"

His face broke into another one of those delicious smiles. There was a dusting of pink across his nose and cheeks.

"Potatoes," he said.

She laughed. "Of course!"

"What can I say? It must be the Peruvian in me. From one potato country to the next."

"And now here? Do you plan to continue the potato conspiracy for world domination on the island?"

He smiled at that and, oddly, she found she loved bringing out the bashfulness and smile in him, this man she didn't even know existed just a couple of days ago.

"It's my little grain of sand to rebuild the island. Potatoes are the perfect food, after all."

"I know," she countered. "I have taste buds, plus, I've seen *The Martian*."

He smiled again, and he looked like he was going to reply but she spoke first. "Are you planning on staying here for good? Tego said his sister was still trying to convince you, and that woman we saw in la Plazoleta asked you about going back to college in the winter."

His eyes widened, as if he was surprised she remembered all that about that conversation.

"I wasn't drunk that night, contrary to what you might think," she said, but this time, she couldn't look at him anymore and turned her face toward the clouds. A flash of lightning crisscrossed the sky.

"I'm still trying to decide," he said.

"What?"

"If what I came here looking for was just a . . . dream."

Madi's ears started ringing with anticipation. Her breath solidified in her lungs.

"What dream?"

He shook his head as if trying to dispel memories too embarrassing to share.

"After my mom died, I had this urge . . . I wanted to find my dad. But so far, there have been no clues. I know he was from Ponce, but nothing more. It's like he vanished from the island and left no trace. But I feel him, in a strange way, considering I never spent time with him at all, you know? It's just so weird that my mom raised me in her Peruvian culture, but it's Puerto Rico that tugs at me."

"You're from here like a coquí, then," she said, smiling at him.

"Like a coquí," he said.

They looked into each other's eyes as if finally they'd found someone they could open up with. Stevie wasn't a psychologist (she hadn't even gone to college), but she was a student of human behavior as Nadia studied the law and Madi studied birth charts. Once, she had told her that sometimes it's easier to tell a stranger things we wouldn't even tell our closest friends because there's no fear of disappointing the other person, or worrying about their reaction. It had been when Nadia and Madi had found out through gossip at school instead from her own lips that Stevie was pregnant. They were seventeen. Madi had been devastated she hadn't been a safe person for Stevie to share this news with, but her friend had explained that talking to a stranger had been easy.

Madi loved talking to people, but she hardly ever opened her heart with anyone, even her best friends. But now with Peter it felt different, and she didn't know why. It wasn't that she thought he wouldn't be disappointed because he didn't care. She knew he cared, but didn't judge, as crazy as that may sound.

She could have spent all day standing by the rail talking with him about life's purpose and expectations, the loss of heritage and the search for help—conversations that went better under the stars and with plenty of wine to loosen the tongue—but heavy, fat drops started pounding down on them. Soon the rain turned into something else.

"It's hail!" Peter exclaimed.

Without thinking, Madi took his hand, and they ran together to the visitors' center, where the rest of the people from their tour were gathered, looking at them.

Chapter 15

Madi was fascinated. It was a storm of biblical proportions. Soon, her fascination turned to worry, though. The sky was falling in chunks.

It poured all the way to San Juan like the rain was never going to stop.

Peter kept reassuring the rest of the passengers that it was only a passing cloud, that this was common in the tropics. But when Mariela had to pull over under a bridge, behind a line of other cars, everyone fell silent.

The sound of rain, usually so soothing, was ominous when the driver couldn't see where she was heading. The roads were flooded, and when they were finally close to the airport, Peter and the other men got out of the bus to help a woman push her Prius to the side of the highway so she wouldn't block traffic and be in danger.

Madi and Heather took turns leading breathing exercises for the rest of the passengers. Audri sat right behind Mariela and next to Peter as the two of them helped her navigate since the rearview mirrors and cameras were useless with the rain.

Finally, when they pulled into the old citadel, the rain abated a bit. Everyone was exhausted after a full day of activities and then the stress of being in danger. One by one, the passengers got off the bus at their respective hotels. The original agreement was that Casa Grande Hotel would be the only stop, but Mariela said she couldn't in good conscience leave the families there without knowing they'd made it to their hotels or rentals safe and sound. So instead, she dropped off each member of the group at their individual destinations. Everyone was very generous with their tip, but the moment felt a little like goodbye to dear friends at the end of summer camp. They'd just met this morning, but the group had a special vibe.

Madi and Audri exchanged numbers with Heather, and they hugged and kissed like best friends, promising to keep in touch.

Mariela headed to Casa Grande Hotel when the stars were starting to blink in the crystal blue sky, clean after the storm.

"I feel like a truck ran me over," Audri said, stretching in her seat. "I think it was the stress of making sure I didn't make things worse trying to guide you."

"You were a lifesaver," Mariela said. She too looked pale and exhausted. She glanced at Peter and said, "You too, nene. This group was amazing, and the tour was great, but the drive about killed us. Literally. Next time we have to offer an overnight option."

"Are there places where people can stay?" Madi asked, interested. The area of the caverns and the observatory had such a good, positive vibe. It would be great to find something there.

But Peter shrugged. "Nothing for a big group, really. There are a few rental homes, but nothing bigger than three bedrooms, three bathrooms."

"I think for that, the closest place would be Dorado," Mariela said. "But the prices there are prohibitive."

"With all the expats snatching the properties?" Madi said, looking at Peter.

"Bingo," he said.

Sometimes at home when she was super homesick for the island, Madi looked up hotels and Airbnbs. The posh hotel in Dorado seemed like a dream, but the prices were too steep for her yoga teacher budget.

The entrance to the hotel was clear, and Mariela dropped them off. "I'll see you tomorrow for El Yunque?" she asked, her eyes bright and intense.

Madi was excited to spend the whole day in the rain forest.

"The tree houses there will be perfect for the retreats you have in mind," said Peter.

"Man, I wish we had a day to just rest, but such is the life of entrepreneur self-employed yoga teachers," Audri said.

"Hopefully, tonight we'll get all refreshed and rejuvenated," Madi said.

"Hopefully," Audri echoed.

"Okay, see you all tomorrow for the private tour. It was nice to spend time with this group today, but it will be less tiring and easier to move around with just the two of you," Mariela said.

Madi got off the minibus. The air was so humid after the rain that her skin felt dewy and happy. "You're not staying here?" Madi asked Mariela as she was ready to drive away.

Their driver shook her head. "I live in Hato Rey, the financial district."

"And you?" Madi asked Peter.

He shrugged. "I live in Cayey, in the mountains, actually, and there's no way on earth I'm driving back until the end of the week," he said. "I'm here at Casa Grande Hotel, too."

"In that case, walk us in, handsome," Audri said, holding Peter's arm for support. Her walking sandals had given her blisters.

Peter glanced at Madi as if to offer his other arm, but she smiled and walked ahead.

Ada, the pretty receptionist, was at the hotel front desk again. At the sight of Peter, her face broke up in a supernova of a smile.

Audri kept walking to the elevators, and Peter said his good nights there and then.

"It's just us so we can start a little later," he said. "What about ten?"

"God bless you, handsome," Audri said.

He looked at Madi and she nodded.

Knowing that Peter was staying at the same hotel had woken up the butterflies in her stomach for some reason. Not that it mattered. The hotel was small, but there were dozens of rooms, and it would be as if he was staying in Cayey for the night.

"I'll take her from here," she said, holding Audri's arm. Her friend's skin was surprisingly hot to the touch, but maybe it was the change of temperature from the bus to the hotel. She didn't mention anything, until they arrived on their floor, and Audri sneezed.

"Oh, my goodness," she said, her voice congested. "What's going on with me? I feel like as soon as the tour was over, I came down with a cold."

"Maybe it's the drop from the high of the day, you know? It was pretty amazing."

"Yes, it was, and I know El Yunque will be even better. I hope tomorrow I'll feel better," Audri said, struggling to unlock her door.

Madi took the key from her hand and opened the door. "Why don't you take a real long shower, and I go down to get you some medicine in case it is a cold?"

Audri nodded. "Good thinking. I never get sick and the one time I'm in paradise my body is like, time to act up!'

"Don't worry about it," Madi said. "I'll be right back."

She thought about dropping off her things in her room next door, but the sooner she got supplies for her friend, the sooner she could take a bath, journal, and do yoga. Her body was clamoring for attention.

The elevator seemed like it was stopping on every floor. It was taking forever to arrive, so she went down the stairs.

When she arrived at the front desk, Peter and Ada were still talking.

Madi didn't have any right to feel jealous. It seemed like when he worked in town, Peter stayed here. It was obvious Ada had a thing for him. He was, after all, one of the most handsome men Madi had ever seen, and they must have known each other for a while. Still, she felt a pang in her lower abdomen.

"Hey, sorry, I don't want to interrupt," she said.

Peter turned to her with surprise that morphed into alarm. "Is everything okay?"

She nodded quickly and then turned her attention to Ada. "Actually, I think Audri's coming down with a cold. Maybe it's just that she's tired, or the change in temperature didn't agree with her. But, I think she has a fever."

His eyes widened. "When she held my arm, her skin seemed warmer than natural. Is she okay?"

"She is. But I thought it's best if I got her some medicine just in case. Is there a pharmacy nearby?"

"Yes, when you go out the lobby—" Ada started saying, already pointing outside.

"No need for that," Peter cut her off. "Sorry, Ada. I have medicine here." He looked at Madi. "In my secret stash." He winked at her.

Her insides melted.

They'd known each other all of twenty-four hours and they already had a secret language of gazes and code phrases. They looked at each other for a few seconds. That electrical, sizzling sensation every time they locked eyes tingled in the air between them.

Ada cleared her voice and said, "Okay. If you need anything else, call the reception and I'll have it delivered to the room." She was obviously making an effort to sound nice in front of Peter, but Madi appreciated it all the same.

"Why don't we bring her some water? And maybe order her some food?" he asked.

He was going to think she could never reject food, and he'd be right. She wasn't even embarrassed when she said, "I could eat a whole pizza by myself."

The corner of his mouth twitched, amused. "Sounds like you feel okay, right?"

Madi knocked on the solid mahogany desk and said, "I'm just tired, but other than that, no sign of a cold."

"Good. Let's go up and then we'll see about soup or something nourishing for Audri. And pizza for you. And for me, too, actually. Lunch was forever ago."

Did this mean he was asking her out to a dinner date? Or was he just being nice?

In any case, she couldn't help smiling at him even though Ada was drilling Madi with laser eyes, but she'd done nothing. She wasn't even expecting Peter to still be around, much less to come to the rescue with his secret stash of medicine.

"Let's go," he said, leading her to the elevator that had just dinged open on the first floor.

She pushed the fourth-floor button and stood in a corner.

This was the first time she and Peter had been alone in a small space. She felt all gross from sweating all day, and then having the sweat dry on her over and over. Her hair must have been a mess and now that she paid attention to her body, she realized she had to go to the bathroom. At least she didn't stink, that she could tell. The perfume that permeated the elevator was musky and woodsy, and mixed with the tinge of hydraulic oil it turned into a sexy scent. She looked up but didn't see a camera or anything. Not that she didn't feel safe with Peter, but her mind flashed to every single sexy scene in an elevator that she'd ever watched or imagined, and chose to play it in fast speed. Her heart started racing as her mind tried to both catch up with and avoid seeing the couples kissing with abandon or doing other things in small elevators.

Wow. She'd never known a frantic tryst in an elevator was a fantasy of hers. A fantasy or a memory from a previous life?

She closed her eyes for a second and instead of fighting the images she let them go over her like a wave. Like the music playing from the speakers.

The elevator music was Enya, of all things, and she remembered Heather's teenagers singing and smiled, amused.

Peter kept looking at her and asked, "What?"

She shook her head. "Nothing. It's just the teens from the tour were adorable."

"Tyce and Mason. They both had a crush on you. Even Mya, their sister, did," he said, uncrossing his arms.

Did he really have to do that? It was like with the gesture his aura expanded so far she could actually feel his energy in every nerve ending of her body.

And why did he have to look at her like she had done anything for anyone to have a crush on her? "How would you even know that? That they had a crush on me?"

He smiled and narrowed his eyes at her. "Because I was sitting right in front of them, and their words were pretty obvious."

Madi was about to object when the lights flickered. The elevator lurched up and down but then it stopped.

"What the hell?" Peter asked, sounding panicked. He'd been calm during the storm and the chaos in the traffic, but now his fear was palpable.

"It's okay," Madi said, her hand flying to hold his. He grasped it without hesitation.

"Do you think Ada is messing with the controls to punish me for taking you away from her?" she asked, trying to tease him and distract him from his fear, but the words sounded way more forceful than she had intended.

He smiled and that dimple flashed in his face. "What? Why would Ada punish you for . . . ?" He paused, and Madi would've given anything to see his expression when it dawned on him that the hotel receptionist had a thing for him. But suddenly, the elevator went pitch-black. If the power had gone out in the building, or heaven forbid, the whole city, when would they be rescued? Madi sent a small prayer to the universe that only the hotel had lost its power, or that it was just a malfunction with the elevator.

"Oh my," she exclaimed, "I hope Audri is okay."

"Audri? She's safe and sound in her room. It's us who are trapped here. What if . . . what if the elevator falls?"

"It won't plummet down the shaft," she said.

No sooner was the phrase out of her mouth that she regretted her choice of words.

"This was one of Nadia's fears growing up and I googled it and I just remembered the phrase," she said.

Peter didn't say anything but then Madi heard a sound like he was gasping for air. The hairs on the back of her neck stood on end.

She didn't think. She followed the sound and with her splayed hands found him in the dark. Or most accurately, her hands crashed against his heaving hard chest.

"Oh, Peter," she said softly, her heart melting for him. "Are you claustrophobic?"

She felt him nodding and then a thread of hoarse voice said, "Yes."

His heart was pounding hard under her hands as he struggled to breathe and try to stay in control.

In the calmest voice she could muster, she reassured him. "You're not going to run out of air."

She knew she had to press the emergency call button to let someone—the receptionist, the fire department, the elevator rescuers—know they were trapped. She hadn't heard the telltale signs of people opening their doors in annoyance to see if they were the only ones without power, which meant it was probably only their elevator. She was grateful this hadn't happened to her when she was alone because her mind was now regaling her with a collection of horror scenes from elevators.

But Peter needed her. His pulse was out of control and his breathing was fast and shallow. The sound of ripping fabric and something small hitting the floor and breaking echoed on the walls. Peter, in his desperation to get air, had ripped his shirt open. "Sorry," he said, his voice hoarse.

Careful not to startle him, she placed her hand on his chest. It was sculpted and hairy and she could picture it perfectly.

"Shhh, is this okay?" she asked.

"Hm . . ." he said, and she took that as consent. As a plea for help.

Helping Peter through his panic attack kept her own fears at bay. She didn't know what she'd do if he fainted here in the dark. He was much taller and heavier than her. If he lost consciousness, she wouldn't be able to hold him up so he wouldn't hit his head against the wall and get a worse injury. She'd learned how to do mouth-to-mouth, but she hadn't ever applied it in a real emergency although she'd been CPR certified since she was twelve when she started babysitting. As she imagined the worst-case scenarios, her own heart rate skyrocketed painfully. If she wanted to help him calm down, she had to start with her own breathing.

"Let's sit on the floor," she said softly.

"Okay."

"Breath with me," she said, once he'd slid down to the floor next to her. She placed his head on her lap and started counting. "In one, two, three, four. Hold one, two, three, four. Out one, two, three, four. Hold one, two, three, four."

He tried, bless his heart, but he couldn't hold his breath. She continued softly counting and breathing with him until he finally caught the rhythm. Once she was sure he wasn't going to pass out, she moved on to the next step to follow.

She'd stupidly left her phone up in Audri's room with the rest of her stuff. But surely, he had his?

"Do you have your phone, Pete?"

Her cheeks warmed when she realized she'd called him by an endearment, but it was too late to correct herself.

He exhaled slowly, and after a few seconds said, "Here."

She probed the darkness with her hand, and then he must have touched his screen because the phone came alive.

"Nice!" she said.

She pressed on the screen for the flashlight and found the emergency button on the panel of the elevator.

A voice crackled from the tiny speaker on the wall. "State your emergency."

She cleared her throat. "Oh, hi. I'm stuck in the elevator at Casa Grande Hotel."

"Are you the only person in the elevator?" the man's voice asked in a professional, calm tone that Madi appreciated.

"I'm with a friend. He's having a panic attack. He's claustrophobic."

There was a small pause. More crackling but no words that she could decipher. Peter's breath became fast and shallow again, probably picking up on her spiking nerves.

"We'll be there shortly," the man's voice finally said.

She turned to Peter, who was sprawled on the floor, his torso half propped against the wall. Even under the super-dim light of the phone, she could tell his skin had a greenish tint. His eyes were closed, and he murmured softly, his white lips moving as if he were praying.

"Do you have anything in your pack that can help you, Peter?"

His eyelids twitched as if he was fighting to open his eyes, and he motioned toward the side where he'd dropped his bag.

"Can I look inside?"

"Yes," he whispered. His sweaty black hair was pasted to his forehead even though the temperature in the elevator was still so cold.

She knelt on the floor and with the help of his phone, she rummaged in the pockets. She smiled when she saw a couple of pairs of rubber sandals. There were menstrual products, baby diapers in a couple of sizes, and several ointments for insect bites and sunburn.

"You sure have a magical stash in here," she teased him, looking over her shoulder to check if he was still conscious.

He tried to smile and seeing him make that superhuman effort made her eyes prickle. How could she feel this tenderness with a man she'd just met? Her soul was in agony seeing him suffer.

In a pocket she found a plastic bag that contained paper bags for barf. She got one. She also studied the label of a little bottle.

"Is this what I think it is?" she asked aloud.

Although she hadn't expected a reply, he murmured something.

She unstoppered the bottle and the unmistakable scent of agua de Florida filled the elevator with its comfort. She didn't have smelling salts or even hand sanitizer. She'd learned that smelling rubbing alcohol helped with nausea. Maybe this would work.

She sat next to him again and poured a little of the perfumed water that always made her think of her abuela Lina on her hands.

She could imagine her voice in her ear telling her everything would be okay.

Madi placed her hand in front of his face. He kept breathing deeply. At first nothing happened, but then he sat up taller. But he must have lifted his head too quickly because he groaned.

"Shhh," she said. "No need to get up until they come break us free. Place your head on my lap again, and we'll wait."

He did as she suggested and kept breathing deeply.

The phone's light winked out, but now that people knew they were here, she wasn't nervous. She combed his hair with her fingers, humming the melody she'd sung since she was a small baby. There were plenty of family videos and recordings of Madi singing a sweet lullaby no one knew where she had learned. He pressed her knee with his hand. At first it tickled, but as the minutes went by, he relaxed his grip and his hand naturally rested on her thigh.

He breathed so deeply that for a moment, she thought he might be asleep.

But then he said, "Thank you, Madi. This has never happened to me before."

"There's nothing to be sorry or embarrassed for. I know you'd have done the same for me if our roles were reversed."

He didn't say anything more, but she knew he was conscious. As conscious as she was of his hand on her thigh, his deep breathing, the temperature of his body rising. Her heart sped up again, but for different reasons.

She would've never considered being stuck in an elevator as a romantic experience, but the air around them got charged again. She knew he felt it too for the way he tried to keep his body still, as if a movement could spark a fire.

"When I was a teen, I had a recurring dream that I was trapped in a cave. When a few years ago, I heard about those Thai boys from the soccer team who were trapped in a cave, I followed the case obsessively. I . . . I couldn't sleep until they were safe and sound."

"But you were okay in the caverns today. Doesn't that trigger your phobia?"

"Weirdly, no. You saw the opening of the sinkhole. We wouldn't have been trapped like they were. But maybe I sensed something today in the bus when were stuck in the tunnel. I hoped no one noticed that I was slowly losing my edge. But just now, I guess it was too much for me. I'm sorry."

"Shh," she said again, her fingers straying from his hair down to his face. His breath hitched, startling her hand away, but he caught it in the air and placed it on his face again. Tentatively, she caressed his face with her fingertips, careful that her long nails didn't scratch his perfect angel face. He had a bit of evening stubble, but the planes of his face were sharp and beautiful. He faced the elevator door, and in the darkness, he couldn't see her close her eyes and imagine every millimeter of his skin. Slowly, her hand moved down to his neck, and she made herself stop on his chest. She rubbed the center, where his heart chakra would be, and she imagined green light blooming and expanding with warmth.

The heat spread from his chest to her, until she felt she was burning up. He sat up, and although she couldn't see his face in the dark, she heard the sound of his lips parting.

"You need some water," she said, turning the light of the phone on again to find one of the bottles they were carrying for Audri. There were no bars on his phone or she would've called Audri to let her know that they were trapped in the elevator and that's why she was taking so long.

He found the water first and opened it. Before he took a sip, he offered it to her.

"You first," she said.

He drank, his Adam's apple bobbing up and down with each swallow and her fingertips itched with the desire to trace the line of his neck. But she fisted her hands to keep herself contained.

"Here," she said, passing him the bottle.

The plastic tasted a little like saliva. His saliva. The thought turned her on in a way that took her by surprise. He watched her drink, and once again, his chest rose quickly and he exhaled in spasms, as if he too was trying to hold himself back.

She made a show of capping the bottle and placed it on the floor. "We have to ration it in case we're here all night."

"Don't say that," he said, and when she smiled to show him it was a joke, he smiled. The flash of white teeth and his red lips made her stomach flip-flop. She didn't know what she was thinking, but she felt the same irresistible pull of the night before. The urge to kiss him or she would die. She leaned in at the same time he did, and their foreheads bumped.

"Ouch!" he said, pulling back a little. "You want to give me a concussion, woman?"

Her lips were pulsating, she could almost taste him. She grabbed the front of his unbuttoned shirt and pulled him closer. His eyes closed softly like butterfly wings, and just as their lips touched, a voice blared from outside the elevator.

"Everyone okay? Señorita, can you hear me?" a man asked in English.

"Peter, are you there?" Ada asked, sounding panicked.

Madi and Peter looked at each other, the same question flashing in their eyes. Should they kiss quickly now or—

But a blinding light pierced through the darkness. Madi had a brief vision of the spectacle the firemen were witnessing. The elevator had been stuck between floors and four firemen and a paramedic looked down at them first with surprise, and then with amusement.

Peter, his shirt undone, on the floor. Madi, her hair disheveled and sweaty, and the perfume of agua de Florida mixed with the scent of their bodies would give the wrong impression.

"It's about time!" Madi exclaimed to save face as she scrambled back to her feet. She offered a hand to Peter, and he took it.

Before the paramedic insisted on examining both of them, they exchanged a look of regret and longing.

Chapter 16

The paramedic, a young man in his twenties with a strong Cuban accent, determined Madi, and most importantly, Peter, were physically okay. The color had returned to his face and other than the ruined shirt, there was nothing else to report.

Physically he might have been okay, but once they stepped out of the elevator, he avoided looking at Madi in the eyes, as if there was anything to be embarrassed about.

"I'll just head to my room, if that's okay," he said in Madi's general direction.

"Do you need food or—"

He shook his head, already walking to the end of the hallway. "I just need a shower and sleep. I'll be fine tomorrow morning. Good night, and thanks."

"Good night," Madi said, waving at him even though he couldn't see her. "You're welcome."

"And you, are you okay?" the paramedic asked.

"I'm okay, thanks. I'll just go check on my friend who was

starting to come down with a cold. Peter and I were bringing her medicine and water when we got stuck. What time is it? I don't even know how long we were in the elevator. It seemed we were there forever."

"It's nine thirty now."

So not that long, but it would take a while for Peter to recover. She hoped he'd be okay the following morning.

In that moment, another paramedic arrived. She was an older woman with cool tattoos of Van Gogh's starry night on her arms. She must have heard Madi because she said, "We can check on your friend very quickly before we go."

Madi considered for a second. She was about to say that she had all she needed when she realized Peter had taken his bag with him—the bag with the secret stash of medicines. In his state, no way would she knock on his door to ask for it. He might already be in the shower by now.

An image of Peter in the shower flashed in her eyes, and she blinked to erase it with no success.

"Actually, maybe, yes," she said, shaking her head. "Maybe it's best to make sure—" A yawn cut her words. Exhaustion had fallen on her head like an anvil in old cartoons. The day had been long, and her emotions had been all over the place.

"Show us where it is," the male paramedic said.

Madi pointed to the door right across the elevator.

"She must not have heard a thing," she said, worried suddenly that Audri was really sick. "I have a key." She fished it out of her pocket. She'd at least had the good sense to grab Audri's and hers before heading downstairs.

Gingerly, she knocked on the door, but no one replied. She gave the paramedics a small smile and turned the key and opened the door. The sounds of the rushing ocean coming out from a phone speaker greeted them. The ambiance was so Zen.

In the bed, Audri slept with a silk eye shade over her eyes that matched her ivory bonnet. She breathed deeply.

"At least she's alive," the paramedic joked, and the other lady sent him an annoyed look.

"Sorry," he said.

The three of them stood by the bed. Madi realized that if Audri woke up and saw her looking like she'd been through a wreck and two strangers in uniforms, she'd have the fright of her life. She didn't want to startle her.

She looked at the woman, who was so competent she understood the situation at once. She moved to the foot of the bed and dragged her partner along.

Then Madi knelt by the bed and took Audri's hand. It wasn't terribly hot, but she definitely still had a fever.

"Aud," she whispered. "I brought you some medicine, mama. Are you okay?"

Audri swallowed and said something so garbled Madi didn't understand.

"Don't be scared, but there's a doctor here if you want her to check on you." She glanced at the paramedic, who sent her a flattered look. "I think it's better to simplify," she whispered.

"A doctor?" Audri moved her eye shade just an inch, and she smiled when she peeked at Madi. "I'm okay, but some ibuprofen would be nice." She then noticed the paramedics, and maybe she took in Madi's look because she sat up higher on the bed. "Are you okay? Did something happen?"

Madi patted her friend's hand. "Everything's okay. It's a long story, but they were right here on this floor and when I mentioned you were feeling under the weather, they offered to check."

"Oh, okay," Audri said.

Madi stepped aside so the paramedics could check on Audri. The whole thing took but a minute.

"It's just a cold, from what I can tell. But if tomorrow the fever is worse, or there are new symptoms, please seek assistance.

But I'm sure that after a couple of ibuprofen and several hours of sleep, you'll be okay," the man said. "What a bummer you're sick on vacation."

"It's actually a business trip but yes, what a bummer," Audri said.

The woman's radio rattled with a new emergency call and after excusing themselves and accepting Madi's gratitude, they left.

"Do you want me to order you dinner?" Madi asked.

Audri shook her head and then winced. "No, thanks, love. I'll go back to sleep as the doctors ordered."

Madi nodded, and she realized she was wringing her hands.

Audri looked at Madi. "Are you going to tell me?"

But Madi could hardly stay on her feet. "Tomorrow. I promise."

She headed to her room. But first things first, she turned the electric kettle on to make herself some tea and ordered food on the app. She had thirty minutes before the food arrived to take a shower and do some yoga to ground herself. The water pressure was deliciously strong, washing away the grime from the day. The scent of her chamomile and lavender shampoo calmed her. But when her fingers brushed her lips, and she thought of the almost taste of Peter's mouth, her whole body felt like it was burning. She wrapped her arms around herself, feeling she was going to fall apart from wanting him so much. For a couple of seconds, she debated what to do. It wouldn't be near as close as being with Peter right now, but she knew from experience that there was no point in pretending she was going to sleep a wink tonight without any kind of release.

Finally, she resolutely walked out of the shower, got her vibrator from her suitcase, and returned to the rushing water. By the time her food arrived, she was way more relaxed than if she'd done her yoga as planned.

After dinner, Madi felt satisfied in every physical way, but not emotionally. Maybe because the day had been so busy and emotional, the memory of Peter's pent-up desire and his feverish lips just a breath away from hers, Madi dreamed.

She was in the dark even though her eyes were wide open. She wasn't trapped, but she was struggling to breathe. In her dream, she didn't know her own body well enough, but a part of her told her she was human, and she was blind. Although her eyes didn't discern even light, she recognized emotions like waves hitting her skin. Someone lay next to her, her lover, crying, pleading for her not to go. Madi was so tired, but somehow, knowing she was close to death, her chest seized for her beloved.

"I'll find you," she gasped. "I promise I will."

Stillness.

A bright light.

More darkness and pressure and the sound of tearing fabric.

And then an urge to rise up to a light and its soft warmth. The sun.

Madi moved her arms like a swimmer fighting to get to the surface, only she was swimming through solid matter. Dirt.

She was a seed, and the sun was inviting her to grow.

But growing hurts, and the earth was safe and comfortable.

Above the surface, the world waited for her. The world where her love lived.

Madi struggled to rise again, and finally she gasped for air.

She sat up on her bed, in the hotel, the clock on the nightstand marking eight o'clock, and the sun of the tropics making her skin prickle.

It had been a dream. Just a dream.

The day before rushed to her in a flood of thoughts and emotions.

Audri. Peter. She had to check on them.

Something vibrated under her sheets, and sheepishly, she marveled at the battery life of her vibrator. But then she realized it was her phone.

Cringing at herself, she untangled it from the bedcovers and looked at the screen.

It was Audri calling.

"Hey!" Madi answered, her voice a little too chirpy for the morning, but it was her stupid self-consciousness of having pleasured herself the night before. She felt like the morning after she'd had sex for the first time in senior year, and how she thought everyone would know she and Jared had done *it*.

"Hey," Audri replied. Her voice sounded like she's just woken up. "Sorry about last night. How boring it must have been for you!"

Madi covered her vibrator with the sheet as if her friend would see it and said, "There's nothing to be sorry about, Aud. How are you feeling?"

"I don't have a fever anymore, but my whole body is sore, as if I ran a marathon and then swam across the Atlantic Ocean. I don't think I can go to El Yunque to check the tree houses today. I'm sorry."

"Mama, no problem," Madi said. She tried to sound upbeat, but the truth was she was disappointed they wouldn't get to check out this place. They didn't have availability for them to stay and experience all the amenities, but the owner was going to meet them and show them around himself.

"To make matters worse, Mariela texted me that she's sick too, so she won't get to drive you," Audri added.

Now Madi couldn't hide her sadness. "Oh, no! Really? Is it the same bug, you think?"

"It sounds like it," Audri said. "She texted the rest of the people from the tour to check if anyone else caught it, but so far, it's just the two of us. Chances are we got it the night we arrived here or it's just a coincidence."

Madi didn't believe in coincidences. It all happened for a reason, even those things that would only make sense years down the road.

She had no idea why Audri and Mariela had gotten sick now, but she was determined not to force things and go with the flow. And instead of staying in the hotel too, or walking around the old city, which was lovely but didn't have what she was looking for, she decided to follow her intuition.

"How about Peter?" she asked. "Is he sick too?"

"Peter's good as new. I talked to him earlier this morning."

"And how did he sound?"

"Perfectly fine. Why? You two argued again?" Audri asked.

"Do you remember last night when I was in your room with two paramedics?"

"It was real?" Audri exclaimed, and then broke into laughter. "Oh my gosh! I thought I had dreamed the whole thing!"

Madi told her everything that had happened after she'd left her room to go get Audri some medicine. She didn't mention how intimate the moment with Peter in the elevator had become. She'd promised herself to keep things professional with him and she didn't want Audri to think she couldn't spend a moment alone with him without wanting to jump him and kiss him. Which was the truth. Embarrassing, but the truth, nonetheless.

Audri didn't seem to notice there were blots in the story, but said, "He's still planning on going with you."

"He'll drive the bus? Just for the two of us?"

"No, he'll take Javier's car. He was heading to Mariela's house to get it when we talked. He must be back to the hotel by now. He said for you to meet him at ten or text him if you didn't feel like going with him. That he understands if you don't feel comfortable going with him."

Maybe he said that because he didn't feel comfortable with her?

"I don't have his number," Madi said, holding her breath for Audri to share it with her without having to ask.

The phone vibrated in her hand, and when she looked at the

screen, she smiled. Audri had sent her Peter's contact information.

Even though she was excited, it took her a couple of minutes to gather the courage to text him. Her last dream had left her tenderhearted, but she had to remind herself that dreams could be visions or predictions, but usually they were just the unconscious unburdening itself, taking the trash out.

Before she texted Peter, Madi got her journal out. She wrote all she remembered from her dream, without gaining a clear understanding or advice.

Advice is what she needed. She sent an SOS to Stevie and Nadia, but then she realized it was still just past six in the morning in Utah, and that it could be a while before they replied. She would get advice from the next best place: her tarot cards.

She'd brough the traditional Rider-Waite. She'd do a simple one-card draw. As she shuffled, she held the question loosely in her mind: "What should I do?"

Before she could even think of the best-case scenario, she pulled the card at the top of the deck. It was the two of pentacles.

"Ah," she sighed.

Balance, priorities, adaptability.

What was her main goal this trip?

Finding a location for the retreats and bringing her grandma's ashes to their final resting place.

What was her priority right now?

Checking out the tree houses in El Yunque, even if Audri was sick. Even if it would be torture to be there with Peter, unable to express all the feelings she had for him.

She'd be a professional businesswoman, the kind that Stevie and Nadia would be proud of. She'd think coolly with her mind and not drive her decisions with her heart, or worse, her coochie.

"The cards have spoken," she said solemnly, and gratefully

put the card back in the deck and placed it carefully inside her purse.

Then she typed and deleted a few messages until she found the wording that worked.

Hey, Peter, how are you? Audri told me that you could drive me to El Yunque for the meeting with the owner of the tree houses. Is that still a go? Let me know ☺ (Madi)

Immediately, three dots danced on her screen. Sweat prickled in her armpits as she waited for his reply.

She put the kettle on again, and when she glanced at her phone, Peter had texted.

Still planning on meeting at 10am at the lobby.

Madi studied the words and punctuation. Did the period at the end mean he was mad at her? Some guys hated showing vulnerability in front of a stranger, a woman. He'd been vulnerable all right in the elevator the night before. Was he the kind that would hate anyone who'd seen this side of him? She hoped not. She hoped that the moment in the elevator had brought them closer, friendlier. After all, she wasn't here to look for a relationship, even if the attraction between them was unmistakable, but a future without Peter filled her with sadness. If they could at least remain friends . . . But, did he want to be friends with her?

She wasn't sure why the text sounded so cold, so curt. Should she ask him directly like Stevie would? Or should she stop catastrophizing the situation? Yes, she should stop jumping to the worst conclusion. She could already feel her mood becoming sour without need.

For all she knew, Peter was smiling just like she had been before he'd replied. After all, he hadn't canceled their outing. She would've still made it to El Yunque on her own, ordering an Uber or taxi, but it was much nicer to go with someone she knew. Someone she trusted. Someone she liked.

"Stop it, Madi," she snapped at herself as Nadia and Stevie would do, and headed to the shower to get ready. This time, she wouldn't bring her vibrator along.

She was a professional, for the love of god!

Chapter 17

Madi was proud of herself for choosing a sensible outfit. She knew that in the rain forest the temperatures would be much cooler than in the caverns, but it would still be humid. Trying to appear as professional as possible, she chose a pair of army green hiking shorts, a short-sleeve white T-shirt, and comfortable black sneakers. She had brought a white hoodie because she'd learned from experience that even if it was hot and humid outside, usually restaurants were gelid, and she didn't want to suffer unnecessarily.

She ditched her Gucci purse and instead packed a backpack she'd bought at Jackson Hole once when she'd visited Jayden while he was hunting with his friends. It had pockets for her wallet, phone, deodorant, and lip gloss. To make the bag less bulky, she took out the pouch where she carried her own emergency stash of tampons and pads (and condoms). She had no need for any of its contents. Her menstrual cycle had been in sync with the moon since her first period. She usually ovulated during the full moon (which would be in three days) and menstruated for the new moon, like the planting cycle.

After checking that Audri was comfy in her room, Madi headed downstairs. Although there was no sign that warned the guests that they could be trapped in the elevator, Madi wasn't about to take risks.

She was sweating slightly when she reached the lobby and saw Peter chatting with the receptionist—not Ada. This was a man in his fifties. Peter must have felt her presence because he suddenly looked up. His face transformed. He didn't smile. In fact, Madi could tell he was clenching his teeth, but his eyes got all sparkly and dancing, like he couldn't hide the fact that he was happy to see her. The corner of his mouth twitched just enough for that dimple of his to indent his cheek.

She was delighted that they matched. His charcoal shorts looked like they were the same fabric as hers, and he too wore a white T-shirt. Instead of a backpack, he had a black fanny pack draped across his chest. A pair of sunglasses was perched on the top of his head.

"Hi," Madi said, standing in front of him.

Taking her by surprise, he leaned in and kissed her on the cheek. "Good morning."

His cologne . . . It undid her.

Madi's breath hitched in her chest. She couldn't get a word out, so she just smiled at him and nodded.

"See you, Rafa," Peter said to the receptionist, who nodded at Madi in greeting, and went back to the ringing phone on the desk.

"Vamos?" Peter asked. His voice, velvety soft, did all kinds of things to Madi.

"Let's go," she replied, and followed him outside.

There was no trace of yesterday's storm. The sky was like polished Murano glass. The bells of the cathedral tolled, marking the top of the hour. Peter headed to a slick black Mercedes that took Madi by surprise. She knew nothing about cars, and as long as a vehicle took her from one place to the other, she never cared what make and model they were. But even she could appreciate this car was nice. Way nicer than the one he'd been driving the night they met. Or at least, the one where he'd put back his emergency stash before they headed down to the Noche de San Juan party.

"Wow," she said when Peter held the passenger door open for her to climb in. "This is special. Thanks."

Before lowering his sunglasses from his forehead, he winked at her. "You're welcome, señorita."

She got in the car and while he walked to his side, she bit her lip to wrench herself from falling back into behaving like an airhead. She didn't know why he was flirting with her, but she was determined to do as the cards had said and keep herself balanced, to keep her priorities straight.

Thankfully, the car was cool, as if Peter had it ready for their trip, and the sweat on her face evaporated quickly. Two bottles of pineapple-flavored water sat in the cupholders in the middle console.

"For you," he said.

"How did you know I love that flavor?" She knew that her eyes were all sparkly too.

"Audri told me yesterday when we stopped at the gas station from Camuy. Ready to head out to the rain forest?"

"Ready," she said, although an hour in the car next to him would certainly be a challenge. Not because she didn't like him. The opposite, actually. She liked him so much, she didn't know how to act. How would they fill the awkward silence? What were they going to talk about?

But again, Madi was preparing for the worst-case scenario when there was nothing to worry about. As soon as he sat in the driver's seat, Peter pressed a button and the radio started playing Bad Bunny. The familiar music relaxed her enough to lean back on the seat and exhale.

"Too bad Mariela and Audri are sick. It would've been fun with them along," she said. "Thanks for not bailing on me, though. I'd have hated if I had to make the trip on my own."

"Of course," he said. "I haven't been in El Yunque in a while. I was looking forward to this since Javier asked me to cover for him. It's actually the main reason I accepted although I had sworn on my honor not to do tours again."

She looked at him, surprised. "Really? I'm flattered!" She had so many questions, and in another situation in which she was intimidated by a guy, she would've swallowed them all, but now she was too curious not to ask. "It looks like you love being a tour guide. Why did you stop?"

He shrugged. "I do love it. I mean, I get to talk about history, food, and people. The trifecta, but doing the same thing every day, like, explaining the same thing can get old. Especially when some tourists expect Puerto Rico to be just like the US, and then they arrive and realize how different it is and are loud about how disappointed they are."

Madi nodded. She had relished in how different Puerto Rico was from the United States. It was really a different country only with a lot of the same businesses and amenities. But she could see how average Americans would get impatient with the traffic, the slower rhythm of life, and the power outages.

"Living in paradise has a cost, as my grandma used to say." She looked out her window at the rushing cityscape.

"I agree," he said.

"And how did you end up becoming a tour guide to start with?"

He smiled and it looked almost like he'd rolled his eyes. "It's a long story."

"It's kind of a long drive," she said, pointing at the GPS that marked a road highlighted in red for the most part.

"Well, if you insist," he said, and shrugged.

She crossed her arms and stomped her foot for emphasis. "I insist."

Oof. His smile. She wouldn't mind being silly—borderline ridiculous, Jayden would say—only to see Peter smile at her that way forever.

"It was kind of an accident," he said, a dreamy look on his face as he looked to the past. "I told you I met Javi in college, and we bonded over our Puertoricanness. Back then, his family was in Florida, and the only ones here on the island were his grandma and his great-uncle. When we graduated, he invited me to the island. He'd promised them he'd bring the diploma for them to see it in person. He was the first college graduate in his family, you see? After some back and forth, I finally agreed to come along."

"Why the back and forth?"

He shrugged again. "I had this hatred toward the island because of my dad, you know?" Peter's knuckles were white as he gripped the wheel. "I know it was irrational, but I hated what my father had done to my mom. Life had been so hard for her, and he took advantage of a girl who was all alone, who had come to the US looking for a better life."

"But she had you," Madi whispered. She had no right to say anything because she hadn't met Peter's mom, or dad. Hell. She hardly knew Peter. But judging by the fierceness with which he spoke about his mom, they must have loved each other very much.

She was right though because Peter smiled sadly in her direction. "Yes, that's what she always said. It didn't excuse what he had done. And to punish him, I blocked everything that came from Puerto Rico, which was kind of hard, to be honest. Until I met Javi, my brother from another mother. So I came to the island with him, and I . . . I fell in love with it. The culture, the food, the air, everything."

Madi pressed her lips. That's exactly how she felt too.

"And it's not that I didn't see the negative things. I did. I saw them too well, but my love for the island was stronger than my dislike for all its flaws. I don't know that I'm ready to make the move permanently, but it calls me. The island calls me."

There was a small pause, and then he added, "The thing is that after that first trip, it's like I had to learn all I could about the island. It was a compulsion to catch up for all I had missed. Before long, I knew more about the history and trivia than a lot of our friends that had been guides and ended up moving to the States. By then I had graduated from my master's program and broken up, I mean, divorced my college sweetheart—Maribel." He swallowed as if just saying her name scratched his throat.

Madi's mouth went dry as her whole body went cold. She had to make an effort not to interrupt him with all the questions in her mind. The D word had shaken her to the core.

Not that she minded that he was divorced. She'd dated a few divorced guys in her twenties. Guys who'd married young for all the wrong reasons and then realized what a commitment they'd made before they were ready.

"The divorce was hard for my mom. She loved Maribel, and Maribel loved her. Then my mom died suddenly. Breast cancer that went undetected."

"I'm sorry," Madi whispered. "My grandma had breast cancer too."

"It's a horrible thing, no?"

Madi nodded.

"After that, I just couldn't stay in Idaho. It was too painful. My mom's presence was in everything, all over the place. Maribel had a baby with her new partner, and then they got married, and now they're expecting another one. I didn't know what my purpose was, you see? I made my peace with us going our separate ways, but I didn't know where my life was heading anymore."

"What do you mean?"

Peter sighed and didn't say anything for a few seconds. "When I was still a boy, I thought I had met the woman of my life, even if she was just a girl herself. I thought we were soul mates, but it turned out to be wrong."

They were stopped at a light, and he glanced at Madi as if making sure she was okay with the narrative. There was so much pain in his expression, a knot formed in her throat. Her whole idea of soul mates was upside down and she was trying to make sense of her thoughts.

Like always, the best way for her to know what she felt was to talk it out.

"Maybe being a soul mate doesn't mean you'll be together forever," she said, more to herself than him, but the words obviously helped him too. The dark cloud in his eyes was gone.

"Maybe," he said with a shrug.

"What happened next?"

He inhaled deeply and said, "Turns out, my mom had a very nice life insurance policy that she'd paid for little by little and then forgot all about it. Typical Cristina. A month after she died, this guy showed up at my house with a check that I would've given anything not to ever receive if it meant having her back. But it was a gift from her, so I could have the freedom to make my way in this life."

"And get a nice car like this one?" she asked. Trying to defuse the sadness or take a bit of it away from him, she placed her hand on his shoulder. Slowly, they'd hunched up as if the load he carried was too much to hide.

The gesture must have worked because he smiled and said, "No! Cars are Javi's thing. We're different. I can't splurge on something like this when I could use it in much better ways. I'll just borrow his."

It made sense. Everything Peter shared about himself with Madi was another puzzle piece that fit perfectly with the image she had of her ideal guy. Too bad he didn't believe in soul mates.

If only she hadn't made a mess of their first meeting. How would this drive be different? Would she be holding his right hand as he drove? Would she have let her hand slide to the back of his head like she was itching to do right now but had no right to? That he had belonged to another woman was eating at her. But why? She'd proposed to Jayden just a few days ago.

"Why did you and Maribel split up?" she asked before she could stop herself.

He hesitated.

"Sorry. You don't have to tell me." She clasped her hands on her lap where she could see them, as far from him as possible, and stared ahead. Water shimmered in the distance up on the road. A mirage. Like all her silly beliefs about love.

He tapped her chin with his index finger. "Don't look so sad . . . Maribel and I were happy while it lasted, but once love ran its course, the best option was to go our separate ways. She wanted to stay in Idaho. I didn't. Little by little, our interests and goals drifted further and further apart. I traveled a lot. She resented that I wasn't home. One day, she told me she was in love with someone else."

"Did she cheat?"

Peter shook his head. "No. Before we even dated, we'd been best friends, and we always told each other everything. The secret was killing her, literally. She lost so much weight. She couldn't sleep, and when I asked her to please tell me what was wrong, the words just came out."

The radio played a sad Bad Bunny song and the lyrics fed Madi's imagination. She could see the whole scene in her mind. A beautiful Maribel explaining her change of heart. Peter hearing the news, devastated, walking out of the house, in the middle of the night.

Madi's heart broke for him.

"What did you do? Were you angry?"

She didn't understand how a woman could fall in love with anyone else while being married to Peter. But at the same time, she admired Maribel for being brave enough to tell him the truth instead of pretending, instead of forcing herself to feel something that wasn't there anymore.

"I was sad, I'm not going to lie," Peter said. "For a while, I thought it was my fault for not trying better. But then, I don't know . . . I saw her with her baby one time, and I knew things had worked out after all."

Madi knew there were two sides to every story, and she would've loved to hear Maribel's version. Did she regret her choices? Did she imagine what life would've turned out like if she hadn't confessed her change of heart to Peter?

"Is that why you don't believe in destiny?"

She crossed her arms, and he leaned in to turn the AC down. She realized her arms were covered in goose bumps and a warmth grew in her chest that he had noticed she'd been cold even when she hadn't.

"I hate the idea that our lives are written, predetermined," he scoffed. "I want to think I have a say in who I become. I'm not a puppet. I want to live my life intentionally."

"So do I," she replied, for the first time voicing the desire that had been growing inside her. She had let life happen to her as she waited for the right time, the right person. Perhaps she had to work for her dreams instead of waiting for them to arrive at her door.

He looked at the cupholder, and before he said anything, Madi uncapped the water bottle and handed it to him.

"Thanks," he said, surprised.

"You're welcome."

There usually was a tension between them, but now the feeling was comfort, familiarity. She liked it. She liked that they didn't have to fill their silences, and that also, they could talk about anything.

Maybe he was thinking along the same lines, because he said, "Tell me more about you, though. Do you think you'll move to the island to head the retreats or are you just looking for temporary places to rent?"

"I don't know," she said, and sighed. They were leaving PR 26 to merge onto PR 3, almost there. A single green peak that was the highest point of the rain forest stood out in the distance. "I've never felt really at home in Utah, but every time I leave—on vacation, I might add—I get literally homesick. It's usually me getting a cold on the second day out of town, not Audri, although I don't think that Audri is homesick. She just caught a cold." She was rambling, and she took a deep breath to rein herself in. "I'm thirty-one, almost thirty-two, mind you, and I've never been anywhere by myself. One of my best friends, Stevie—"

"The Japanese Peruvian."

"Yes, we established that," she said, rolling her eyes at him. "Well, Stevie, she's been everywhere in the world. She started traveling solo when she was eighteen, but Utah is her home base. Nadia is more like me, but she likes Utah. She's settled there for good. But I've never felt like I belong there, and yet, I always resist leaving. I craved coming back to Puerto Rico, but I resisted it somehow. Maybe bringing my grandma's ashes here would make her loss more final, definitive, you know? But now I'm here, I don't really know how I'll leave at the end of the week. Life here might be hard, but it's hard everywhere. I might as well live where I feel at home."

She hadn't known she felt so strongly about where home was for her. A home away from her parents and the rest of her family. Now she was on a roll.

"I think that for someone to lead the retreats, they have to be local. They have to know the culture and people, the vendors and neighbors. That way, the revenue from the retreats can also help the people on the island."

He looked like he was trying to make an effort not to roll his eyes.

"What?"

"Tourism doesn't really help the island as much as they say, you know? The Boricuas get employed in the service industry but the profits go back to the mainland."

Madi thought for a second. Her heart pounded, trying to

push out the words forming in her mouth before her mind vetoed them. "What if the retreats and workshops were targeted for the locals, by a local."

She didn't dare say that by local, she meant *her*, but she hoped he could read it in her eyes.

"Now you're talking," he said, with a smile that flooded her with light.

But then it was like he thought of something, and a cloud crossed his face, making it somber.

"What?" she asked again, and this time she didn't hold herself back and placed her hand on his.

"What about your friends?"

She sighed. "That's what's hard for me too. My friends . . ."

She knew that if she told Nadia and Stevie how much at home she felt in Puerto Rico, they'd pack her bags for her and wish her the best, on the one and only condition that she kept a guest room ready for them to visit every other month. But, she didn't know if she had what it took to uproot herself.

Or would she really be uprooting? If anything, it would be coming back to the place where it had all started, coming back to her roots.

"I don't know why I don't feel the same way about Argentina," she said. "That's where my bio father and my dad are both from. I love it. I've been there. But I feel at home here. Does it make sense?"

"It does," he said, adjusting the AC vents away from Madi. He continued, "I've been in Peru, and Japan. I feel like I'm more Peruvian when I'm in Lima. No one bats an eyelash at my name or asks me where I'm from. No one asks about my accent."

"Your accent in Spanish is lit," she said, which earned her a big smile.

"I have the annoying trait of picking up accents. If I spend too much time with Chileans, I speak like a Chilean." He said the last section in the most striking Chilean Spanish.

"In your defense, Chilean accent is super catchy. Cachai?"

He smiled at her gratefully.

"No, really," she insisted. "Your trait is wonderful. It's a superpower. You're like a chameleon!"

"My grandpa used to call me Lagartijo, a lizard," he said, his voice wistful.

Lagartijo and Lagartija, what were the odds?

"In Japan I stand out a little more because my skin's darker than most people's there, and my Japanese is rusty, to say the least," Peter continued. "But the Peruvian and Brazilian Nikkei community, the diaspora, is huge in Hamamatsu. I've made a lot of friends through the years. After the first day, I forget I wasn't born and raised there. I can navigate the streets as if I remembered them from another life . . ."

He chuckled as if he'd said the most ridiculous thing, but the words struck Madi in her soul. "I know that doesn't make any sense, but that's how I feel. It's different in Puerto Rico, though. It's new and fascinating. It's like I want to consume the island to keep it inside me so I'll remember it even after I'm gone from this world."

Madi held her breath to try to calm her racing heart. He was just echoing her feelings.

By then, the car was cruising in a neighborhood of stucco houses with Pico El Yunque as a background so majestic it seemed like an artificial backdrop. Madi's hands prickled with excitement. She imagined bringing people to experience this beauty, to help them reconnect with nature and their inner selves.

But to help others, first she had to help herself, that know-it-all voice said in the back of her mind. To silence it, she increased the volume of the song playing on the radio.

"You like him, huh?" Peter asked, raising an eyebrow as if he'd discovered something unique about her that intrigued him.

She flashed him a smile, shrugging. "I know it's Bad Bunny because his voice is, like . . . unique."

Peter nodded. "That's a way to put it."

"Most times, I have no idea what he says though."

They were laughing by the time the GPS told them they'd arrived although they were in a crossroads with no signs to tell them where to go.

"Are you lost, tour guide?" she teased him.

"Hmm," Peter said. "I never get lost, but . . . Give me a sec here."

He looked around but it was lush trees to the right and more lush trees to the left. Then, he turned left.

"Are you sure?" she asked.

He halted the car, making it lurch.

She laughed. "I was teasing you. I think it's this way, too. See? There's a bakery truck heading in that direction. I have a hunch it's making a delivery to the tree houses."

"A hunch, huh?"

"Yep, my lizard brain speaking to me."

Up on the winding road, the image of the truck flickered in and out of the trees, but it was definitely there.

He looked at her with admiration. "You're a clever, clever woman."

Madi had been working on not needing external validation for years. She was doing better now than she had last year or even a few months ago, but still, satisfaction bloomed in her lower belly and filled her to the tip of her toes and the top of her crown. She imagined she had light coming from her eyes, so she kept her gaze ahead.

And a few minutes later, they arrived in front of an island cabin with solar panels on the roof and glass windows all around. Small signs pointed to Paradise, Bliss, Nirvana, Paraíso, Elysium, Eden. The bigger one led to Gokuraku. Madi looked in its direction and saw a cabin built like it was part of a giant tree's canopy. She guessed the signs were the different names of tree houses.

Peter parked and Madi's nerves about representing Reyna

and Audri returned. She didn't want to ruin this for them. She didn't know if she had the skills to negotiate and ask the right questions.

As if he could hear the wave of the anxiety cresting over her, he said, "You're going to do incredible. You'll see."

She winced and looked down so this time he wouldn't see the self-doubt darkening her face. "I hope I don't let Reyna and Audri down. They're . . . such power businesswomen, and I feel like they should be the ones here."

"Hey," he said, taking hold of her hand. "Didn't you say that everything happens for a reason?" Softly he rubbed his thumb over her knuckles. "You're the one here and you're going to be wonderful."

If anything, she appreciated the vote of confidence. "Thank you. For everything, Peter. I'm glad I didn't have to drive here on my own."

Then, just realizing that they were far from everything, she asked, "Will you wait here for me? Or . . ."

It was too much to ask for him to hang around all day, but her phone didn't have signal, and if he left, then she'd be stuck here—

"Hey," he said again, pulling her up from her downward spiral. "I'll be here. And who knows? Maybe I can come along to the excursion?"

"Really?" She hadn't dared to ask this of him. "Are you sure?"

He smiled softly. "I love to get pointers from fellow guides. In the meantime, I'll be waiting here. You go do your thing. You're going to nail it."

Her heart fluttered with the rush of adrenaline and the confidence he was sending her. Before she faltered, she leaned over the console and kissed him on the cheek.

Taken by surprise, and in a reflex, Peter placed a hand on the back of her neck. The gesture was so tender and protective, that

Madi closed her eyes to imprint this second on her heart, and then left the car and headed to the main office.

"You must be Madison," said an American man who looked like a young version of Robert Redford. If Stevie were here, she'd be a puddle. Of the three amigas, she was the one who had a thing for blond, tall, cocky-bordering-on-arrogant men.

Madi, instead, sensed her defenses come up like a shield the moment they shook hands.

"Hi, you must be Jeremy."

She tried to keep her face straight, impassive. But Jeremy was living proof of their conversation on the way here. An outsider acting as the face of Puerto Rican tourism, while Puerto Ricans were relegated to service positions.

"I am Jeremy, yes. Nice to meet you," he said. "Audri called me this morning. I'm sorry she got sick. I was looking forward to meeting her too."

"I know," she said in a breathy voice that she had to rein in if she wanted to be taken seriously. "Today I'm her eyes and ears. I'm ready to be dazzled."

"When Audri told me about her beautiful Puerto Rican friend who was coming in her place, I was prepared to be dazzled by you, but I have to confess, her words didn't do you justice."

Madi felt her smile freeze on her face and the light dim from her eyes. So it was going to be like this . . . She didn't want to play the ditzy Latina.

"Tell me about you," he said. "You don't have a Puerto Rican accent in English! I mean, I've lived here for a year, and I've been surprised at the sharpness of Puerto Ricans, you know? Like, it's not coming the right way, but I've learned there's usually a lot of substance under the good looks."

He had a boyish demeanor and a smile that he used like weapons, and now that Madi knew this about him, she felt more comfortable because she knew just how to deal with men like him. Men who thought she was a bimbo because she had big boobs, a big booty, and liked to smile. Men who thought that anyone who wasn't a white, cis, rich man was inferior.

"I might say the opposite is also true, many times," she said.

She kept smiling as he worked out the meaning of her words, and she saw them sink in, and a light of understanding turn on in his eyes. He now knew she wasn't someone he could bamboozle with empty compliments.

He clapped, and said, "Good. Let's head to the conference room and go over numbers, and then we can tour the property. I think you're going to love how cozy the tree houses are." His eyes scanned her up and down, and she willed herself not to blush, and succeeded. "I see you're ready for a hike. Smart girl."

Madi liked it better when Peter had called her clever woman.

"In fact, my business associate Peter will come along the tour with us. He's an expert in the industry and I trust him."

In that moment, Peter walked into the lobby, looking like a real-life superhero.

Jeremy didn't seem to love this plot twist, but there was nothing he could say.

"Peter, thanks for joining us," Madi said, waving him over. "Just in time. We were going to start going over numbers." She turned toward Jeremy and said, "Shall we?"

Jeremy fumbled for a beat, but then he said, "Of course, come in, please." And directed them to the conference room.

Chapter 18

A couple of hours later, after Madi drilled him on costs and revenue and flow charts and his five-year plans, Jeremy called for a break.

"Let's take some time for lunch so you can appreciate the resort fully, Miss Ramírez, sound good?"

After the first few minutes of the meeting, he had stopped directing his questions to Peter and now referred to her as Miss Ramírez. Madi's confidence soared, but she kept her composure and looked at her watch and notes for a few seconds of suspense.

Then he glanced at Peter and said, "That's okay for me. Are you doing okay, Peter?"

"Super," he replied.

Visibly relieved, Jeremy left the room to give instructions to his assistant.

"You're killing it!" Peter said.

She leaned on the chair and groaned. "I'm exhausted! Thank goodness for prescription deodorant because otherwise I'd be drenched."

Peter narrowed his eyes at her. "You need to stop doing that."

"What?"

"That thing you do when you find even the single most diminutive negative thing to put yourself down. You're amazing, Madi. Own it."

He sounded like the rude astrology app she'd deleted a few weeks ago when it kept telling her things like "Stop doing that self-destructive thing you do."

But Peter had a point.

In that moment, Jeremy walked into the room, his face still scarlet from being put under such an interrogation, and smiled. "Follow me to the main terrace. I think you'll enjoy the view there."

"Thanks," she said.

She and Peter followed him up a set of modern metal stairs to the roof of the cabin. Vines crisscrossed the top and enormous ceiling fans turned lazily. There wasn't a need for a sounds-of-nature track because the rushing water, daytime coquís, and tropical birds were perfect.

There was a scattering of round tables and a couple sat in a corner. The man and the woman both looked in their late twenties or early thirties, and although they were in paradise, the vibes pulsating from them screamed "trouble." They had that influencer look, and they were both immersed in their phones, without even looking at each other.

"Enjoy your lunch," Jeremy said. "I'll meet you in about an hour for our tour around the park?"

"Sounds perfect," Madi said, taking a sip of her fresh lemonade—no alcohol in this type of setting. She wanted to remain present, calm, and in control.

Jeremy checked in with the couple. "The honeymoon still magical, Cooper family?"

Madi tried not to look, but from the corner of her eye, she saw the guy shrug while the woman turned on a megawatt smile and said, "It's the best! Thank you!"

Peter winced at the fakeness of her high-pitched voice. When he and Madi locked eyes, they both suppressed smiles.

For the rest of the hour, they were captivated listening to the couple bicker over everything. From the way she picked at her salad, to how he gulped down his margarita. By the time their lunch arrived, they were full-on fighting.

"You know what, Spencer? I'm out of here! This is going exactly how I thought it was going to go."

"That's the only thing we agree on, Steph! For the first time all week, you're finally saying what I've been thinking the whole time! I'm going to text my mom right away to start the annulment. What a nightmare!"

Madi held her breath. She hated confrontations, and for a second was nervous the argument would transition from a verbal fight into a physical one.

Especially when the woman, Steph, threw a napkin at her husband (ex?) and stormed off.

The guy finished eating his lunch and drinking his margarita to the last drop. Then, he stood up, and coolly walked off, his chin high, shoulders thrown back, as if he had finally rid himself of a weight that had been crushing him down.

Madi and Peter both had been frozen at the harsh vibes coming from the couple.

Before heading downstairs, the man turned toward Peter and said, "Don't marry her, man. The magic dies. Love is a lie."

Madi scoffed and Peter flipped the guy off.

He and his (ex) wife left behind a heavy atmosphere like grease. It even started smelling like sulfur to Madi.

"Wow," she said. "That's just sad."

"Actually," Peter said, and he raised a hand to guard off Madi's reply. "Hear me out." He laughed. "It is sad, but it's better they know now that they don't belong together than waste years trying to make a relationship work. I would know."

Madi's stomach clenched. Suddenly, she'd lost her appetite. It wasn't that she didn't agree with Peter in a way, but she believed in love, and it was never fun to see a dream die.

"Hey," he said in that way of his. "Why are you looking sad? At least you're not them."

She shrugged. "I know. It makes me sad. I just imagine that they had all these illusions for what life with each other would be like, and then, when they're supposed to be the happiest, it doesn't happen."

"Maybe that's the problem," Peter said. "They had all these illusions and expectations instead of going into the relationship clear-eyed and accepting of each other. They thought they could change the other, perhaps, and when that didn't work, then, they gave up. Are you going to tell me they didn't know that she picks at her salad or he gulps down margaritas like they were Gatorade?"

Madi smiled at that. "Maybe they just met and eloped."

Peter laughed, but not in a mocking way. "You're such a romantic." It didn't sound like an accusation but a compliment, and Madi felt herself blush.

"Is that so wrong?" She looked up at him, kind of holding her breath for his answer. Were she and her friends really the last romantics in the world? Nadia had her happily-ever-present with Marcos, and she had had a long-term relationship with her ex since high school. What was so wrong with her that no guy wanted to spend quality time with her, and ran at the first suggestion of commitment? But she wasn't going to ask this aloud and have her heart broken when his look of affection turned into pity.

"It's not wrong at all," he said. "You know? My mom was a romantic. She raised me to be a gentleman. Hold the door open, pay for my dates, always make sure I get consent before . . . you know? But, maybe I'm unlucky but the women in my life have kind of taken advantage of that. I hate to say it, but some women do love the bad-guy stereotype, and I don't want to be a jerk, pretend to be something I'm not so I can be in a long-term relationship."

"Is that what happened to you?" she asked.

The air between them got electric. She knew she'd asked something he was more defensive about than having a panic attack in an elevator in front of a stranger.

He nodded. "When I was young, I wanted to believe in true love too. Maybe I've been going about it the wrong way, though. Maybe there isn't 'one' person who's right for me. Maybe there isn't just one person for each human. The way I figure, if I try to be the best human I can be, it will work out with whoever I choose to be with. Thinking there's only the 'one' can be . . . paralyzing. Because how do you know? I already made that mistake once."

"But looking for that person can also be exciting, because you don't know when you're going to find them. And when you do, then, it's like finally arriving at a destination, you know? You're complete and then continue on a journey that you started together at the beginning of the universe. Together, we—I mean, hypothetically—can face anything because at least you found 'your' person."

He smiled sadly at her, unconvinced. "Maybe. I hope you find that person, Madi."

Madi lowered her gaze. She wanted to tell him that if his initials were right, he might be her person, the one she'd been looking for all her life. But she'd risked everything when she proposed to Jayden and he rejected her.

Never again would she strip herself of all her defenses.

She drank the rest of her lemonade just as Jeremy's assistant returned.

"Miss Ramírez, Mr. Tokeshi, I'm Yara, ready for the tour?"

Madi got up from her chair and, sending Peter a determined look, said, "Yes. I'm ready to see the whole property."

* * *

Before they got on the UTV that Yara was going to drive around, one of the bellhops ran toward Madi and Peter.

"Excuse me, sir," he said. He couldn't be older than eighteen and looked like a high schooler wearing his school uniform for work. "Is the black Mercedes yours?"

Peter hesitated for a second, but Madi nudged him. "Yes. That's our car, Peter."

Peter nodded and the boy sighed in relief. "Oh! I've been trying to find out because we have a truck delivering construction material for a remodel, and 'acho! I didn't want it to get blocked, so I was thinking, is it okay if I move it to a different parking lot?"

"Sure!" Peter said, and threw him the keys.

The boy caught them in midair, and said, "Thanks!" And then, as if he remembered something, he added, "Just in case, here's the valet parking ticket. Not that you'll need it, but just in case. Here you go."

He gave Peter the ticket and dashed back to the parking lot in front of the office where Jeremy was waiting. The boy threw him the keys, but Jeremy didn't catch them. They couldn't hear how the manager berated the boy, but they could tell by the way the boy hunched his shoulders that the man was laying it on thick.

"Ouch," Peter said.

"What a jerk," Madi added.

Yara, their guide, kept her opinions to herself, but by the way she pressed her lips, Madi guessed that Jeremy wasn't very popular among the employees, which was something to consider. The resort numbers were fantastic, and a collaboration with Reyna's world-renowned retreats would be profitable for both sides, but Madi wasn't going to ignore her gut feeling that Jeremy was someone to watch.

She put her comments in the back of her mind to tell Audri and Reyna later.

Yara turned the engine on and took off along a well-tended path through the lush foliage of the rain forest and started giving them an account of how the resort was a sanctuary for many species of flora and fauna, not all autochthonous, pointing at iguana specimens lounging on a fallen a tree. As if trying to make up for the bad impression Jeremy had given, she was enthusiastic and knowledgeable. Perhaps she was just relieved to be away from the stringent manager, or she just loved being out in the dazzling beauty of the rain forest.

"Contrary to popular belief, iguanas aren't native to the island," she said. "They were brought from Central America. Since they don't have natural predators and breed rapidly, they have pretty much overrun every corner of the archipelago."

A dense cloud enveloped the jungle, but the light breeze cooled down Madi's face and blew her hair in her eyes. Automatically, she pulled it back in a knot on the top of her head, but when she was going to tie it with the scrunchie she usually kept on her wrist, she realized it wasn't there.

In a flash, she remembered she had taken it off along with her many bracelets before she showered and then had stashed it all in her suitcase without taking the elastic back. But when she let her hair fall, internally berating herself, she saw Peter's cupped hand in front of her. He offered her a scrunchie like it was jewel. The white silky fabric matched her top way better than the pink one she usually wore.

"What? How?" she asked, looking at him, her mind racing to figure out how, number one, he'd guessed she needed a hair tie, and number two, that she preferred scrunchies that didn't damage her hair.

He just smiled and shrugged, as if saying, *I got you.*

"Thank you," she mouthed at him and the way his eyes lingered on her lips made her tingle as if he'd touched her.

"You're welcome," he said, his resonant voice sending ripples all over Madi.

"What's that?" Yara asked, glancing over her shoulder at Peter.

Peter leaned in a little closer to the driver's seat so Yara could hear him. "I was just thinking how exciting it must be to see a different scene every day as a tour guide in the rain forest."

"Oh! I remember Jeremy told me you're a guide in San Juan, right? I hope I do well enough. Anything I've missed? What do you think so far?" she said. Madi couldn't see the girl's face, but the tips of her ears had blushed.

By now, Madi was aware that Peter's magnetism was irresistible for most people they encountered, and Yara wasn't an exception. But she was professional and respectful.

Peter said, "You're doing great. I don't have any experience on this side of the island. I mostly stay in the metropolitan area and the west. Out on the island, really. I've been looking forward to this tour. You won't believe me, but I've only been to El Yunque once before, and I don't really remember much."

Then he turned to Madi and added, "Javi brought me the first day I was on the island. I was jet-lagged, and honestly, hung over."

"A lot of our clients arrive here after partying in San Juan," Yara said, a smile in her voice. "Now, be ready to be enchanted." She took a sharp turn into a path that Madi hadn't noticed coming up and Madi gasped with delight.

Enchanted was an understatement. Yara was the perfect guide, and for the next several hours, she showed them the secret gems that were out of the way for average tourists and a treat for Puerto Ricans who rediscovered their island each time they ventured out.

Unsurprisingly, a couple of hours in, they'd learned not only about nature and the resort, but also about Yara, who was outgoing and personable.

She had a degree in organizational development, but she couldn't find a job in anything other than the service industry. She applied her knowledge and poured her whole soul into pointing out all the best spots in El Yunque, the only rain forest in the US territory.

Madi had come dressed for a professional meeting, and even though she'd anticipated she'd be hiking (hence the sneakers and shorts), she hadn't imagined how much she'd want to get into the waterfall or the natural pools that beckoned to her.

Like any good tour guide worth her salt, Yara sensed her wishes. "We will stop up here for a bit for a little picnic." Once they stopped next to a natural water hole. By the sound of the rushing water, there must have been a waterfall nearby.

Yara grabbed a cooler and a couple of rolled towels from the back of the UTV and left them at a picnic shelter surrounded by ferns and wild orchids. "You can swim if you want to. I'll be in the vehicle if you need me."

"Thanks," Peter said, grabbing a bottle of water and a can of Coco Rico he offered to Madi.

Like a kid on Three Kings' morning, her whole face lit up. "Oh my! I haven't had one of these in forever! I'd forgotten about them!"

Peter popped the can open and handed it to her. The sweet bubbles of the coconut soda tickled her tongue. "This soda hits different in Puerto Rico with this amazing landscape."

He smiled and pointed toward the water with puckered lips. "Let's go swimming? I'm melting."

"I don't have a swimsuit on." Madi sighed, once again, regretting not having planned better. A swim right now would be heavenly.

"Jump in as you are."

"I won't spend the whole day in damp clothes!"

"Isn't this fabric fast drying?" Peter said, rubbing the edge of Madi's shirt with his fingertips.

It was. But before she could reply, he headed toward the edge of the small pool shaded by palm trees and ferns. Agile like a lizard, he climbed to a rocky outcrop that served as a jumping platform. In an instant, he'd already taken his clothes off and laid them on a rock.

"Easy for you to say," Madi said, trying not to stare at his body. "You're a guy. You can just take off your shirt, but I don't want to wear a damp shirt all day. A white shirt, at that."

He watched her with a devilish look and said, "I dare you to take it off! Just wear your underwear. It's like a bikini anyway! I won't look."

Madi laughed nervously, but he wasn't joking. He jumped before she made up her mind to join him. In the seconds he was underwater, she considered her options.

At first she told herself there was no way she'd be so unprofessional and take her clothes off and swim in her underwear. But then . . . why not? Peter wasn't a creep, and there was no one else around. She didn't know when or if she'd be back to El Yunque. She wished she'd brought her swimsuit or wore it underneath, just in case. She was on an island, for crying out loud!

Finally, Peter's head broke through the surface. He shook his head, sending diamond droplets all over, and when he saw her, he called back at her. "You're still there? Come on, Madison! Just jump in with your clothes on! We're only alive once!"

The way he said "Madison" convinced her.

All her life, she'd been looking behind, trying to remember past lives, or a dream from her childhood. She'd lived for a day in the future, never really living in the present, enjoying the moment.

If what Peter said was real, that this was really all we got, no previous lives, no promise of another chance, she would regret not swimming in a private natural pool in the most beautiful place she'd ever been.

She climbed up to the rock from where he'd jumped and left his shoes and shirt. He was still swimming the opposite way. She'd surprise him.

She took off her T-shirt, shorts, shoes, and socks and placed them on top of his. The rock was so hot on the soles of her feet that she hopped to the edge. From this height, she got a surge of fear. What if the water was shallower than she expected? What if she fell and hurt herself? Or if he thought she was ridiculous?

But what if she had fun?

At least she was wearing matching, sensible underwear. From a distance, no one would know the set wasn't a white bikini. There was technically no difference other than people's perceptions. Besides, there wasn't anyone else but Peter to judge, and so far, she'd felt safe with him. It's not like she was going to post a picture on social media, or anything like that.

Madi had to experience the essence of the resort, and to do so, sacrifices were necessary, she told herself. She was only doing it for professional reasons.

She took a deep breath, and mid-exhale, she jumped.

She only caught a flash of green from the vegetation around them, and Peter's surprised, delighted face, before she closed her eyes just as her feet touched the water and she plunged deep into the pool. After a second or two, she opened her eyes and marveled at the crystalline fresh waters. She was always afraid of the salt burning her eyes in the ocean, but now, she wanted to snap a picture with her eyes and keep it in her memory forever. She wished she were a fish like in her most memorable dream in which she'd been a koi. Her hair, somehow free from its knot, splayed around her. She saw Peter's legs as he swam toward her. She grabbed the scrunchie before it sank deeper into the pool and deftly placed it on her wrist. She kicked up and treaded water to rise to the surface.

She was smiling when the sun touched her face like a kiss.

"Brava! I didn't think you'd do it!" Peter exclaimed, swimming near her and looking at her in a way that made Madi feel like she was on fire although she was in the water. Little droplets hung on his long, dark eyelashes, and his mouth was red and plump. He had tiny freckles across his nose and cheeks, and Madi lifted her hand to brush his skin softly.

Even in the water he was still taller than her, and when he looked down at her face, his gaze went beyond, and his face reddened so fast it would have been funny if the tension between them weren't so charged.

"Oh, Mads," he said, turning his head away. "Your top is undone!"

"What?"

The scrunchie wasn't the only thing that had malfunctioned. To her horror, when she looked down, she realized that her bra was barely hanging on. The bra must have come unclasped when she lifted her arms to get the momentum to jump far from the rocks.

"Ay Dios mío!" she shrieked, and swam away from him as fast as she could, which wasn't fast at all. The pool was too deep for her to stabilize herself while she re-clasped her bra. She was already tired of treading water and trying to avoid her breasts from breaking free from the bra's flimsy hold on them. She couldn't stop laughing as she imagined what the whole thing must look like to an outsider.

What if someone was watching the whole thing? She sobered up quickly.

She had to ask for her help.

"Peter! Come here!" she yelled over her shoulder. "The least you can do is help me now!"

"The least I can do? I told you to jump with your shirt on!"

"And I told you I wasn't going to wear a damp shirt for the rest of the day!"

He was already swimming in her direction while they pretended to bicker.

Her mind flashed to Sunday when she'd be on her flight back to Salt Lake, Peter-less, and her eyes stung with stupid tears. She hardly knew him. They'd never even really kissed. Now, he was a couple of feet away from her, laughing at her, with her, and she already missed him. As was her habit, Madi catastrophized everything.

"I can't tie it myself. Help me," she said, gasping for air with the effort of keeping afloat. She had excellent breathing technique and was flexible from the yoga she'd practiced most of her life, but her cardio could use some help.

Then, she felt his approach like his aura had touched hers. She shivered a little when she felt Peter's fingers on her skin.

"Stay still," he said, fumbling with the bra clasps.

"I can't! If I do, I'll drown and I'm not spending the afterlife as a ghost with an undone bra!" she said.

He tried to clasp the hook, but he was laughing so hard his fingers kept slipping, brushing the skin on her back. She didn't even want to imagine what he was picturing.

"Peter, this isn't a good look on you. I thought you'd have experience."

"Undoing bras, not hooking the clips together," he said.

His breath brushed the back of Madi's neck. Every nerve ending in her body got electrified.

"Done," he said, his hands still on her back.

She cleared her throat and tried to fix her features along with the front of her bra, which had hitched a little, before turning toward him.

Just millimeters from him, the energy from his body reached her in magnetic ripples. The water was a perfect temperature, smooth and silky over her skin, but her nipples were taut through her bikini top—her bra.

Peter must have felt something too. His arms were covered in goose bumps, but his eyes were clear like the pool.

The sun filtered through the palm trees and ferns, turning everything golden. Turning Peter into a dream.

She wanted to swim to him, hold on to his neck, wrap her legs around his waist, and kiss him until she forgot about the past or the future.

But if this was all she would ever get with Peter, these few days in the whole of eternity, she didn't want to ruin it with regrets. Because if he wasn't the love of her lives, it would be too painful to know he was with someone else even if they stayed friends. The memory of the kiss and whatever it led to would haunt her forever. Nothing would ever compare, and she couldn't set herself up for failure.

"Race me to that tree?"

Peter, his lips parted, his eyes intense, shook his head as if he needed help to come out of a spell.

He smiled and that dimple flashed in his cheek.

"Deal!" he replied, and took off swimming before she could react.

"Cheater!" she yelled, but he was laughing, already halfway to their goal.

Chapter 19

The whole way back to the resort, Yara drove in silence, smiling at the furtive glances Peter and Madi sent each other. She hadn't made any comments when they returned to the road where she was waiting, and had put her vape pen away in her pocket. But she had totally noticed their wet clothes, or more precisely, his wet shorts, and Madi's dry clothes. It didn't take a genius to guess that she'd gone swimming in her underwear. But she didn't say anything, which made the moment sweeter for Madi. It belonged only to Peter and her.

She was glad she had taken off her shirt and shorts, because when she put them back on, they held the warmth from the sun, and smelled a little like Peter.

On the rest of the island, the sun wouldn't set for a while, but in the sanctuary of the rain forest, it was already twilight.

It would be a long drive back to San Juan to get ready for the last couple of days in Culebra. Peter had suggested they could stop at a restaurant in Loíza, so she could see how the area had grown and developed for both tourists and locals.

"Loíza!" Madi exclaimed. "There's so much to do and such little time! I wanted to go to Ponce and Cabo Rojo. I wanted to see the bio bay in La Parguera—it's one of only five in the world! And I wanted to go to las lechoneras in Guavate—even though I don't eat pork! But there's so much to see and so little time."

"Next time you come visit, right?" Peter said, telling her so much with his eyes she could only nod.

They arrived at the resort, and Peter tipped Yara for the wonderful tour. They exchanged numbers so they could collaborate and refer clients to each other. Javier would need people to help him in the tour company when Peter went back to working in la finca, and she was always looking for extra work to complement her salary at the resort.

But when Madi and Peter headed to the valet parking, Jeremy was waiting for them with a strange expression on his face.

"Something happened," Madi said.

Peter took a glance at the hotel manager and agreed. "I hope everything's okay," he whispered. "But let's not jump to conclusions."

Jeremy cleared his throat and smiled in a way that made the hairs on the back of Madi's neck stand on end. "I trust you had a great time with Yara?"

"The best," Madi replied. "She's an encyclopedia of knowledge about the rain forest, and she's amazing with people. Patient, pleasant—"

"Discreet," said Peter.

Madi had to avoid his eyes so she wouldn't blush guiltily, although they'd done nothing forbidden or wrong.

At least their hair and clothes had dried on the drive back to the resort.

Jeremy cleared his throat and said, "There's been a little mishap with the car."

Madi's stomach dropped.

Peter's color drained from his face. "What? What happened?"

Jeremy rolled his eyes, and said, "I asked Iván, one of the bellhop boys, to get the key to move your car earlier today."

"Yes, like Yara, he too is nice and personable," Peter added, obviously trying to make a point that he'd liked Iván. "Something happened to the car then?"

"Well, yes and no," Jeremy replied. Madi wondered how she'd ever thought he looked like Robert Redford. "I moved the car to a different parking lot, but I . . . locked it before taking the keys out."

There was a brief pause in which Madi felt both relieved and at the same time, alarmed. Peter was going through a similar process. He sighed loudly as if he could see exactly what had happened.

"We got locked out, is that what you're trying to say?"

Jeremy nodded. "I'm so sorry, Mr. Tokeshi. It's never happened to me before. I have no one else to blame but me."

"We can unlock it though. I'm pretty sure Javier has a spare key in a magnetic compartment," Peter said.

"Really?" Madi asked.

"That would be a lifesaver," Jeremy said.

"Javi locked himself out the first day he had the car, and had to wait for me to drive an hour to get him the spare key. He bought the magnetic box that same night."

"Let's go check," Madi said.

The dusk was glorious in the resort, and Madi had a fleeting wish to see how the rain forest looked at night. The coquís were serenading them in earnest, as if they knew Madi would be going back to Utah in a couple of nights.

The car was parked under a flamboyán tree in full bloom, the crimson flowers an explosion of colors. Without preamble, Peter got on the ground. He fumbled in the underside. "Got it!"

"Whew! What a relief," Jeremy said. Sweat had beaded on his forehead and he dried it with a dainty linen handkerchief.

Peter opened the box, and to Jeremy's dismay, the compartment was empty.

"Shit," Peter said, glancing up at Madi. Now he looked mortified too.

Madi, true to her determination to go with the flow, tried not to panic. "Are you sure it's the only magnetic box? Maybe he has more than one to confuse thieves?"

Peter, back under the car, said, "I don't see any other boxes. I could call him . . ." He looked at his phone, crestfallen. "If I had a signal."

"We can use the landline in the office," Jeremy said.

A few minutes later, Peter walked back outside, shaking his head.

"You didn't get through?" Madi guessed.

"I did," Peter replied. "But the empty key box isn't a decoy for potential thieves. He locked himself out last week and forgot to put the spare back in the compartment."

"Bummer," Madi said.

"Bummer indeed!" Jeremy said. "But maybe we can find a rock and smash a window?"

Peter stared at him for a second and then laughed. Fakely. Madi laughed too. Jeremy joined in a little too late, his face the color of putrid yellow leaves now.

He was sweating through his linen shirt.

"We could call a locksmith?" Madi asked. Surely there was a civilized way to do this?

Peter and Jeremy exchanged a look.

No one was coming up to El Yunque. Not the cops. Not a locksmith.

It was a Thursday evening in the summer.

Madi and Peter turned toward Jeremy. This was his doing.

"I can totally give you a ride to San Juan, and then tomorrow—"

"We have a full day heading to Culebra," Madi said.

Then, Jeremy's face lit up. "I have a brilliant idea! We had a cancellation in the honeymoon suite." He rolled his eyes, obnoxiously. "The honeymooners will be divorcees by next Monday. But the thing is, their tree house is available. Wouldn't it be amazing if you stayed and experienced the resort at night, which is one of the best times to appreciate its splendor anyway?"

The more he spoke, the more Madi's body heated up. She didn't dare look in Peter's direction. But at the same time, she loved the idea.

"Tomorrow the rest of your party can pick you up on your way to Culebra. You're hiring a private boat or are you bumming it on the ferry?"

Madi didn't know the details of their plans. After all, Audri had been in charge. But surely Peter knew.

"We . . . they, I mean, our party chartered a boat." He finally turned toward Madi. "We can call Audri and Mariela for them to pick us up on the way there."

"But I don't have any clothes," she said, appalled.

"I have something you can wear tonight in the car," Peter said.

"The locked car?" Madi replied.

Peter hid his face behind his hand.

Jeremy coughed, a faked cough that didn't deceive anyone but reminded Madi and Peter he was still there. "I'll excuse myself for a second to give you some privacy to discuss the particulars," he said. "I know it's inconvenient since you already had a reservation in San Juan, but I promise you won't regret staying over. We'll make this worth the inconvenience."

He practically ran inside the lobby.

Madi's skin was throbbing from the sun she'd caught in the afternoon although she'd made sure to put on sunscreen several times. She wasn't about to ruin her complexion after being a guinea pig for Audri when she was learning how to do laser skin treatments.

"I'm sorry," Madi said.

"It's not your fault, Mads." Peter sighed. "But . . . are you sure you're okay with this? He's under the impression you and I are together . . ."

Madi bit her lips to hide an inconvenient smile. "I know . . ."

Peter looked like he was holding his breath. "So, you want to stay?"

She glanced at him and looked away before he could read her mind. "It might be fun."

Yes, it might be fun, which was the last of her problems.

It was unprofessional. Sharing the room with Peter might be a test that destiny sent her to see if she could resist the temptation of being in the same room, and not . . . doing anything.

She couldn't even conceive the idea of forming the words "have sex" even if he couldn't read her thoughts.

But in these few days, Peter had learned how to read her like a book, like she read her tarot cards, or the vibes people sent her.

"I'm okay if you're okay," she said.

He made a motion with his hands. "I mean. We're both adults. How bad can it be?"

Chapter 20

"This is Gokuraku, our most special tree house," Jeremy said.

"Gokuraku? Heaven in Japanese?" Peter asked. His Adam's apple bobbed up and down.

A luxurious cabin named after heaven built into a tree. Madi gulped too.

"Yes, each one of our tree houses is designed after a different version of heaven from different cultures," Jeremy explained. "Japanese culture places a big emphasis on baths to relax. So much so that a version of Japanese heaven on earth is a hot, steaming bath."

Peter and Madi exchanged a look.

Jeremy continued, "This tree house has a state-of-the-art audio system. Organic bamboo bedding and towels. All the designer toiletries you might need." His cheeks went bright red when he glanced to a discreet black box on the nightstand. The lamp light shone on it just so that the embossed letters that spelled EMERGENCY LOVE STASH popped out as if someone had screamed them in their ears.

Jeremy continued gliding through the room, showing off all its charms. The view from the balcony was majestic. There was an extra-large, old-fashioned hammered copper tub for two already set up. The steam rose in rivulets from the water covered in flower petals. Lit candles surrounded it and infused the air with a sexy scent that went all the way to Madi's head and made her insides melt, just imagining being in the tub. With someone. The someone across the room from her with his arms crossed and looking like he'd reached heaven, just not in the circumstances he'd planned.

It's not like she was going to pull out her vibrator for the occasion. It was in San Juan anyway. At least it was stashed in her suitcase where Audri wouldn't accidentally see it.

A bottle of champagne sat in a bucket next to a low table set for two.

"I know you have no clothes to change into, and I want you both to be as relaxed and comfortable as possible. There are matching silk robes in the closet, and here is a gift certificate for the store downstairs. It's blank. You can grab anything you need. This is all my own fault, after all, and I want to show how regretful I am."

He smiled toothily and his pain was so sincere, Madi smiled back.

"But I believe everything happens for a reason," he added before walking out of their tree house.

The door clicked behind him, the echoes reverberating in the room.

Madi and Peter looked at each other and after an agonized moment, they both started laughing.

"Listen," she said, when she could catch her breath. "I can take the sofa. I'm smaller than you, after all."

"Absolutely not," he replied, vehemently.

Madi's mind went in circles. Like Jeremy had said, everything happened for a reason. Did this mean that the reason was for her to prove that she wasn't going to let herself be swayed by her heart, or worse, other body parts?

Someone knocked on the door, and they both said, "Come in!"

A middle-aged man with a thin mustache came in pushing a room service cart. The scents made Madi's stomach growl. Lunch and their little afternoon picnic had been ages ago. And now, hungry, exhausted, and nervous, she knew she'd better give her body something to calm it down.

There was steamed rice, and sushi, and oysters, even. Mochi and wine.

A perfect pink orchid was wrapped around a white one. Everything was sensual and pleasing.

This was a recipe for disaster.

Noticing the looks on Peter and Madi, the waiter was confused and concerned. "Everything okay? I can send for something different if you—"

"No, it's perfect," Peter rushed to say.

"Thanks," she said, and tipped the waiter.

After the man left, Peter sent her an annoyed look.

"What? You tipped Yara, and I can't let you play the hero every time we're together. After all, I hired you to come along with me."

The corner of his mouth quirked. "That sounded . . ."

"Weird?"

"I was going to say *hot*."

"Peter, you're killing me!" she said once she realized he was joking.

"Relax, girl," he said, coming up behind her and massaging her shoulders. "What did Audri tell you to do that first day at breakfast?"

She swirled so fast the movement caught him by surprise and startled him.

"You heard that conversation?" She hid her face behind her hands. She was so embarrassed he'd known about her obsession with finding the love of her lives all along! What must he think of her? But maybe it was better that he knew why she'd run the night of San Juan when they had almost kissed?

He gently pulled her hands away from her face. She had taken her shoes off and he hadn't. He was so much taller than her that he could still not see into her eyes, and softly lifted her chin until she couldn't hide anymore.

"Shh," he said. "It's okay. Really. It kind of helped me understand you better. By the time we talked in the caverns, I wasn't annoyed or hurt anymore."

"You shouldn't have eavesdropped on our conversation. Peter, did no one tell you that was rude, not to say immature?" She felt like crying, but it was also a relief that he knew. He knew about her obsession with the love of her lives, and he'd still gone along with her and her attempt to be friends.

"I know. That's my bad boy showing, though."

She playfully shoved against his chest but one of her nails caught on the fabric of his shirt, hurting her.

"Ouch," they both said.

"You're a bad boy, no matter what you think," she teased him.

He stepped closer to her, making her breath hitch. "And you're a bad girl, Madison. I know more secrets."

She sent him a pointed look through narrowed eyes.

He bit his lower lip.

"Come on, tell me. What do you mean I'm a bad girl?" she asked, her voice husky with nerves as she took a tiny step toward him, closing the distance between them. As if they'd done this a million times before, Peter placed his hands on her waist, and she rested one hand on his chest. The fingers of her other hand brushed his mouth like she'd fantasized for days. When he exhaled, his breath made her break out in goose bumps.

He took a deep breath, and his eyes dancing with audacity, he leaned in and whispered in her ear, "I heard you last night."

The words echoed in her every cell. She lifted her face boldly. Shamelessly met his eyes. "*What* did you hear?"

He smiled and bit his lip again. "Our rooms at the hotel share a wall. A thin wall, I might add." He swallowed. "Last night, after I showered, I heard your shower." He leaned closer and softly kissed her from the base of her neck all the way back to her ear. "Every sound, every moan. Every time you said my name."

Madi, her eyes closed, offered the rest of her throat. She never wanted him to stop those small, tiny kisses that were setting her on fire and making her legs turn into jelly.

"Whisper your name like this? Peter," she murmured against his ear, bracing against his arms, which she had been dying to run her hands over. His skin exploded in shivers. "Peter," she repeated.

He lifted her chin again, and her mouth watered in anticipation. But if he thought she was a bad girl, he was going to get a surprise because he didn't know what was coming his way. She leaned back, and said, "Not yet."

She walked away from him, their arms stretching until only their fingertips touched. "No. Don't go," he pleaded.

But she was only making sure the door was locked. With the windows open, anyone passing by might get a show, and she wasn't about to risk anyone walking in on them.

"Good idea," he said, and followed her around the room as she turned the lights off. With only the glow of the candles, Madi stood in the middle of the room.

This wasn't what she had set out to do when she agreed to come to Puerto Rico, or when she'd met Peter. It was the complete opposite of what the tarot had told her to do.

Balance. Priorities.

But if she was honest with herself, what could take precedence over love? She didn't know if there really was an eternal love, a love of all her lives that she had to find in order to be happy. What she knew was that there was something special between her and Peter now. Today. In this moment.

They were two consenting adults in a beautiful tree house in paradise. If she didn't do this, she'd regret it forever.

Slowly, she took her T-shirt off. She caught the trace of the scent of sunshine, sunscreen, and sweat, the most intoxicating perfumes ever created.

Peter walked toward her. He placed his warm hands on her waist and this time, finally, they both leaned in for a kiss.

At first, it was sweet, slow, and tentative. It was like arriving home after a long day of working hard and being beaten by the world. It was like falling into bed after a long journey, your limbs trembling with exhaustion. But it was worth it when you finally found the person who guided you on.

Peter.

Her person.

Madi's eyes prickled with sudden tears, and she closed them to savor this moment forever. She pressed herself closer to him, as he pulled her hair from the scrunchie. It cascaded all the way down to her hips, and he pressed his head against it and breathed her as if he'd spent centuries craving this moment.

Their kiss turned fiercer, hungrier as their tongues glided against one another, and his mouth then moved on down to taste her neck and below.

Madi wasn't thinking anymore. She let herself flow. She lifted his shirt and when she placed her hands on his stomach, he moaned. "I . . . Madi, I don't want this to be something fleeting. I can't—"

She stopped his words with another kiss. If this was fleeting like a shooting star, then it had to be the brightest one in the dark sky of their lives. Something so blindingly brilliant to make the past, fumbling around alone, worth it. Something so pure and incandescent that seared into their eyes so they saw that light even in the darkest night.

She pulled his shirt off, feeling the planes of his chest and back, leaving her mark, biting, scratching, tasting every inch of him.

He lifted her as effortlessly as if she didn't weigh more than a feather, and she wrapped her legs around his waist. He headed to the bed, the most non-authentically Japanese piece of furniture in the room.

Madi was in a heaven she could have never imagined or planned for, and as long as she was next to Peter, she didn't need a name for it in any language.

Later, Peter watched her, his head propped on his elbow, both trying to catch their breath. The moon was almost full and as it rose over the tree canopy, its silver beams fell right on the bed, like a heavenly blessing.

"Do you think they tested the exact location of the bed for the moon to fall like this?" she asked him.

He smiled although his lips were swollen for their frantic kisses and her bites. "It must have taken a lot of testing for that to happen. I hope whoever was in charge had fun." Then he narrowed his eyes in that way before he said something irreverent. "Do you think it was Jeremy? He seemed particularly proud of the design of this room."

She laughed and hit him in the shoulder with the back of her hand. "Ow," he complained. "You bit me there!"

She turned to kiss him where his tender skin was bruised. "I actually don't think anyone human planned it. It's too perfect. I think it was destiny. And I think it's destiny that brought you and me to this moment."

He gazed at her with those soft, velvety brown eyes like moth wings. "And also each of the decisions we made to this moment. I need to believe I had some agency in the matter."

"Of course we had agency. But destiny dipped her toe in it. Now tell me, what decisions did you make for destiny to bring you to me, Peter Tokeshi?"

The corner of his mouth tugged up enough for the dimple to pock his cheek. "To start with, deciding to come to Puerto Rico. Agreeing to sub for Javi. Staying a little later at La Sirena for you to bump into me just as I was leaving. And then . . .

throwing caution to the wind and the promise I made never to have a casual relationship like this?"

Madi's breath caught in her chest. She didn't want this to be casual, a one-night stand. For her, entering a relationship had always been under the clear understanding of going all in for eternity. But that was the one point that had always freaked out all her boyfriends. Even Jayden after she'd put her ego aside and proposed had rejected her. She wanted to tell him that this didn't have to be casual. She had no idea logistically how it could work. It's not like she could jump on an airplane to come see him every weekend, and he was literally tied to the land with the farm. He wouldn't leave what had taken him so long to build and grow.

Be in the present, that inner voice told her. The inner voice that sounded like no one but herself. Her higher, wiser self when she was young and still unscathed from so much heartache and disappointment.

She had him now. And now had to be enough, however fleeting the moment was.

His stomach growled, and hers echoed. They were synchronized just like they had been minutes ago when they'd crested the wave of pleasure that had washed over them.

"I guess this is a good time to recharge energy if we want to use up the box," she said, gesturing to the condom wrapper discarded by his head.

He mocked outrage. "I'm not a machine, Madi!"

"We have oysters." She pulled him by the hand and relished in the feeling of his eyes sweeping over her body. Her curvaceous, plump, larger than stylish body she'd tried to contain all her life.

"I could just eat you all night," he said, and his voice was raspy and breathless.

"You can do that too . . ." she said. She'd almost added the endearment "mi amor," but stopped herself just before her tongue got her in trouble.

They ate, and then fell into each other's arms back in the bed, in the tub, on the sofa, and in the shower. By the time the birds started singing in the trees and the sun peeked through the canopies, it looked like a hurricane had gone through the room.

"I'm not one of your machines, woman," Peter joked again, mumbling in Madi's hair when the phone in the room rang.

She turned to answer because when she saw that it was almost noon, she imagined it would be Audri calling to let her know that she was on her way, or worse, almost here. She didn't want to give her maybe-almost business partner the wrong impression, although once she found out Peter and Madi had shared the honeymoon suite, it wouldn't take a genius to put two and two together.

Peter threw his arm over his eyes and pretended to snore. Madi playfully kicked him to be quiet, and he snored louder.

She cleared her voice, and picked up the phone. "Hello?"

"Hey, Madi," Audri said. "We're about half an hour out. I just wanted to give you a heads-up." Familiar music sounded in the background. The Bad Bunnification of Audri seemed almost complete.

"Perfect!" she said, sitting up in bed. "I'll wait for you in the lobby so you can take a look at the premises if you want."

"It's okay," Audri said. "I trust your judgment. Besides, the boat captain will be waiting for us, and he charges by the hour."

"Perfect then. How are you feeling? You sound much better than yesterday."

Audri laughed, although not amused. "I feel like I was reborn. I don't know what kind of twenty-four-hour bug that was, but wow, I hope I never experience that again. Hey, before I forget, I have your luggage and the urn in the trunk."

Madi exhaled in relief. "Thank you, Audri. You saved me having to go back to San Juan for that."

"Of course," Audri said. "It's one of the main reasons I want to see Culebra. Your grandma traveled all over the world, and for her to want to rest forever there, it has to be something pretty special."

They hung up, and Madi fell back on the pillow.

Peter watched her pensively.

"Ready to go back to the real world?" he asked.

Now it was Madi who draped an arm over her face. But it wasn't enough to block all the responsibilities coming back to her. "Not really, but, life's like this. It keeps going."

She was about to get up, and he grabbed her arm and pulled her back into an embrace. She let herself melt in the scent of his skin, sticky with sweat and saliva from all the lovemaking. His chin was scratchy, and his hair stuck in all directions. He'd never looked more handsome.

Madi's chest hurt realizing that she loved him.

How would she ever go on knowing this wouldn't happen again?

But she had to. She loved him enough not to derail his life so it would match hers. She had no right to do that.

It seemed that deep, life-changing thoughts circled his mind too because he said, "Listen, it's not like there's no phones or WhatsApp or even airplanes. It's the twenty-first century, after all."

But the directions of their lives were in opposite ends of the world, and she didn't know how to be responsible and practical and bend space and time to still be with him.

"Let's run to get some overpriced resort wear before they arrive," she said. "We have a blank gift card, after all."

Half an hour later, after a shared shower that left Madi glowing without needing any makeup, they grabbed the coolest clothes available in the shop, and they went down to wait in the lobby.

Mariela's car slowed down next to the curb a few minutes later, and Jeremy joined them to see how the previous night had gone. Luckily, Audri and Mariela were still out of earshot, but Madi wanted to derail the conversation before they got out of the car.

"It was . . ." Madi said in her breezy voice.

"Relaxing," Peter said.

"Revelatory."

"Unforgettable."

Then Peter looked at Madi and said, "Life-changing."

"Hey, Madi! You survived the night in the rain forest!" Audri said, planting a kiss on her cheek.

"That I did," she said, glancing at Peter and widening her eyes dramatically.

He smiled softly and hugged Mariela, who still looked a little peaked from her cold.

"Here are the keys, nene," she said. "Next time, check before you lock the car. You know how Javi is."

Jeremy had the decency to clarify, "It was me who locked them out of the car. Thank goodness, it all ended well."

"Thank goodness," Madi said, worried that he'd continue talking about them sharing the suite.

"I'll talk with Madi and Reyna, and we'll be in touch with you shortly," Audri said, shaking Jeremy's hand. "Thank you for your hospitality."

"Thank you," he said, and bless his heart, kept his mouth shut.

"We should go," said Mariela, glancing at her watch. "I'm not sure if the captain has other trips chartered, but I don't want to keep him waiting."

"Sure," said Peter, unlocking the Mercedes and turning the AC on.

Madi hovered between the two cars, and then, in a voice meant to convey that she was making a sacrifice, she said, "I'll ride with him to keep him company."

"He looks like he didn't get any sleep last night," Mariela said.

Madi almost choked. "I think the mosquitos drove him nuts all night."

Audri and Mariela exchanged an amused look, and Mariela said, "Those mosquitos must have had long nails and big mouths to leave those marks. Poor Peter."

"Poor, poor Peter!" Audri added.

Red-faced, Madi got in the passenger seat with him.

Chapter 21

Most of the tourists heading to Culebra on the public transport had left in either the six a.m. or eight thirty ferries. A regular passenger ferry and a cargo one left roughly every two hours. Madi remembered taking the ferry with Abuela and becoming seasick on a day the waves were bravas.

But today, a shiny boat with the name *Pipona* waited for their group at the dock. Like every other detail of the trip, Audri had arranged this, and she and the captain, a weathered Puerto Rican man named Filipo, shook hands as old friends.

"Nice to meet you," he said as he shook hands with the rest of them.

Madi was quieter than usual, not really subdued, but solemn. She hugged the urn with her grandmother's ashes close to her chest as if it were a life ring, the one thing preventing her from drowning. All her life, she'd thought this day would never come, but here she was, almost in Culebra.

She was at peace that she'd finally keep her promise to her abuela.

Even though she tried not to be too obvious, her gaze flickered to Peter every few seconds, as if a part of her was afraid he was going to disappear, and another part just couldn't take enough of looking at him.

It seemed to be the same for him.

While Audri and Mariela prattled nonstop about all kinds of details about the boat, the captain, his history, and other things, they sat side by side on the second level and gazed toward the sea.

"This Caribbean blue," Madi said.

Right on cue, Peter hummed the Enya song and they both smiled.

"I hope Heather and her family had tons of fun," Madi said. "They were good people."

"Yes, they were," he said.

Filipo had prepared a cooler with all kinds of drinks. When Audri told him she didn't drink alcohol, he replied, "I remember you said that, but I have light beer for you, too."

Madi and Audri exchanged an amused look.

"It's alcohol all the same, Filipo," Mariela intervened.

The man couldn't comprehend that someone didn't drink any alcohol at all. Madi knew they'd be joking about this for years to come.

The trip was only about thirty minutes, and before Audri finished her Coke Zero with lime, they'd arrived at the dock in Culebra.

On the way, Peter had explained to her that the island is geographically part of the Spanish Virgin Islands, way more similar geologically to St. Thomas than the main island of Puerto Rico. He couldn't get out of tour guide mode, it seemed.

At the dock, they rented a golf cart, which was how the tourists moved around the island. They could've rented a car or mopeds, but Madi wasn't getting on a moped, and golf carts were easier to park and cheaper, since gasoline on the island was so expensive.

Everything was more expensive here in Culebra. The food was twice as much as it was on the main island, and they only bought enough supplies for twenty-four hours.

They checked in their rental, a small house in a neighborhood of larger stucco houses. After they changed, Peter was ready to take them on a tour around the main hostels and hotels that would match what Audri and Reyna had in mind for the retreats.

But Madi's heart wasn't in it.

All day long, Mariela and Peter drove them and waited for them to scout the locations, but her mind was elsewhere—her childhood dream, the previous night with Peter, the looming days without him.

Finally, after six, they returned to the rental. It was only a couple of blocks from Flamenco Beach.

Audri was getting ready for a massage and a nap, and Mariela was going to the town to visit a friend from school she hadn't seen in years. Later, they were going to see the Culebra Wildlife Refuge together.

Madi had hours ahead of her, and she wasn't sure how to fill them. The pool in the complex was beautiful, but she didn't want to waste these precious hours inside a facility.

"You could keep your grandma's promise now," Audri said. "Tomorrow, we leave early in the morning. I hope we get to come back soon. Sorry we ran out of time. You told me this place was special, but I hadn't really understood how beautiful it is. I'm speechless."

"I'm going to head to the beach now," she said. "I'll probably stay out until late, so you don't have to wait for me. I want to wait for the full moon to rise, and then I'll say goodbye to my grandma's ashes."

"Sounds good," said Audri. "Please put sunscreen on and bring mosquito repellent. Filipo said the beach gnats are vicious."

Madi packed her safari backpack and went downstairs. Peter stood in the doorway, gazing toward the beach. The sun cast him in a golden light. Madi watched him in silence to remember him like this for the rest of her life.

If love at first sight wasn't a thing, and what she felt for him wasn't really love, then she vowed to build the kind of relationship that would allow her to feel true love eventually.

"Hey," she said.

He looked over his shoulder and smiled. "You ready to head out?"

She nodded. The invitation for him to come along was at the tip of her tongue, but she was afraid he'd reject her. And her battered heart couldn't take any more of that.

He swallowed and brushed his hair out of his face. "Long day, huh?"

"Yes," she said. "Are you going to rest too? It's nice and quiet in the house. Finally, you get a break from us."

Peter watched her in silence as if he were debating something. They'd planned the itinerary weeks and weeks ago, and Madi liked to fly by the seat of her pants. This was not his thing.

But then he said, "I'll drive you if you want. Unless you want to be alone?"

Madi crossed the distance between them on her tiptoes like she was gliding. She hugged him. "Thank you! I thought you'd never ask."

He kissed the top of her head and they headed out to enjoy the golden hour in Culebra.

Madi held on to his hand as the golf cart climbed up a hill, passing a cemetery of whitewashed crosses that glinted in the sun.

"I want to show you something amazing," he said.

When they arrived at the top, the turquoise view brought tears to her eyes. Sometimes when talking about tropical places, people said, "Different island, same shit." There were even shirts and mugs with the saying people could bring as joke souvenirs to their loved ones back home.

But Madi knew this place was like no other. Her heart, her roots, and her essence were more in Culebra than on the main island.

Her backpack with her grandma's urn was firmly secured in the back seat. When Peter stopped in front of a house perched overlooking the ocean, she got out as if she knew exactly what this place was.

There was a plaque next to the front door that said CASA DE LOS SUEÑOS.

"There's an open house only today, and when Javi told me about it, I knew you'd love it," Peter said, leading her in.

"I love it already," she said.

"Wait until you see inside. It's a dream."

Entranced, Madi walked from room to room as if she were coming back home after a fun but exhausting vacation. The house was exactly what Madi had envisioned when Reyna had first started talking about destination retreats. It was an old Spanish colonial place with views to the ocean and the natural reserve from every window. The kitchen was wide open and still warm, like it missed hosting a big family over the holidays. The best was a patch of land where fruit trees grew next to a garden plot overrun with weeds now.

If she strained her eyes to glimpse into the future, Madi could almost see a version of Peter working the fertile ground, and herself, leading a group in meditation and yoga, the crash of waves and the cry of birds all the soundtrack they needed.

"What do you think?" the real estate rep, a middle-aged man, asked.

"I think it's lovely," Madi replied.

If Stevie, a consummate saleswoman, were here, she'd scold Madi for wearing her heart on her sleeve. But she couldn't curb her enthusiasm. She liked what she liked. She loved who she loved, even when being impulsive ended in heartbreak. But the truth was, Madi loved being who she was.

"Are the owners renting?"

The man shook his head. "No, unfortunately, they're only considering offers to buy."

"They're not open to rent long term either?"

"I can ask, but they're adamant on finding the right people who'll love this house as much as they loved it. They don't want investors that will turn it into yet another Airbnb."

"You know them?" Peter asked.

The man smiled as if he were reminiscing. "'Acho! I was born and raised here in Culebra and I've known the Rexach family all my life. The kids moved to the States one by one, and the grandparents held on as long as they could after Maria. But things were too hard for them. They finally moved in with a daughter in Orlando. Doña Gloria had a dream that the perfect couple would come along, and she says she'll know who they are when they arrive. Old folks get persnickety like that sometimes."

"They sure do," Peter said.

Madi couldn't speak. Her heart started racing at the mention of Doña Gloria's dream. When the realtor walked back inside the house to give her and Peter some privacy, she said, "You made this appointment just for me?"

She was moved by how much he knew about her and her dreams. More than any other boyfriend or significant other. Even more than Jayden, who'd known her for years and who never got her.

"When I heard you talking to Audri that day in the hotel, I knew exactly the house that would be perfect for you. I knew it was this one because every time I come to Culebra, I too feel like it speaks to me. I knew you'd like to see it."

"But Reyna and Audri aren't going to buy it."

Peter held her hands as they stood outside, the wind tossing Madi's hair like it was a living thing. "But you could."

"I said I would become a recluse in a beach house only if I couldn't find the love of my lives," she said, teasing him.

Peter's eyes softened and still holding her hands, he said, "Imagine. It would be your house. You could rent it to them for their retreats. You could partner together, or even better, you could do your own thing, your own way."

"Like a community center for the island," she whispered like she was dreaming aloud.

He looked at her with so much trust, but her doubts were louder.

"I don't know if I can," Madi said, shaking her head. "I don't have the business knowledge."

"Stop saying that," he said. "You held your own in the meeting with Jeremy. You're a local, or a returning one. That's exactly what the owners want. They don't want to sell to an expat who'd turn it into a rental and charge an exorbitant amount per night. Madi, you're perfect for it."

She wanted his words to be true. Again, she closed her eyes for an instant. She could see herself as if this had already happened in another life. Maybe it was another chance?

When she opened her eyes again, Peter's eyes were full of stars, with so much faith in her. She stood on her tiptoes and kissed him softly.

"Only if you're here with me." That's the only way she could do it.

Her heart drummed all over her body. If he rejected her, she wouldn't ever recover.

But Peter kissed her again, and whispered in her ear, "I'll be here with you."

They stopped to buy sandwiches and drinks and headed to Flamenco Beach to wait for the moon to rise. The sun was perfect, soft and buttery as they took pictures by the war tank the US Army had left behind and nature and the locals had reclaimed. It was now covered with colorful graffiti promoting peace. Shells and algae decorated it like garlands.

Madi knew she'd remember each of Peter's smiles and looks, how he laughed when the waves tossed them, and the joy when a school of colorful fish weaved through their legs. But she still wanted to keep physical memories of this afternoon and took pictures from every angle as they planned the future together.

A Thursday evening in the summer, the tourists had left.

Flamenco and its glory belonged only to them. They placed a towel on the powder-soft white sand. Madi sat against a palm tree heavy with fruit, and the beach grape leaves rustled softly in the gentle breeze. Peter rested his head on her lap, and she combed his raven black hair with her fingers.

Madi from a week ago, brokenhearted and lonely, would have never believed this present in a million years. What would her neighbors Carmen and Sadie say when she told them? This would be a validation for all the cheesy love stories they weaved in their minds.

"Did you see the patch of land for a little finca?" he said. "We can plant potatoes. I'm sure they'll grow well here. And other nightshades, and vegetables."

"Will I have room for my witchy herbs?"

"All the herbs for my witch," he said. "I saw some lemons and grapefruit trees and I could make you garden boxes next to them."

"We can ask Tego and his sister to sell us an orange tree to start our grove here, our little familia," she said, going along with his fantasy.

He gazed into her eyes and rose on his elbow to kiss her. "A little familia for now, and then we'll open our doors to our guests and help the island with our grain of sand."

"That's how you build monuments," she said. "A little grain of sand at a time."

For hours their ideas became more and more farfetched, but

it was freeing to share her fantasies with someone who wouldn't laugh at them or her.

"I'm thirsty and hot," he said, after a while.

She pulled him in an embrace. "Thirsty and hot is my favorite kind of Peter."

She couldn't wait to meet all the versions of Peter. Hopefully, she had not only a lifetime but many more forever and ever.

They ran to the water as the sun gifted them a sunset that all the special effects in the world could not re-create. The water was calm like glass and still so warm, Madi wondered if this was a dream, but not even her most vivid ones had made her feel so alive.

Once they were refreshed, Madi went out to gather flowers and leaves for her offering to the sea. Peter set out on his own.

After a while, he came back carrying his own gift. He had used his T-shirt as a bag to gather the shells he'd collected for her.

"What do you have there?"

"This." He'd found a conch.

"I've never seen one in real life," she said, placing it against her ear. The ocean rushed inside it.

"You can blow it like this to call all the sea spirits and fairies," he said, and blew the conch that made a sound like a dying goose and made them laugh.

The stars had started to come out as the sky turned purple, indigo, and then dark blue. The moon rose from the water, a disc of untarnished silver light.

"I'll be nearby if you need me," he said, knowing that she needed privacy for this ritual she'd planned since she was a little girl.

He walked toward the empty cabins, leaving Madi alone to say her goodbyes.

Just out of reach of the waves, she made a circle with the shells he'd gathered. She didn't have candles, but the moon and the Milky Way provided their own light. She placed the urn in the center, sat on her heels, and breathed deeply.

She remembered the dream she'd had so long ago but that was still so vivid in her mind. Like Abuela Lina had said, just because something happened only in dreams, it didn't mean it wasn't real.

Similarly, though she'd only met Peter a few days ago, what she felt could be true love. All too well, she knew that relationships can't live off good sex and good vibes. There was so much work involved. And she had worked hard in her relationships, too hard, like Jayden had told her when she'd proposed.

Why was she resisting this wonderful thing she had with Peter only because it had come to her so unexpectedly?

She didn't want to think she'd been born to be all alone in this life. It would be too cruel if she cared more about what people said about her for rushing into a relationship with Peter than following her heart and having her happily ever after.

She wanted to ask her abuela for confirmation, for a sign that she was making the right decision in moving back to the island, buying this property, starting a life with a man who was practically a stranger.

She remained in prayer, the ocean barely whispering next to her, reaching far enough to kiss her naked feet with its warm caress. The wind tangled her long, loose hair, but it brought no words from the beyond or other lives, or at least none that she could decipher.

But she felt peace.

And when she opened her eyes, she felt him nearby. The knowledge that he respected her even though he didn't understand how she could be certain about other lives without tangible proof filled her with joy.

What other confirmation could she want?

"Thank you, Abuela," she said. "Rest in peace. Go back to the ocean that you love."

Her feet had gone almost numb under her. She rose slowly, grabbed the urn, left the lid on the sand, and walked as far into the ocean as she dared.

She didn't want to think of marine creatures swimming in it. The crystalline water only reflected the sky, so she couldn't see where she walked, but she advanced powered by faith.

Also, she knew that on the beach, Peter waited for her, that he was watching over her.

When she felt ready to stop walking, she scattered the ashes. For a second, she worried that the waves would toss them on her.

But she needn't have worried. The tide flowed away from the beach, and she blinked and the cloud of dust around her was gone.

She went back to the beach, her hair and her white gauze dress tight against her when she walked out of the water. Peter looked at her like she was an apparition. The Milky Way was a snake of mist and stars over them, and she knew it was impossible to see the bioluminescence with the moon so bright, but she could swear the sea was glowing. Droplets of light dripped from her arms, legs, and hair.

"It's done," she said, and a sob rose in her throat.

He had her in his arms until her heart stopped pounding. She looked up at him and the whole sky fit in his eyes. He was more beautiful than she could ever imagine. And he was kind and didn't care that she had a head full of crazy beliefs.

"You're fucking gorgeous," he said, and leaned in to kiss her. "You're a goddess and my atheist soul will worship at your feet forever."

She took him back to the water, where the ocean held them up while they loved each other.

Chapter 22

Sometimes, the morning waters drown the magic from the night before. But when Madi woke up next to Peter, in his bed of the rental they shared with her boss and his boss's cousin, she felt like the whole galaxy shone from her eyes.

She felt incandescent and complete, a supernova pulsed inside her. She wanted to bottle this feeling forever; it was like a supercharged Florida water.

Peter never let go of her hand on the way to the dock, as Culebra fell behind them, in the boat where they ate the breakfast Filipo had prepared for them.

Audri and Mariela smiled knowingly, and if they thought Madi and Peter were unprofessional, they never said so.

On the drive back to San Juan, in Javier's car, Madi indulged and held his hand, or placed hers on the back of his neck as she had wanted to do from the first moment she saw him. She couldn't keep her hands away from him. Knowing that even if they spent the rest of their lives together, she'd have to go back to Utah to set things in order, even the thought of being apart from him for those days or weeks hurt. It was physical, like holding her breath, or opening her eyes in the ocean.

"Do you think you'll have to head to Idaho sometime soon?" she asked, not able to help herself anymore.

He winced. "Not really." He sighed, as if he was trying to move things around in his calendar but didn't see how. "There's no rush, Mads. The paperwork for the house will be a while anyway."

"But I can't even imagine not seeing you for months and months," she said.

"We can meet halfway through," he said. "Florida would be fun."

She wasn't so sure, but she didn't want to act crazy and impulsive. There was a way for spontaneity, but she didn't want to rush things between them and ruin everything.

She had to remind herself that they had now, they had today. The present was enough. It was the only thing. Dreading the future was making the present bitterer than it needed to be. Her flight wasn't leaving until the following day anyway. They still had tonight. They still had forever to get to know everything about each other and be surprised every day.

In the meantime, they tried to crunch a thousand dates and conversations in an hour drive. Their favorite colors. Favorite music. First loves, heartbreaks, crushes, dreams. All about their dreams. They couldn't get enough.

When she was little, the drive back to San Juan had always seemed to stretch into impossible lengths. Now, even though Peter took every detour he could think of, they arrived in the old city sooner than she was ready for.

"Don't look so sad. We have tonight," he said, pressing her hand. "We have to make it unforgettable."

"I'm kind of worried about the walls in the room, though," she said, when they were trying to decide if they were spending the night in his or her room. "I don't want Audri to hear."

"We'll give her earplugs," he said.

"Brilliant. She'll never suspect why!"

They were still laughing while they got out of the car and walked into the lobby.

Ada, the receptionist, seemed friendlier with Madi. At least her smile looked sincere. She gave Peter a bunch of referrals to pass on to Javier for when he was back in town in a couple of days and returned the room key to Madi.

"Audri and Mariela arrived about half an hour ago. They were starting to worry something had happened to you," she said with a curious look on her face.

"Really?" said Madi, avoiding Peter's gaze in case she started laughing. She felt giddy with joy. "We must have hit rush hour right after them."

"I think we did," said Peter.

Ada nodded, apparently convinced by their excuse. "There's a special surprise for you in your room, Miss Ramírez. I hope you enjoy it," she said.

Thinking back on the royal treatment at the tree house resort in El Yunque, Madi got excited. Maybe they wouldn't even need to leave the room for dinner or drinks. She didn't want to share Peter with anyone else for the rest of the night all the way into the morning.

Slowly, they climbed upstairs. Although now neither one would hold back their kisses or anything else in the elevator, they weren't eager to be trapped in it. They must be the only guests who were scared of the elevator because they didn't cross anyone else. In the perfect humid gloom of the staircase, they stopped at every landing to kiss each other. By the time they arrived at the fifth floor, they were out of breath and not for the stairs. Bruise-lipped and impatient to tear his clothes off, Madi opened the door.

At once, she felt there was something off.

The TV was on. An American football game played, which couldn't be the romantic surprise Ada had hinted at. But then she saw the socks on the floor and heard the toilet flushing.

Someone was here.

"Did she give me the wrong room key?" Madi asked.

"Madi?" a man's voice resonated in the room.

Instinctively, Peter stepped in front of Madi to shield her with his body.

The bathroom door opened, and a tall, blond man with piercing green eyes stood looking at them as if he'd seen a ghost. No. As if he'd seen a crime. He placed a hand over his chest.

"Jayden?" Madi asked, but her voice sounded all wrong. There was no trace of the softness she tried to mold her tone to when she spoke to him in the past. The love she had thought she felt for him was nowhere. In fact, all she felt was annoyance.

Instead of greeting her, or even noticing her presence, Jayden glanced at Peter, took a twenty-dollar bill from the pocket of his pants, and put it forcefully in Peter's hand. "Here. Thanks for bringing her bags upstairs."

Madi felt like time suspended. She could practically see the motes of dust dancing in a sunbeam entering through the open window.

She registered Peter's joy crumbling to ashes, and he turned to her in disappointment. His mouth twitched, but no words came out of his lips. Those luscious, delicious lips she wanted to spend all her life kissing.

"You can go," Jayden said, stepping toward Madi, and planting a slobbering, rough kiss on her lips.

Madi didn't close her eyes. She wished she had. Because before she could wrench herself away from Jayden's arms and lips, Peter walked out of the room.

The click of the door closing was like a shot piercing through her soul.

Chapter 23

Madi didn't regret her choices.

She had lived a life true to herself for the last couple of days, finally leaving aside the fear of letting people down. But she had never wanted to hurt Jayden.

He might not be the love of her life. He might have really hurt her when she kept saying he wasn't sure she was *his* one, and when he said no to her proposal, or worse, when he laughed at her and told her to grow up and be realistic.

No matter what she had told Nadia and Stevie after Jayden had broken her heart, she didn't hate him. She didn't want him to suffer.

And now he sat appalled on the bed, the crumbles of the Doritos he'd eaten as he waited for Madi stuck on his white shirt, the skin on his forehead breaking out in a heat rash.

It turned out Jayden *really* was allergic to humidity.

And still he had made the trip to Puerto Rico to surprise her and propose with the ring of her dreams, which now sat next to the TV.

Jayden's team was losing.

She grabbed the remote and turned the screen off.

The silence that followed thundered in her ears. Adrenaline from expecting to spend the rest of the night with Peter, and then the shock of seeing Jayden had ratcheted up her body temperature. She felt like steam was coming out of her ears and crown chakra.

"What do you mean you moved on?" Jayden asked again, his voice a monotone.

"Jay," she said, sitting next to him. "You can't expect me to still be waiting for you when you rejected me and went on your trip. I saw your stories of you golfing with your ex-girlfriend."

"But that was before I realized that it was you who I wanted. I texted you and you never replied. I . . . wanted to do something spontaneous to get you back. I came here, after all. Isn't that what you wanted?"

That had been exactly what she wanted.

Before she met Peter.

"You told me *I* was the love of your lives. You told me *I* had the right initials and all."

It sounded so childish and ridiculous when he said it like this. But she had told him that. She had held on to that ridiculous notion, to everyone's detriment, especially hers.

She had almost ruined everything with Peter because at first, she couldn't see beyond the fact his name didn't match her vision for this life, not to say anything of eternity.

Jayden had done nothing wrong, but seeing him like this solidified her knowledge that he wasn't her one either.

"What do you mean, Madi? If it's because you slept with the bellhop guy, I guess, oh well. I don't love it, but we can move past that. I did after all sleep with Claire, but like I said, I realized I had made a big mistake letting you go."

Madi's breath had caught in her throat. There was so much to unpack in all he had said she didn't even know what to start with.

"First of all, Peter isn't the bellhop."

"The tour guide," he said, throwing his hands in the air. "I don't care. I mean, don't get me wrong, from what I could see, he's good-looking. But . . . a tour guide? Mads, you can't be serious."

"I'm going to come back and buy a house here and open a yoga retreat—"

"How?" he scoffed again. "Worst business plan model ever. You'll be broke in less than a year. When things get hard, because they will, the rose-colored glasses will crack. Remember the last hurricane? This island is held by toothpicks and rubber bands! When that moment comes, Bruce Lee there—"

"His name's Peter," she said. She didn't want to raise her voice, but it was hard to sound rational and composed with that infuriating expression on his face.

"Peter? He looked Asian. Whatever," he said, shrugging and rolling his eyes. "What I mean is, I will take you back."

Madi sighed and she placed her face in her hands like the whirlwind of thoughts in her mind was too heavy for her neck to hold.

He must have misunderstood her gesture, because he ruffled her hair like she was a disobedient child.

She wasn't a child.

She wasn't an airhead.

Was it too much to ask to be loved with her crazy notions of love and all?

Jayden knelt in front of her and, popping the ring box open, he asked, "Madison Amor Ramírez, will you be my wife until death do us apart?"

Blood rushed in her ears as the last several days flashed in her eyes. Each kiss and look from Peter, each word, and sharing their dreams last night making love under the stars, resonated in her skin.

A romantic gesture and a proposal were all she had ever wanted.

But now, she wanted the rest, what Peter had shown her was possible.

She was a different person. If she accepted Jayden, forever and ever, she would replay her time with Peter.

It wouldn't be fair to anyone. Not Peter. Not Jayden. Not herself.

"Jayden," she whispered.

He held her gaze, as if willing her to just say yes. He smiled tentatively and her heart broke for him. He wasn't used to rejection. But he would survive. And hopefully he would learn. And when he met the love of his eternities, the joy and love and relief would be so great that he would thank Madi for saying—

"No, Jayden," she said. Her voice was firm and sure. "I won't marry you."

She almost added "sorry," but she was done lying. She was done minimizing her feelings to make other people comfortable. What she wanted was an epic love story, and there had to be a loco to her locura, to quote the great Bad Bunny, whose lyrics she could finally understand.

Jayden got back on his feet, and his knees creaked. She held his hand to help him up.

"I can't believe this shit," he said in a cold voice that froze her with fear.

Madi knew that some men, when hurt or humiliated, became violent.

Jayden had always been civil and respectful—in his Jayden way—to her. But she was suddenly scared.

She stayed as still as she could. After a few seconds, Jayden groaned. "Fuck!"

"What?" she asked, on the verge of tears.

He didn't say anything for a few seconds. Finally, he said, "I'm sorry, Madi."

There were so many things he should apologize for, but she didn't know what he was referring to.

"I'm sorry for scaring you. It wasn't my intention. Hell, it hurts that you said no, but . . . I love you."

"Jay?" she asked, because he sounded on the verge of tears

himself. Jayden who prided himself in showing no emotions. Whose mother said hadn't even cried as a baby.

She hugged him, and to his credit, he didn't try to kiss her or convince her to change her mind.

In a way, she loved him too. They'd shared this short, brief, wonderful life at least for a bit, and their time together had led Madi to Peter.

"Thank you," she said, and kissed him on the cheek. "Thank you for this. You're a good man, Jay."

He kissed her forehead, and before leaving her room, he said, "I wish you the best. Be happy, Madi."

Chapter 24

When Jayden left her room, and she composed herself enough, Madi went to Peter's room next to hers and knocked. No one answered. In a panic, she texted him.

She told herself to remain calm and not act like a caricature of the stereotypical airhead, impulsive Latina. But Peter never texted back. She called him once, and her call went to voice-mail.

Her fears were confirmed when she went back to the lobby, and Ada told her that he'd left with his suitcase about an hour ago, and that her "friend" had checked in a different room. So basically, right after leaving Madi's room, Peter had fled.

She was too heartbroken to cry. She went over the whole sequence, and she didn't know what else she could've done or said to avoid this disaster. She had to speak with Jayden. How could Peter not realize communication was the number one priority so they could start the rest of their lives together without a stain in their past?

But he hadn't given her the chance to explain.

She went to her friend.

Audri listened to her in silence, and said, "Maybe it's just like you told Jayden. Peter might not be the love of your lives either. Maybe his role in your life was helping you realize many things."

"Like what?" she said, blowing her nose with a tissue.

"You tell me?"

Her first impulse was to say that she'd learned that she kept making mistakes. But that wasn't true. She had learned that above all else, she had to love herself. That until she had embraced who she was, with all her flaws and beauty, she hadn't really felt loved by anyone else.

She cherished that knowledge like a talisman, like one of the crystals in her collection. It was a jewel that had cost her a lot to earn.

She didn't know what Jayden's plans were, but she had a flight to catch. She thought she had felt heartbreak the night before, but it was nothing like seeing the outline of the island, la Isla del Encanto, get farther and farther away from the airplane window.

The Madi who returned to Utah was very different from the one who had left only a week before.

"See you soon, love," Audri said when her sister picked her up at the airport. "Are you sure you'll be okay on your own?"

"I'll be okay. Stevie and Nadia are picking me up," she said when Audri got in her car. "Thank you for everything."

They kissed on the cheek.

"I'm stopping by at Reyna's tonight, but I'll come home tomorrow," Audri said, and waved goodbye.

In the past, Madi would've hated the company of her own thoughts, but now she relished them. She knew what she had to do.

A few minutes later, Stevie and Nadia picked her up, and they too sensed the change. There was a cloud of melancholy clinging to Madi, but they seemed to know she needed time to process what had happened.

"We had planned a girls' night at your apartment, since Audri won't be there. We can let you rest tonight and then we can catch up later?" Stevie said after a nudge from Nadia.

But Madi had missed her friends, and she needed their advice. "I have so much to tell you. You won't believe it."

The delivery from Cancún Querido arrived just as the three amigas walked up to Madi's apartment. Obviously, Nadia had been in charge of coordinating everything.

They sat down to eat, and Madi told them the story, leaving some parts out that belonged only to her and Peter, even if he'd decided to run from her life.

"I have the money I was going to invest into Grounded Yoga, but I'm buying this house in Culebra instead. I know you two will think it's a crazy idea, being so far from my family, in a place still trying to recover from the last hurricane, but I know it's the right choice."

Even without Peter, the house already felt like her home.

"I hate that you'll be so far," Nadia said, pouring some of her trashy favorite refresher in her glass. "But I love your idea, Madi."

"You better save room in your house for us. It sounds like paradise," Stevie said, her eyes shining with longing.

It hurt to look at her dear friend, because she reminded Madi so much of Peter.

"I promise you can move in with me any time you want," she said. "That is, if the paperwork and everything else goes through."

"Send good vibes to the universe," said Nadia, lighting a candle right then and there.

The candle and their good vibes worked, because the paperwork did go through. Madi hadn't heard from Peter again. He'd vanished from the island like he had been an apparition. But she could still feel him on her skin and lips, and at night, she relived their nights in the tree house and Flamenco Beach. In the mornings, she felt like something was missing in her heart, and she let herself cry.

A few months later, when the mountains were already covered in snow, she got an envelope from Jayden.

At first Madi was going to throw it in the garbage, but her curiosity was stronger than her desire to leave things with him in the past. She opened it and realized it was a wedding invitation.

For his wedding. Jayden's.

To none other than Ada, the receptionist from Casa Grande Hotel.

Her phone rang before she caught her breath.

It was Audri.

"Hey," said Madi, unable to take her eyes off the photo. They looked radiant. They had that glow she imagined she and Peter had when they were together.

"Are you okay, sweetheart?" Audri asked softly.

Madi sat on the stool of her almost empty apartment. Packed boxes, carefully labeled in Nadia's perfect handwriting and Stevie's spidery one, were stacked all over the place. She was moving to Puerto Rico, to Culebra, in a week, after her yoga entrepreneur's seminar in Idaho Falls right during the winter solstice.

"Are you calling about Jayden?" she asked.

Audri laughed, and Reyna's laughter echoed in the background.

"That is a plot twist I never saw coming," Audri said. "Are you okay?"

Madi twirled her hair with her index finger. "You know, destiny is a funny thing. I'm happy he found his love in such an unexpected way."

"I'm proud of you, Madi," Audri said.

There was a pause, and then Reyna spoke. "When are you leaving for Idaho Falls, babe?"

Madi looked at her calendar. Not that she had everything planned to the minute, but she'd discovered it was true that it was easier to be organized and accountable when she knew exactly what she wanted to do and a way to remind herself.

"I'm leaving at ten. It's about six hours to the hotel," she said, visualizing the map in her mind.

"It might take you a little longer to get there with the incoming snowstorm," Reyna said.

Madi groaned. "Snow the whole day? Ugh! Good thing I'm getting out of here soon."

"Do you want me or Audri to come along? I know how much you hate traveling on your own."

Madi smiled. She considered for just a second. Just one, but she dismissed the idea. She didn't hate traveling on her own anymore. After all, the partner who'd been along for this ride since the moment she took her first breath and would still be around until she took her last (hopefully many, many years and adventures in the future) was none other than herself. She had learned to love her own company.

"Thanks, Reyna. But I'm okay. I'm prepared and ready for this. I need to do it on my own."

"Okay," Reyna said. "Please call us if you change your mind."

Madi knew she wouldn't, but knowing people cheered for her, even from afar, was one of the best feelings ever.

Madi squinted but there was no use. She couldn't see anything through the thickest, biggest snowflakes in the history of winter. Enya sang "Caribbean Blue" from the speaker of her car, but the ethereal voice of the fairy queen of excellence wasn't enough to calm her nerves.

It wasn't even five p.m. on I-15, but the freeway was a parking lot. She was still hours away from Idaho Falls, and the winter solstice seminar she had enrolled in. To manage her little farm slash yoga retreat destination, she was going to learn more than breathing techniques and yoga positions. But if the storm became worse, she'd have to pull over and wait it out, or even better, check in a little hotel along the freeway and head over in the morning when it was safer.

She wasn't really scared.

If she got stranded in the snow, she was ready. It was amazing how in this area, where people were supposed to be used to dealing with this kind of weather, every single driver seemed to freak out when the first storm swept through the valley.

Her body was in her car, where she struggled to keep warm, but her mind and soul were on Flamenco Beach, under the Milky Way, in the arms of a man who now only lived in her dreams.

If only she had the chance to explain.

If only he hadn't run.

A light blinked on her dashboard, and at first, she had the impulse to ignore it, but then she realized that she was running out of gas.

She had meticulously planned her route, but the storm that had caught everyone by surprise had added a couple of hours to the journey. She knew she had to stop for gas sooner or later if she didn't want to panic in the middle of the stretch that had no gas stations for miles.

Madi inched toward the nearest freeway exit to get gas.

As soon as she got out of her car, the wind whipped at her face. When she turned her back to it, a gust snatched her beanie from her hair.

"Hey!" she yelled, conscious that she was getting mad at the wind. "I need that!"

She knew she could buy another one at the conference, but she liked this white one that Nadia had knitted for her.

Nadia, an accomplished lawyer, had gotten into knitting to be more mindful and had gifted Madi the first product of her labors. Yes, it was misshapen, but it was the love and meaning behind it that Madi appreciated. She wasn't going to let the wind take it from her.

She made sure the gas dispenser was firmly secured to the car and followed her hat. It was flying to the gas station entrance as if someone was carrying it with an invisible hand.

What if this was a sign of the universe? What if there was a runaway truck, one of those gigantic semis, and if she didn't follow this sign, she ended smashed under its wheels?

Madi decided to trust the universe and go with the flow.

Well, that seemed to be anxiety more than the universe speaking, but she could use a hot tea and a visit to the restroom, anyway.

She walked toward the area with logs stacked on top of each other where the hat had gotten stuck. She was looking at the ground because the snow was falling harder than ever. When she lifted her eyes, she stopped in her tracks.

The wind howled in her ears, but the rush of her blood was deafening as she had the most vivid déjà vu of her life.

He was walking in her direction.

Tall, and resolute, his hands in his pockets as he defied the wind and snow to get to her. He had a dark beanie, but she knew that underneath, there was a thatch of the silkiest black hair. Her fingertips prickled with the memory of combing through it as she moaned his name.

He wore a dark parka with the initials JR.

They stood in front of each other, oblivious of the snow and the wind, and the looks from truckers and drivers trying to find shelter in the smallest, most out-of-the-way gas station Madi had ever seen.

"Peter," she said.

His face broke in a smile. "Madi? Is it really you?"

She nodded, but before she could ask what he was doing here, he gathered her up in his arms. She held on to him after waiting for him for eons.

He was here. It wasn't a dream.

She pulled back an inch and traced the JR initials embroidered on his jacket. It didn't matter that the initials of his name weren't JR, but she had to know.

"Why are you wearing this jacket? Did you change your name or something?"

The corner of his mouth quirked. "You silly, silly girl." He kissed the tip of her cold nose. "I didn't have a winter jacket, and grabbed a random one from the closet in the cabin I'm staying at." He sounded like he could hardly believe what he was saying.

The wind roared around them and her hoodie snapped back, freeing her mermaid hair.

"My beanie," she said, reaching out for her hat, which wasn't really hooked to anything and was just lying on top of the logs, impervious to the storm raging around them.

He took it from her gloved hands and placed it back on her head.

"I can't believe this," he said. "I'm . . . are you real? Am I dreaming?"

"Do you see me?"

He nodded.

"Do you feel me?" she asked, standing on tiptoes to kiss his lips.

He inhaled as if he wanted to get her essence inside him. "Yes."

"Then it doesn't matter if it's a dream," she said. "But please be real because I never want to wake up."

"I'm real," he said. "I'm here."

And he kissed her. They were so far from the island, but he still smelled of saltwater and bonfire.

"All my life I searched for the wrong thing," she whispered against his lips.

He tilted her chin up with a finger and held her gaze. His eyes danced with amusement. "You really think? Every step, every decision we ever took made us who we are, and it brought us together. Would you go back and change anything?"

She searched his face and the memories of so much heart-break and disappointment flashed before her. And then, the incandescent light of having met him, of loving him, eclipsed the rest.

It had been him all along. And he had been worth it.

He was staying in a little cabin not a mile away. He'd come to Idaho to pick up seeds that had just been approved by the Department of Agriculture to be transported to Puerto Rico. He hadn't been sure where he'd plant them, but he knew he wanted to take them to his island, where he was moving permanently.

He'd been looking at their pictures from Culebra, when he'd fallen asleep.

He never slept during the day. But this time, he'd dreamed.

In his dream, Madi was calling him from the gas station. Her heel had snapped, and she needed him to come help her right now. He'd woken up startled and rushed out to find her.

He'd even packed an extra pair of boots in the back seat just in case.

"I never expected that it would be you. The real you," he said, snuggling against her naked neck in his bed. Faux fur blankets kept them warm, and a fire crackled in its grate as he told her the story with wonder.

"I knew that if I didn't at least go, I'd wonder forever if maybe I could have helped someone in distress. I never imagined it would be myself who I'd been saving from misery." He kissed her like she was made of honey. "Madison, I don't even want to imagine what could've happened if I hadn't gone out, about you driving alone in the snow, and me here moping like an idiot. I'm sorry I left before you could explain. I didn't know what to say, so I never called. I'm glad someone took pity on me and shook me by the scruff of my neck."

She sat up and watched him like he was made of the stars of her memories.

"You're really here, love of my lives," she said, and kissed him on the spot on his neck she knew drove him mad.

Epilogue

A year later

Tomorrow, the first group was arriving from the main island for their first yoga retreat. Who knew what stories each person would bring with them? Who knew what new stories they would take back to their corner of the world?

Nothing had happened as Madi and Peter planned. But they wouldn't change anything. She was still learning how to manage a business, but she had good intuition because she listened to her gut. Peter could revive even the most barren of soils. He had a magic touch.

Their little island, ravaged by storms, bad government management, and gentrification needed so much of everything. Madi had joined the municipality council and yesterday they'd hired two new teachers and a doctor. She was teaching a yoga class at the high school and Peter was teaching gardening. Sometimes, the work ahead seemed insurmountable, and what they did so little. Together, she and Peter had whitewashed the house and fixed the roof.

The potato seedlings were sprouting. The power had gone

out earlier after a light rain, but if it didn't return, they had the generators. They would do, for now.

Things in Culebra weren't the easiest, but anything was better with Peter by her side.

Each little action was her grain of sand to make this world a better place, to fill it with love.

She had a purpose, not that she had needed one to feel complete, but she was grateful she'd found it, back in the land of her ancestors. Madi looked at the turquoise ocean and smiled.

Madi had polished the plaque in front of their house that read CASA DE LOS SUEÑOS until it gleamed.

Today she'd learned a new recipe for vegan mofongo. The roosters she'd rescued from the neighbors' chicken coop lorded over the yard, pecking at the dirt.

She marveled at the twists and turns life took.

If she hadn't stopped for gas that day in Idaho.

If she hadn't listened to her heart.

"Ready, mi amor?" Peter asked, his hands still dusty with dirt from their finquita. Their own piece of land by the sea.

"Ready," she said, and grabbed a Moscow mule to watch the sun set into the horizon just as a perfect quarter moon waited patiently to rule the sky. It wasn't the solstice or the equinox, but each day had its own kind of magic.

Regular days were a gift, and magical in their own ordinary ways.

She didn't look at the sky for shooting stars to wish upon. She had all she ever wanted right beside her.

If anyone asked her about her theory of eternal loves, Madi would say that she didn't know if there really had been other lives with Peter. She didn't know if after their last breaths on this beautiful earth there would be another chance.

Today, each moment was life. It was all she *knew* she had. She treasured each day, each lifetime with him. And she was making the most of it, with the love of her lives.

Acknowledgments

Thank you, Linda Camacho, my superagent, for your trust in me, for your patience, and for your support. We make a really good team! Thank you to my family at Gallt & Zacker Literary.

Thank you also to Norma Perez-Hernandez, my dear editor, for the chance to tell this story and set it in Puerto Rico. All my gratitude to the Kensington family: Jane Nutter, Carly Sommerstein, Kristine Mills (what a beautiful cover!), and freelance copy editor Gary Sunshine.

Thanks to Bad Bunny for the soundtrack of my days and my dreams. Every song from *Un Verano Sin Ti* inspired me and encouraged me!

Thanks to my friends, las incondicionales: Giselle, Luciana, Mariana V., Mariana S., Ana, Alejandra, Nayla, Tania, Denisse, and Veeda. Las quiero, chicas!

Amparo, I adore you, compañera y amiga!

Thanks to my Plot Twister Sisters: Kalie, Megan, Ellen, Jennifer, and Jill.

Thanks for my VCFA family and Las Musas.

260 • *Acknowledgments*

Finally, thanks to my children: Julián, Magalí, Joaquín, Areli, and Valentino. Everything I do is for you.

To my family in Argentina and Puerto Rico, los quiero y los extraño todos los días!

Most of all, thank you to the love of my lives, Jeffrey Allen Méndez, for the beautiful life we've built together, for our children, and for giving me Puerto Rico. Te amo.

I'm not Puerto Rican, but I love the country and its people. As I finish this book, Puerto Rico is trying to recover from Hurricane Fiona, after the destruction of Hurricane María and Hurricane Irma. I'm inspired by the fire in the Puerto Rican people in the island and the diaspora. Thanks for taking me in as one of your own, and I hope I make you proud.

Visit our website at
KensingtonBooks.com
to sign up for our newsletters, read
more from your favorite authors, see
books by series, view reading group
guides, and more!

Become a Part of Our
Between the Chapters Book Club
Community and Join the Conversation

Submit your book review for a chance to win exclusive
Between the Chapters swag you can't get anywhere else!
https://www.kensingtonbooks.com/pages/review/